SHIFTER

BOOKS BY J. C. MCKENZIE

Embrace the Flame

The Carus Series
Shifter (Shift Happens)
Beast (Beast Coast)
Demonic (Carpe Demon)
Cursed (Shift Work)
Carus (Beast of All)

Obsidian Flame
Dangerous Dreams
Dangerous Liaisons
Dangerous Decisions

That Old Black Magic
The Good Griffin

Standalones
Immortal Throne (with Harper A. Brooks)
Call of the Deep (The Shucker's Booktique)
Stormbound (Be My Love)

SHIFTER

J. C. MCKENZIE

COPYRIGHT INFORMATION

Shifter

Contact Information: jcmckenzie@jcmckenzie.ca

Cover Art: Olga Sauchenia

Publishing History:

First JCM Publications Edition, 2024

First Black Rose Edition, 2014 (*Shift Happens*, Wild Rose Press)

ISBN: 978-1-990143-53-3 (print)

ISBN: 978-1-990143-54-0 (ebook)

To Scott,
with every breath and beat of my heart.

You're entering the creative domain of a Canadian author. There will be a combination of British and American spellings, a combination of measurement systems, and maybe even a little French thrown in to spice things up.

This series contains explicit language, open-door spicy scenes, ghosts, violence, gore, torture, PTSD from past SA, threat of SA, murder, assassinations, sociopaths and narcissists. This series also contains death, grief, and loss.

Please read with care.

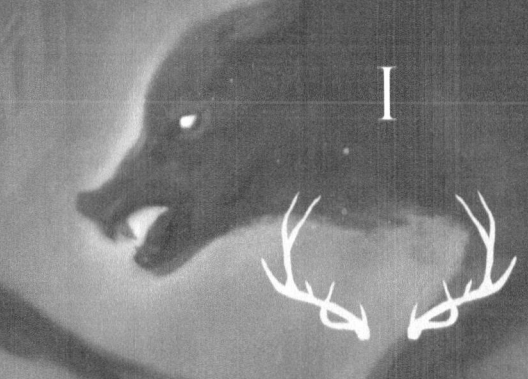

A human? Not what I expected. Tall and muscular, Clint Behnsen's broad shoulders made a girl want to take up mountain climbing. With slicked back hair the same deep sable as mine, and a dark Armani suit, he announced his wealth like a red flag to the lowlifes in the sleazy downtown Vancouver club. A good looking man in his prime.

A shame I had to kill him.

I leaned my tall frame against the sticky bar and pushed my boobs out, hoping to draw my target's attention. The smell of booze and desperation assaulted my senses while strobe lights flickered all the colours of the rainbow. A man stepped away from his buddies to stand beside me.

"Hey, babe. What's your name?" he shouted over the music. His breath hit the side of my face in little punches of air.

"Andrea," I said, keeping my gaze on Clint. I didn't

have time to deal with losers, especially ones sporting lopsided faux-hawks. He wore a charming smile, but one sniff of his narcotic containing sweat, I pegged this guy as a moron in seconds. Having heightened senses and animal magnetism might give me a professional advantage, but at times like this, it was a liability.

Mr. Faux-hawk's eyelids drooped in a lousy attempt at bedroom eyes. He looked more like a sedated patient from the psych ward. He leaned to the side and looked at my butt. "Your ass is pretty tight; want me to loosen it up for you?"

Gross! My muscles tensed as heat flushed through my body. *No man should speak to a woman like that.* A low growl escaped my lips, and the man's spine straightened. I wanted to embed my fist in his face. I turned my full attention to him and my eyes tingled, telling me they'd partially shifted to reflect the animals within.

He froze, his eyes widening.

Prey recognized predator. The man grabbed his drink and scurried away, quickly engulfed by the gyrating throng of dancing norms.

"Glad you got rid of him." A singsong voice pulled my attention from the fleeing man's back. Prey should never run. I squeezed my eyelids shut and took a deep breath in, resisting the urge to give chase, before turning to the woman.

Mel?

Invisible arms squeezed my chest as all the air whooshed out of my lungs. Stomach acid burned my throat. The room tilted and my vision narrowed until an awful memory, one I tried to suppress, overtook it.

Sweat, mixed with the acrid scent of blood rolled off the pack women huddled in the corner of the room. Naked. Waiting their turn. Hair plastered to their faces. My friend Mel mouthed our mantra, "Survive."

I took a long, controlled breath in. The woman behind the bar wasn't Mel, but she could've been a body double, down to the hourglass figure and big blonde hair. I shook my head to clear the horrible image she triggered.

I hadn't seen Mel since I broke free.

"Um...You okay? Can I get you something?" The blonde quirked her finely plucked brow. How long had I been staring at her?

"Rye and cola, please," I mumbled and shelled out a twenty-dollar bill. After slapping the money on the counter, I grabbed my drink and moved away from the bar to one of the nearby tables before she could give me any change. Time to focus on my assignment.

Stashed below an expensive hotel, I surveyed the bar known to locals as the Dirty Dungeon, and thought of Clint's reasons for slumming. He had enough money to go to any number of the higher-end clubs, just down the street.

So why here?

I drummed my fingers on the table top. Maybe he planned to meet someone? So far, he'd strutted around the club with his guards, establishing his presence without accomplishing much—except picking up women and looking good. Real good.

Whatever Clint did to piss off my employer had transpired in the past, because I'd watched him all day and unless getting laid in triplicate now constituted a crime, he'd been a law-abiding citizen the whole time. Typically, I went after preternatural beings, or supes, that broke the rules set by the Supernatural Regulatory Division.

Why would the SRD place such importance on this norm?

I finished my drink and left the empty glass on the table. My employer's motives didn't matter. Not my job to question, and time ticked away. A twenty-four hour deadline with virtually no information. *Awesome.*

With a relaxed stride, I dodged the obstacle course of men who gathered in the club like packs of wolves, ready to hunt down vulnerable women with low self-esteem and a penchant for making bad decisions. Plumes of smoke billowed around their heads and caught in my lungs as I made my way across the dark room toward Clint. He stood near the second bar at the back of the club and recounted some sort of hunting story. I heard him say, "prowl," and "caught a few." The loud pumping bass and the obnoxious drunks screaming at each other made it difficult to make out more, even this close, but Clint's tale probably didn't involve any four-legged herbivores.

"May I buy you a drink?" I purred in my best sexy voice when I reached him.

Clint turned his head and gave me the once over. His smouldering gaze assessed and dismissed me in seconds. "I prefer blondes."

Of course you do. With jet black hair, gray eyes and a skin tone hinting of a biracial background, I'd look ridiculous as a blonde. Wrong colouring. A lesser woman would've been discouraged by Clint's lack of enthusiasm, but not me. I wanted this over. Pushing my lips out into a pout, I played with a strand of my hair and pushed out some of my animal magnetism to curl around him. "I can change your mind."

Gorgeous shoulders shook as he chuckled. "Glenfiddich," he said. "Neat."

Good choice. Thankful my so-called-charm worked, I nodded at the hovering bartender and held up two fingers. "I'm Andy."

Clint grunted in response. I took a gamble approaching him, but after spending the last hour across the bar trying to lure him to me, I had to accept my attempts at body posturing and hair flipping had failed to capture his attention.

The bartender placed the whiskeys on the bar and I stepped over to slip him some cash and grab the drinks. When I eased past the guards, the urge to hip check the ones standing in my way rose up. It would be so easy. Their norm scents swirled around me, bolstering my confidence that this would be a simple hit. It better be. Tonight was my deadline. No one missed an SRD deadline.

I sidled over and gave Clint his drink. He dipped his chin and clinked my glass.

"Boys night out?" I nodded at the guards. They surrounded me and Clint, rigid and stiff, moving only their eyes to track the flitting patrons of the club. They failed miserably at looking casual.

Clint appraised my cleavage before answering. "You could say that."

"Are you from around here?" Small talk was not my thing. No need or desire to get to know my targets. The less I knew the better. I hoped Clint would take the bait quickly and ask me to go upstairs to his room.

Clint's eyes narrowed.

Crap. Did he glimpse my motives? I let out more of my magic and wrapped it around him.

Clint swallowed the amber fluid slowly. "Are you?" he asked.

"It's my sister's wedding this weekend." The whiskey burned down my throat as I sipped it.

His eyebrows rose and he looked around. "Why are you here? Shouldn't you be obnoxiously drunk trying to stuff dollar bills down some man's thong?"

I smiled. "Strippers are tomorrow. Tonight, the bridal party is tying bows around useless gifts most guests will throw away."

"And you're missing out on that?"

"It's not my thing."

"Tying bows?"

"The whole wedding thing." I looked at him through my lashes and dropped my voice. "It's not what I want."

He hesitated. His gaze took another look at my breasts and then he leaned in. "And what do you want?"

"I thought that would be obvious." My attention dropped to the area below his belt and lingered. Guys always liked it when they thought I was checking out their junk.

Clint reached out slowly and brushed a finger down my cheek, trailing it along my jawline and then the side of my neck. All the while his gaze focused on my face. Like he could look inside my head, find one of those colourful cubes, and solve it. Despite his handsome features and strong stature, my skin wanted to crawl away from his touch. I sucked the nausea down. I had an act to follow and this guy would be dead soon.

"Such beautiful skin," he murmured. His finger slipped down my chest until it reached the top of my dress. He followed the neckline, making a path to my cleavage. "Flawless." He hooked his finger into the dip between my breasts and tugged on the cloth.

I stepped closer and angled my face up. "It bruises easily." My voice came out ragged and breathy, as intended. *Should've been an actress.*

Clint's face darkened and his mouth slowly lengthened into a lascivious smile. I'd seen the bruised flesh of the blonde bimbos he preferred. His needs were not a secret.

"Did you have something in mind?" he asked. Taking both our drinks away, he placed them on a nearby table. His hands slid to my waist, anchoring me in front of him.

I leaned up and nipped his jaw, close to his ear. "I'm done talking."

His chest rumbled. He looked over my shoulder to the guards. "I'll be upstairs," he said.

"Maybe you should wait for Wick," one of the guards replied, his voice a deep monotone.

I frowned into Clint's chest. This Wick didn't sound like someone I wanted to wait for. Cupping Clint's groin, I whispered, "I don't want to wait."

Clint chuckled. "Three's a crowd," he said to the guard. "I'll be upstairs." He took my arm and led me to the elevator.

When the doors to the lift closed, Clint used a card to access his floor. I detested this moment the most. I needed my target hot and heady with his blood shunted to the lower half of his body. I didn't need or want him to think.

Time to put on my big-girl-acting panties. Turning toward him, I smiled slowly.

Clint raised a brow. "How impatient are you?"

I slammed him against the wall, making the elevator shake in answer. Kissing him roughly, I said, "Consider this foreplay."

I didn't worry about being gentle. This big boy liked it rough. His tight grip on my ass hurt and my lips swelled from his teeth and hard kisses. He grabbed a handful of hair at the nape of my neck and pulled. My head snapped back to see his hooded, hot gaze. His other hand pulled me against his body. The hard ridge of his pants, tented from his arousal, pressed against me. He started to grind.

Dry humping in an elevator. Just another day at work.

The elevator dinged and the doors opened. I pushed

Clint off my body with a fake show of modesty and straightened my dress. It didn't worry me that I acted out of character. He wouldn't notice at this point and I hated swapping spit with targets.

Clint chuckled and pulled me out after him.

"The penthouse?" I asked. I already knew which room he stayed in. Despite the seedy state of the bar in the basement, the hotel had nice rooms, very nice rooms, at very high prices. Even the rich liked to slum and this establishment provided the perfect environment on site.

Clint's smug smile answered my question and he unlocked the door by swiping his card. Swinging it open, he gestured for me to enter before him.

"Nice," I said and walked in. The floor plans I'd downloaded from the internet earlier this evening had given me a precise idea of the layout. With my arms stretched out wide, I twirled around the room. Nothing wrong with feeding his ego. The more he thought about himself, the less he thought of me. I headed toward the balcony.

"What are you doing?" Clint asked.

"Opening the patio doors," I said, preparing my escape route.

"Not exactly large enough for what I had in mind." He undid his tie, pulled it off, and nodded toward the enormous king sized bed in the middle of the room.

"I like fresh air," I said.

"Are you warm?" He stalked toward me. "I will be."

He smirked and pulled me toward the bed. "What about people hearing?"

I licked my lips. His attention flickered to them and focused. I knew what he wanted me to ask— hearing what? Instead, I said, "I like the idea of people hearing me scream." I leaned up and bit his plump lower lip. "You are going to make me scream, aren't you?"

"You have no idea." He cradled my face and kissed me, smashing his mouth hard against mine. Of course, I had an idea. Images surged up of bruises along the necks of some of Clint's earlier conquests. The marks would've matched Clint's fingers if anyone bothered to check. The SRD might have their own reasons for wanting this bastard dead, but after watching him all day, I rapidly developed my own.

Clint pulled at the clingy material of my red dress until it started to tear at the seams.

"Rip it," I murmured as I dragged my teeth along his neck. "Make it hurt."

He smiled and jerked the dress hard. It broke apart immediately, no doubt leaving red marks where the cloth bit into my skin. I winced into his chest, then tore his shirt from his body—a classic pain diversion technique I picked up on the job years ago. Clint clawed at my bra. I let him. I needed to be naked and he needed to be distracted.

Pounding at the door froze us both.

"Clint," a deep voice boomed. "You fucking idiot. I'm coming in."

My pulse jumped in my throat. Crap! I didn't want any witnesses. Clint better tell this guy to get lost. If he didn't... I pinched the bridge of my nose. Now was not the time for a headache.

"I'm busy, Wick. Go away," Clint snarled over his shoulder.

"I got a call from the boss. We have to leave. Now," Wick growled. "Either you open this door, or I'm breaking it down."

My heart ramped up a bit in my chest. No! If he took Clint away, I'd never get another chance at him. I'd have to do this now, and fast.

Clint and I sighed in unison, but for entirely different reasons.

"Didn't want an audience?" Clint asked. He squeezed my breast, leaving angry red marks where his fingertips dug in, before turning toward the door.

"You have no idea," I purred, admiring his back.

Nice and exposed. My headache instantly dissipated.

It happened quickly. The flash of pain and the familiar coil of muscle and fur rippled through my body as I shifted, my change to a large mountain lion complete when the door burst open.

"Why do I smell..." said a large blur of a man at the door. My attention wasn't on him. This was my chance. I wouldn't get this close again.

Clint spun in slow motion toward me, too late to react. My feline body uncoiled, pouncing on him. I closed my eyes and enjoyed the feeling of my teeth sinking into the soft tissue of his neck. I ripped it out in a large chunk. Clint made a gurgling sound as blood sprayed across the room.

Whirling in the air, my paws hit the floor and I leapt toward the balcony.

"Shoot her," a voice snarled. I smelled wolf. *Goddammit.*

Leaping from the balcony, I spread my limbs out and willed the shift again. Paws stretched and shrank into feathery wings. The air took hold and the exhilaration of flight lifted me. I soared away in victory. Aloft in the dark night. Free.

The wind rippled under my wings as I headed toward the park.

An unexpected burst of pain blasted through my right wing. *Wha...?*

They shot me.

My breath caught and a sudden coldness hit my core. The air whistled past feather and bone, spiralling my body out of control as I plummeted toward the ground. My heartbeat thrashed in my ears, and my lungs locked as I fought to correct my alignment, somehow managing to aim my damaged body toward the forested park area the hotel bordered.

The sting of snapping branches and the intense pain of the bullet wound vibrated through me before I felt the cold, hard impact of the ground.

2

Cold spring air laden with the rich loamy smell of earth and sweet cherry blossoms scraped my lungs as I sucked it in. The muscles around my chest constricted like a synched-up corset and made breathing difficult. I couldn't do it fast enough to fill the empty feeling inside. Slowly, I drew in more air, one breath at a time, one stabbing pain to the heart at a time. The clamp around my lungs slowly released and the tang of pine and fresh blood flooded my senses.

I pried my eyelids open and winced. Dirt caught and scratched my eyeballs. My tear ducts kicked into over-drive and I fluttered my lashes against the damp ground, trying to get the muck out. Sharp pebbles dug into my face. I lifted my head and brushed them away. Blood covered my hands. I sat up and held them out, spreading my fingers. The blood stuck to my skin, partially dried and muddled with grime. Mine? Clint's?

My upper arm throbbed. An angry swell of damaged

tissue surrounded a gaping bullet hole. Though shifting would've healed the wound a bit, it still burned. I twisted my arm back and forth to look at the injury more closely. At least it had gone straight through. I prodded around the tender damage from the bullet's exit and winced.

A deep boom thundered overhead. The night sky glared at me, dark and ominous. Storm coming. Time to go. Locals nicknamed this city Raincouver for a reason.

Pulling my feet under my body, I straightened slowly to a standing position. My shoulders and thighs ached like I'd been in a football training camp. A dank earthy taste filled my mouth. I turned to the side and spat out dark brown soil and pebbles, leaving my mouth dry and gritty. I ran my tongue over my front teeth and spat again.

The forest remained silent—too silent. Only wind whistled through the leaves.

At least I didn't have to worry about witnesses. A naked woman covered with blood, face planted into the dirt tended to make the news. My body sometimes shifted back on its own during sleep or when I lost consciousness. I didn't know why.

The wind changed direction and a new smell hit me. Wolves. They must've seen where I landed. I needed to get out of here, and fast. A ripple of pain travelled down my body and my sleek feline fur replaced naked flesh.

Another crash of thunder rocked the air, followed by a streak of lightning. The storm moved closer. My claws dug into the sodden bark as I scampered up the nearest tree, moving with as much grace as my injury allowed, through the canopy, tree to tree. I could *trust* my strongest and most agile form, the mountain lion.

A wolf howled in the distance, punching through the silent night—to the south. Another answered to the east. They were closing in. No doubt they also came from the other two directions, but remained silent. That's where they wanted me to go—herding me, hunting me as a pack.

That was fast. A Werewolf pack on call? From the beginning, nothing about this assignment seemed right. Maybe Clint hadn't been so normal after all.

Then what was he?

During The Purge, a series of natural disasters and deadly viruses had swept the world. As the fragile human population declined, the death defying presence of the supernatural led to one preternatural group after another getting exposed—Werewolves, Vampires, Fae, Demons, Skinwalkers, Witches, Angels, everything from our dreams to our nightmares. Pandora's Box had opened.

Now one of the most vicious and tenacious of those groups tracked me.

I leapt to another tree. The bullet wound lanced pain up and down my front leg. I ignored it and moved on. The Werewolves owned my scent now and they'd hunt me to oblivion. How did they tie in with Clint?

Never mind, no time to think about it now. I needed to outmaneuver them.

I turned east to where I'd left my car by one of the many park exits for a quick escape. If I could drive away, it would give me enough time to heal so I could shift into a falcon and fly. The Werewolves couldn't track me then. Managing to weave through the leaves along the branches with a few wobbles, I made my way to where the trees thinned out near the end of the path below, the exit gate only half a football field away. Sniffing the air revealed no one upwind.

The tall grass in the undergrowth rustled. A twig snapped downwind. My breath caught.

Rodents scurried across the trail path. I exhaled. No wolves in sight.

Shimmying down the tree, I got close enough to the ground to jump. Pain shot up my arm. My fur rippled from the discomfort. I hacked in response and limped toward the exit.

Thunder rolled, followed by an instant downpour of rain. A lone shape emerged from the dark in front of me. A growl bounced off the pathway. Too late, the wind changed again. Werewolf. Female.

Another one of my forms pawed inside my head.

Let me out, she said. *I'll take her.*

I shooed the voice away.

My sleek feline body coiled, pain forgotten, survival instinct taking over. Ears back, I hissed in response. *Bring it, bitch.* The shewolf answered my challenge and slunk down the path toward me, teeth bared, fur slicked down by the heavy rain. Her gaze darted back and forth, no doubt looking for her pack. When she tilted her head to call them, I sprang.

My body slammed into hers. We tumbled and rolled, body over body, fur over fur. She yelped when I sank my teeth deep into her back. Blood flowed into my mouth and coiled around my tongue. Wrapping my forelimbs around her, my sharp hind claws raked against her back and legs as I kicked, shredding open her skin. The smell of her blood saturated the air. She spun around, forcing my jaw to release its hold. I tried to bite down again and failed. Stronger than a natural wolf, she threw me off. I landed with a splash and slid along the path, now only twenty feet from the gate. The shewolf staggered, then collapsed in a bloody heap. She'd recuperate eventually. I needed to move.

I turned from the damaged shewolf and sprinted toward the parking lot.

Three more wolves stepped out of the dark shadows. The wolves slipped through sheets of rain, the water pelting against their fur and the path at their feet. I pulled up short. Water and blood ran down my shaking leg. My pulse thundered in my ears. I hissed at them.

They gave no warning and leapt in unison, one large furry motion. One landed on me, while the other two flanked my body before attacking. Teeth clashed and claws ripped. Sharp needles of pain lanced across my back, under my hip and along my shoulders. I rolled and thrashed around, trying to break their hold. One clawed at my back, latching on with its teeth. Another held my back leg between its sharp teeth, tearing skin. The last circled around, looking for an opening. The bitter scent of blood consumed the air, mingling with their excitement and the canned ham smell of my desperation.

A roll of thunder vibrated the air and the wolf on my

back loosened his grip. I bucked him off, sending him flying into the others. My chance to escape. I only needed one. I ran.

They sprinted in pursuit, so close their fangs brushed my ankles. It tripped me, making me stagger. But I recovered. My mountain lion could outrun most supes. I kept moving, dodging their attempts to bring me down. I hurtled past trees and hurdled over fallen logs. I stumbled into a clearing and froze. The scent of more wolves in front of me slammed into my nose. A trap.

I spun around. Too late. The wolves behind me closed in, but didn't attack. They didn't need to. More of their pack poured into the clearing from the forest, surrounding me.

Dizzy and weak, I assessed my situation. Not good. *Let me out*, my other form whined inside my head. *Let me take them.*

Stronger and more agile, my mountain lion stood a better chance against the angry Weres, so I ignored the voice and focused on the wolves around me. Their jaws snapped open and closed, flashing teeth that gleamed in the moonlight, and sputtering a frothy spray of saliva, but they waited. Their snarls and growls formed a solemn backbeat for the erratic hammering of my heart. *So this was it*. Werewolf dinner. *Fuck.* I cursed Feradea, the deity responsible for protecting Shifters, and braced for impact.

A large black wolf trotted into the clearing to confront me. He had a white-tipped snout, white boots and mitts and would have looked cute had he not been the most intimidating Werewolf I'd ever seen. Standing tall and solid, power rolled off of his body. His eyes bore into mine. I sniffed the air. The strong Werewolf scent of rosemary swirled around me, strong and seductive, laced with sugar. A weird fuzzy sensation spread out from my chest. *Whoa*.

Alpha.

My other form growled low, demanding release, straining against my skin. The energy of the wolves built —layers upon layers of excitement and impatience. The air pulsated with anticipation. They could sense the imminent kill.

Let me out! My other form repeated, throwing her power against my built up walls, howling in defiance.

When the energy of the Werewolves surged, I finally released her. My wolf form flowed out fast, wiping out the feline in little more than a heartbeat. Smaller, weaker and the size of a natural wolf, a Shifter in this form was no match for a Werewolf, especially a dominant one. I had time to meet the eyes of the Alpha for only an instant before the pack leapt forward. My limbs shook. It went against every instinct ingrained within me, but I rolled onto my back—submissive.

I squeezed my eyelids shut and waited. Every muscle tensed. But the pack never reached me. Popping my eyes back open, I stared at the smooth belly of the Alpha standing over my prone body, snarling a warning to his pack. All tension flowed out of my body in an unexpected release. My head felt suddenly light.

Holy crap, it worked.

Maybe I should thank Feradea. I relaxed, granted respite for the time being. There would be repercussions for my actions, but they'd have to wait. The adrenaline left my system, and the toll of my injuries consumed my body. As my vision faded to black, I wondered how I would escape the mess I'd just surrendered myself to.

3

When the haze weighing down my senses cleared, I realized I lay naked in a strange bed, which smelled of wolf, man and floral dryer sheets. I'd woken up dazed in a stranger's bed before, but this was no wild night out after binge drinking—no hung-over, vaguely attractive frat boy passed out beside me, and no slinking out the door to do the walk of shame before he woke up and asked for my number.

The coppery taste of blood clung to my mouth. I ran my tongue through my teeth repeatedly and swallowed, but it did little to clear my palate. I moved my head back and forth. A small whimper escaped my lips. I needed to test exactly how poorly everything operated. Wiggling my toes and fingers, I decided my body functioned, though stiff and sore.

Better than dead. Opening my eyes did nothing to dull the throb of pain.

A dark shape moved to my left. Startled, I sat up in bed and instantly regretted it. My brain smacked against the inside of my skull and convulsed. Clutching my head, I squeezed my eyelids shut and sank back into the soft pillow with a groan.

"Easy." A man's voice splintered the silence.

The glare of sunlight filtered through the glass and burned my retinas. I squinted and took in my host. He sat by the window. The opaque drapes billowed out behind him, surrounding his body in a white glow as a strong wind gusted into the room. With blond hair cut short, chiseled features, and broad shoulders, a present day Norse God returned my appraising gaze. Attractive, to put it mildly. Though sitting, I could tell he was tall from his long, muscular legs stretched out in front of him. He sat relaxed, wearing dark jeans moulded to his body and a plain blue t-shirt with NAVY in big white block letters. His irises caught my attention, not blue like the Norse, instead, rich, chocolate brown.

The wind carried his scent to me; rosemary with an underlying tone of sugar swirled around, embracing me like a long lost lover. I stiffened. The Alpha.

"How are you feeling?" His voice rolled over me, hinting at subtle power, chilled whiskey poured over warm cream. It sounded familiar.

"Like I was in a dog fight."

"You were." His lip quirked as he looked me over. "Better than dead," he echoed my earlier thoughts. "But you are healing slowly."

Though comfortable in my own skin, in my several

skins, the way he looked at me now made me wish I had clothes on. I pulled the thin sheets up, over my bare skin, and crossed my arms over my boobs. Shifters and Weres were used to being naked around others. Few held insecurities regarding their physiques because we all had great shapes from our increased calorie burning. Shifting took a lot of energy, and like it or not, shift happens.

The Alpha's dark gaze tracked every move I made, sending my heart spiking, and not out of fear. His Alpha power pulled at my wolf. I suddenly wanted to get closer and touch him. And that was absolutely the last thing I should do or want to do.

"I'm not a Were," I said. "The question is why I'm healing at all. Why wasn't I ripped to shreds?" I dreaded the answer. I'd submitted to an Alpha and in pack culture that gave him power over me. What he'd do with that power caused me the greatest concern. Not being a Were, I could break his control, but... A shiver racked my body. But I didn't want to go through that again.

He shifted his weight in the seat. "When you are better, you will be asked some questions." All Shifters and Weres could scent a lie. He spoke the truth, but he said it slowly as if avoiding something.

"By you?" I asked.

He relaxed. I wouldn't have noticed if I hadn't been keenly watching for a reaction. Not the right question then. "I would like you to answer a few of my questions before you answer Lucien Delgatto's."

Frowning, I tried to place the name. Then it hit me. "The vamp?"

"The Master Vampire of the Lower Mainland?

Yes, *the* vamp." He sounded amused.

"What does he want with me?" My brain hurt. My target had been a norm and my timeline short. I hadn't wasted time researching the local supes in the area. I'd taken a cursory glance, of course, and knew a bit from living nearby, but now I regretted my haste. I didn't know how Clint, the Alpha and Lucien linked together and I needed to figure the connection out. I had a feeling my health depended on it.

"That will become apparent. I am not to speak more of it," he said in a flat voice, not sounding thrilled about the situation. The formal phrases and his occasional inability to use contractions gave him away as an older Werewolf. Maybe a couple hundred years old? Some Werewolves found adapting their speech to current times more difficult than Vampires. Go figure.

"You're following orders out of the goodness of your heart?" Somehow I found it unlikely. Alphas were a law unto themselves.

His jaw tightened. "I follow orders because I have to. He's my master."

"But you're an Alpha. The leader of a pack."

"His animal to call is a wolf." He bit it out. A vein in his forehead puckered out, pulsating.

Clarity hit me like a three hundred pound wrestler with a grudge. A Master Vampire's word reigned absolute over his subjects. And as his animal to call, this Alpha and all the wolves in his pack, fell into that category. Now I knew the connection between him and

Lucien. But how did Clint factor into everything? I glanced at the Alpha. He couldn't go against Lucien's orders even if he wanted to, which meant I wouldn't get any more information out of this Werewolf.

I lay back in bed with a groan. "Is that why he wants to speak with me? Another minion to add to his horde?"

The Alpha leaned in. "He did not ask me if you were a wolf."

My ears perked up.

"I would hold closely to one of your other forms when you speak with him."

Exactly what I planned to do. "Why would you protect my identity from him?"

He shifted his weight, his gaze cut away. "He has enough wolves enslaved to his purpose. He does not need another."

Truth, but again I had the impression he left something out.

"What are your questions?"

He smiled and leaned back. "Your name?"

I laughed. Normally this would be an easy question to answer, but as a government assassin, my identity remained one of my biggest secrets. "Andy," I told him.

He straightened in his chair. "Short for Andrea, I assume?"

"Only if you're my mother."

He chuckled.

"And you are?" I asked.

"My apologies. I should have introduced myself earlier. You can call me Wick."

Clint's guard. The one he hadn't waited for the night I killed him. Another piece to the puzzle, but it still didn't tell me how Clint fit in with the Werewolves and Vampires. I leaned forward. "Short for Wicked, I assume?"

Wick laughed out loud. "Short for Wickard, my last name."

I settled back against the soft pillows. "Fairly easy round of questioning,"

"I'm not done."

"My last name is off limits," I stated, anticipating what he would ask next. Staying invisible and nameless comprised one of my most important job requirements.

His lips twitched. "That wasn't it, but I can easily find out."

"With your superior telepathic skills?"

"I have many skills, but that is not one of them." His knowing look made me want to fidget with the blanket. I suppressed the urge, very aware I lay in a bed which smelled of him. It was rare for me to react to a man this way, and it bothered me.

I looked around, mainly to break the eye contact and take in more of the room. The walls, painted a sage gray, gave the room a serene sanctuary feeling. A painting of rocks in a hazy forest hung in the centre of the main wall, decorating an otherwise unadorned room. The space had a tranquil quality. A large dresser, overflowing with large articles of clothing smelling of Wick, told me this space belonged to him.

Good mate, my wolf huffed.

What the heck? Where'd that come from? My wolf hadn't spoken like that since Dylan. And boy, had she been wrong. I shushed her and focused on Wick's chocolate eyes.

"What are you?" he whispered.

A norm would've missed his question. I jolted in the bed and my attention zoomed back to his face. "That's a rude question."

It wasn't really. There were a lot of possibilities and eighty years post Purge, we were all "out of the closet" so to speak. Most supe groups were relieved to be out of hiding after centuries of censorship. I wasn't. A price existed for such exposure. I felt like my date had walked out of the restaurant and left me with a bill I couldn't pay.

Wick shrugged. "We're both supes. It's a moot point."

"A Shifter." I squirmed, the urge for clothing palpable. But it would be a sign of weakness to admit being uncomfortable naked in his presence. Not wanting to give Wick any further control over me, I bit my tongue.

"With three forms? A cougar, a..."

"A mountain lion," I interrupted.

The corners of his mouth twitched. "Sweetheart, from what I heard about your performance last night, you are worthy of both names."

I gave him a flat stare and ignored the increase in my heart rate.

"My apologies." He cleared his throat before continuing. "A mountain lion, some sort of bird..." He paused

27

to give me the opportunity to enlighten him. I didn't. He forged on, "And the most delectable gray wolf."

If my wolf could purr, she would have. *Good mate,* she repeated.

I fidgeted under his gaze. The way he said delectable made it sound like I was some sort of chocolate sundae. My cat hacked, not impressed.

"How is that possible?" he asked.

I shrugged. The hell if I knew. He stared for a while, most likely trying to gauge whether I would say more on the subject or not. My skin itched to run. I'd rather have one of my canines pulled out by a dentist school dropout than elaborate.

"Where are your feras?" He changed tactics.

"Now that *is* a rude question."

Wick shrugged.

Shifters bonded to animal familiars, known as feras. Every Shifter I met bonded to one and only one. The bond allowed Shifters to take the same shape as their fera. These animals accompanied Shifters through life and communicated with their Shifter through the bond. They were magical and once bonded, lived as long as the Shifter. I always wondered how bear Shifters managed to stay concealed during the pre-Purge era. They must've lived in rural areas. A black bear couldn't stroll around the city unnoticed.

Of course, if I'd grown up with the lore passed down from generation to generation, I'd know all about it, but all my information came from the internet. I'd been born during the first year of the Purge, when gun-toting norms took out an estimated ninety percent of Shifters by offing their feras. Those volatile years also claimed the life of my birth parents. Or so the adoption agency claimed. Working for the government gave me a different perspective of the *truth*.

I hadn't walked into the forest to find one animal. I found three. But something went wrong during the bonding process. One touch and they evaporated, as if my soul sucked them into my body. I had no feras to walk with me through life and keep me company, save the voices in my head.

I wouldn't answer Wick's question. Couldn't. Asking about a Shifter's fera was a sensitive topic. The death of the animal meant the death of the Shifter. They were every Shifter's strength and every Shifter's vulnerability.

No one had ever witnessed my multiple forms and lived to tell the tale. Until now. The exposure of my secret made my heart sink in my chest. I couldn't take out a whole pack of Werewolves and everyone they told. Social media was a bitch.

"Fine," Wick said. "I'm sure we'll spot them eventually. They'd be safer inside with us."

I clamped my mouth shut, willing myself to remain silent. He didn't need to know I had no physical feras.

Wick stood up and stretched. His shirt pulled up a little and revealed a taut six pack. I had the biggest urge to lick them.

Not the appropriate response. I should be thinking about incapacitating him to escape.

He peered down at me. "It goes without saying that you will be guarded at all times." He shut the window and locked it with a key. "All the windows in the house are Were-proof. You'll injure yourself more if you try to break through them."

I grunted and shut my eyes. Of course, imprisoned in a Were house. These buildings were pretty damn close to indestructible and near impossible to break out using strength—a must for house training new Weres. They could get pretty uncontrollable. Good thing I never counted on brute force to get me out of trouble.

"Is there anything I can get you?" he asked.

"Clothes," I said without thinking.

A shadow passed over me. My eyes flew open. Wick leaned in and placed a hand on each side of my head. Bracing his weight, he bent closer. A smile tugged at his lips, now inches away from my own. His white teeth flashed. "Nervous?"

"You wish." Butterflies danced the mamba in my stomach. Oh God, he totally nailed it.

His face darkened and he lowered his body. His peppermint breath brushed my face. "You should be."

A shiver ran through my body at the promise in his words.

4

Looking good enough to dry hump, Wick leaned against the hallway wall with his arms crossed when I emerged from the bedroom. After providing me with the unofficial uniform of Weres and Shifters everywhere—sweatpants and a t-shirt—he'd been a gentleman and opted to wait outside while I changed. Ridiculously large on me, the clothes smelled of Wick. He masked me in his deliciously rich scent, marking me as his to prevent his pack from attacking.

My cheeks grew warm. I'd submitted to him in wolf form. Did Wick protect me out of obligation as the Alpha, to keep me in one piece for Lucien or because he had other designs on me? Ones that involved limbering up and a whole lot of nakedness.

Get a hold of yourself, woman!

While I thought of Wick's potential motivations, I'd enjoyed the privacy to dress. There'd been nowhere to go anyway, save the ensuite bathroom. A pleasant surprise.

By the time Wick left me to change, I needed to *go*. Badly. Damsels in distress never had inconvenient bodily functions, such as a full bladder, in any of the novels I read. This convinced me either I was not a damsel in distress or those books were full of shit.

Probably both.

Then I realized Wick had never asked me about my employer. Did he know I worked for the SRD? Did he assume? As an SRD agent exacting justice on behalf of the government, I should never be held against my will. But some supe groups were so anti-authority, they'd as soon kill me as release me. Did Wick fall into that category?

If Wick wouldn't ask, I wouldn't tell.

Now standing outside the bedroom, I continued to ignore Wick to look around. The hallway revealed four doors, solid oak, stained dark, hiding whatever lay beyond. Carpeted stairs led down to another level, probably equipped with an interrogation room. The air smelled crisp and clean with a faint scent of pine cleaner.

Wick cleared his throat and nodded at the stairs. "Shifters first." His warm voice caused my body to start walking before I processed what he said. Fucking alphas.

He's probably checking out my ass. Part of me wanted to put more swagger in my step, a little fuck-you-for-looking, but the other part didn't want him to think I tried to impress him. A stiff and stilted march resulted. When I looked over my shoulder, Wick's serene expression gave nothing away. His chocolate brown attention appropriately fixed on my face. When our gazes locked, he raised his eyebrows in question.

Shaking my head, I went back to my march. The landing at the base of the stairs opened to a large living area filled with natural light. The large bay windows clamped shut, probably for my benefit, left the air stale. The serene taupe colour scheme of the room, accented with crisp white trim and dark espresso furnishings, belied the wild nature of the resident. Wick's house, without a doubt, his scent imbedded everywhere, in everything.

Three members of his pack sprawled in lounge chairs and on a large L-shaped couch. And they were his, each with their own unique scent mingled with Wick's. At our entrance, their bodies tensed and straightened. I wrinkled my nose. A norm might detect the faint smell of shampoo or soap, but nothing more. Werewolves never wore scented perfume or aftershave. It assaulted their senses more than it did mine. To a Shifter's nose, or a Werewolf's, the room smelled full of wolves—wet dog and rosemary.

"Why isn't she dead?" asked a woman with a menacing look curled up in a large armchair.

I gave the East Asian woman a flat stare and looked her over. She sported short black hair spiked up. The black painted nails and sour expression gave the impression she hadn't progressed past her years of teenage angst. Her pale skin had no wrinkles and she looked around twenty-five, though hard to tell with Werewolves. Her scent gave her away as the shewolf I had mauled to get to the gate.

"Why aren't you?" I asked.

She growled and repositioned herself in the chair, getting ready to spring.

"Ladies," Wick's voice warned.

We both grunted and then, realizing we had the same reaction, glared at each other. The other two wolves in the room remained seated. Their relaxed posture could fool a norm, but they tracked every small movement of mine.

A short black man with piercing amber irises assessed me with open hostility. I could smell his hatred from where I stood. He was solid, built like a tank.

The other Werewolf, a lanky caucasian male with flaming red hair and ice blue eyes, had a face faintly speckled with freckles. He didn't give off any anger, but he rose from his seat and placed himself between me and Wick.

"Let me introduce you to some of my pack," Wick said. The other two stood up to join us. Wick pointed at each one and named them.

"Ryan." The ginger nodded to acknowledge his name.

"Ryan is my second," Wick explained.

"John." Wick pointed at the black man who clenched his jaw and balled his hands into fists. What was his problem?

"...and Jess." Wick's voice softened when he spoke her name.

"That's Jessica to you," she said in a hard flat voice.

Wick didn't look alarmed or reprimand her; instead, his lips tugged up at one corner. He had a soft spot for this one.

Biting the urge to flip them off, I ground my teeth and managed to bite out, "Pleasure."

From Ryan's snort, I knew my tone came across sarcastically. It wasn't a delight to meet them, not at all. My chances of escape decreased severely with their presence. In a one-on-one fight, I'd put money on my mountain lion against a Werewolf any day. But three? I knew my limits. I was outnumbered and outgunned.

"This is Andy." Wick gestured to me.

"That's Andrea to you," I added, proving I could be equally as childish.

Wick exhaled loudly, but he didn't make any comments about my mother.

"She will be our guest for the next couple of days while she mends," Wick said.

"Guest?" Jessica asked in disbelief.

"He means prisoner," I said. A spade was a spade, after all.

"She will be treated as a guest..." Wick restated before I had a chance to add anything. "But she will be guarded at all times and not allowed to leave."

"So a prisoner minus the torture and uncomfortable accommodations?" Jessica's flat tone made it clear she disapproved of the distinction.

"Yes," Wick said.

"Christine's not going to like it," John said.

"Christine doesn't have a say," Wick replied.

Who the fuck's Christine? Not liking the sudden hollow feeling in my chest, I swallowed and kept silent.

"What happens in a couple of days?" Ryan asked, his voice a husky rasp.

"She goes to see Lucien."

All three of Wick's Werewolves flinched. Ryan shot me a sympathetic look and John didn't look as pissed off as before. Jessica's face transformed into an expressionless mask. She looked away.

My stomach knotted and my throat constricted. *Great.* Meeting Lucien now made the top of my *Things I Don't Want To Do* list.

"And then what?" Ryan asked.

Wick sighed and shrugged. "We'll see."

I didn't like the sound of that. If I came out of the Lucien meeting alive, I planned to go on my merry way. Tra-la-la.

"I need to go to work to check on a few things." Wick paused and looked around the room. Satisfied with what he saw, namely the lack of escape routes if I had to guess, he continued, "You three are to remain here and keep a close eye on her. The doors and windows stay closed and locked at all times."

Jessica's head snapped up. "Why?" she demanded to know. "It's already stuffy in here."

"Because I said so." Wick spoke softly, but the dominance in his voice rolled across the room. I felt it and I wasn't pack. Jessica's body snapped to attention. I all but expected her to roll on her back and expose the soft, vulnerable tissue of her belly and neck, or start licking his face in supplication.

She merely nodded and Wick appeared satisfied with her response. Too bad.

Wick turned to me and his hand flashed out. I flinched, expecting a strike, but he gently ran a finger down my cheek. Looking at his tense mouth, I knew he'd seen my reaction, but he didn't comment on it. Instead, his body relaxed and he spoke softly, not soft enough to keep it from the others, but enough to give a pretence of privacy. "Behave."

A shiver ran down my spine as if thousands of leaf-cutter ants danced along it.

Wick straightened and gave his pack members one last meaningful look. "Ryan, I would like a word with you before I go."

Ryan nodded and followed him out of the room. To avoid checking out Wick's backside, I turned to face the two Werewolves in the room who openly despised me—the gruesome twosome—and no visible escape routes.

5

The stare Jessica cast me before sitting down on the chair irritated me, like an ill-fitting sweater from a used clothing store. Instead of offering me her exposed back, she opted for a backwards stride to make it to her seat. It looked ridiculous.

John chose to stand off to my right and pace, back and forth, like a model with OCD and a limited runway, casting wary glances in my direction every third or fourth step. Burnt cinnamon wafted off him in waves. He was pissed.

"I understand why you don't like me, *Jessica*," I said, emphasizing her full name. "I kicked your ass, after all."

She bared her teeth in response.

"I hurt your pride, but if I'm to be a *guest* here, let's get one thing straight. I did nothing you wouldn't have done in my place." I gave her a pointed look before continuing, "Except maybe spare your life."

Jessica looked away. It told me all I needed to know.

If I'd collapsed, bleeding out and vulnerable, she would've killed me.

"But you..." My attention shifted to John. "I have no idea what's up your ass."

He stopped pacing. "Jess is my mate."

Understanding came faster than I could say, "fuck my life." If I'd been male, John would've mauled me to death. Or tried. Female Werewolves were rare and cherished by their packs. For some reason, few survived the initial change. Some claimed the pain was too much, but that never sat right with me. Women had to have a higher pain tolerance. Hello, childbirth.

I'd always figured the second X chromosome in females wouldn't tolerate the lycanthropic viral DNA and imagined some epic genetic battle between the two where they both ended up self-destructing.

Regardless, few female Weres existed and I'd yet to meet one not mated or in a forced union. My eyes narrowed at John, my anger rising at the thought. "By choice?"

"Our wolves chose each other." He didn't sound bitter; his tone came across more confused, like he couldn't fathom any other possibility. I could.

"True, but there are true mates and there are..." I trailed off, trying to stem the surfacing memories.

"Forced unions," Jess spoke softly. Something in the way she spoke made me look up. Our eyes met and mutual understanding passed between us. "John is my true mate, Andy," Jessica said. Her words came out soft and slow. I didn't correct her on my name—not after that look. "All the couples here are. It's not that kind of pack," she explained.

I turned away from her knowing gaze. Though I'd only known him for less than an hour, Wick didn't seem like the kind of Alpha to support forced unions. He'd given me privacy and space. But, Dylan hadn't seemed like the forced-union-type at first, either. Nausea gnawed at my guts and I slammed a door on that memory before it could surface. Nothing boiled my piss faster than thoughts of Dylan.

A photograph on the wall caught my attention, and looking for a distraction, I walked up to the picture of Wick skydiving in a bright blue and yellow suit. He wore a look of sheer joy as he beamed into the camera. I smiled.

"So what in The Purge are you?" John crossed his arms over his chest. "You're not a Were or Wick's pack magic would have healed you faster."

"I'm a Shifter."

John apparently didn't get the hint from my flat tone. I'd finished answering his questions. "Don't smell like one," he said.

Shifters normally smelled human with a faint hint of the animal form they took. Not me, though. A Shifter once told me I smelled of the forest. He demanded to know what I was. When he lay beneath my claws with his life bleeding out of him, I told him I had three forms and no physical feras. He'd called me *Carus* before he died. If he hadn't been a target, I'd have rushed him to a witch coven, paid the healing fee and demanded answers.

No amount of Google searches had clarified what

Carus meant. All I could find, besides an aging porn star with an interactive website, was *Carus* meant *beloved* in Latin. What an odd thing to call the woman who killed you. When John grumbled, I shrugged at him.

"I don't understand why we're housing you and letting you heal. We should've been allowed to rip you to shreds," John stated.

"Oh, John, why don't you tell me how you really feel?"

John paced, a scowl plastered on his face like clown make-up.

Jessica looked a little shocked. "John..." she started.

"It's what Lucien will do to her anyway," he snarled. His mouth opened into a mean toothy smile.

I flinched. Werewolf males were so dramatic, but he spoke the truth. I heard it in his words and smelled it in the air.

"There are some questions he needs answered first, apparently," I said.

John grunted. "What information of value could you possibly have?"

My feras howled inside my head. I did not like the implication I lacked gray matter, or significance. Being dumb enough to enter a relationship with Dylan had made me a bit sensitive on anything regarding my IQ. Some might say *overly* sensitive.

"Careful, John," Ryan spoke as he entered the room. "Keep poking the beast and it's going to bite."

"I'm not afraid of a little pussy." John sneered.

I meant to respond with a witty remark, but a low

hiss came out instead. Hmm. Must be angrier than I realized. John tensed and whipped around to face me. No time like the present to assert my dominance. Werewolves had a distinct pecking order in a pack. John would keep pushing me until I submitted or dominated. And I was nobody's bitch.

Dominate, my wolf demanded.

Kill, my cat hissed. She had no patience for dominance games and lacked subtlety.

I bared my teeth and let my canines elongate. Most Werewolves lacked the control to do the same. Only the strongest could pull off a partial shift. Yowling, I let out the high-pitched call hikers dreaded to hear when alone in a dense forest—Werewolves too, apparently. They all tensed. They could only override so many instincts of their wolves, and a mountain lion trumped lone wolf in the wild.

Figuring I made my point, I told my cat to settle and closed my eyelids to rein her in. When I opened them, three wary wolves in human clothing stared back at me. *Great*. Putting them on edge was probably counterproductive to any escape attempts—and there would be escape attempts—but I needed to establish my place first.

Ryan cleared his voice. "Well, that's settled. How about some cards?"

"Cards?" A strangled sound choked out of my throat in disbelief.

Ryan shrugged. "Daytime TV makes me want to stab myself with a fork. There're only so many paternity shows I can handle." He nodded at John and Jess. "And sitting in a room watching these two lovebirds moon over each other is worse."

Muscles I hadn't realized were tense, relaxed. The idea of playing cards certainly beat dominance games or torture. I reached my hands out and stretched them for what I hoped would be hours of cards instead of less enjoyable prisoner activities.

Ryan's attention darted to my hands. "And maybe some sparring afterwards."

"Isn't that a little dangerous? I might hurt you," I warned.

"I might like it," Ryan countered, flashing his teeth. His flirtation gave little doubt to his unmated status, but my wolf yawned.

"Maybe some sparring," I agreed. My wolf's opinion wasn't the one that mattered most. I liked him. He'd let me fight. Hell, anything to take my mind off of what Lucien planned to do to me in the not-so-far-off future.

6

Sweat dripped down my face and stung the tiny scratches on my neck. Under fluorescent lights in the stale smelling dungeon of a basement, I circled Ryan, wary of his every move. He was good. His fluidity gave him away as an older Werewolf. The various forms he'd demonstrated over the last half hour of sparring required time to learn and master. Some people threw cash at dojos, buying black belts from money-grabbing establishments. Ironically, those schools tended to be the more high fashion outlets instead of the less than savoury ones that spent little time or money on appearances.

Ryan didn't buy his black belts. And he had more than one, his technique crisp, clean and perfect.

Of course, he had lots of time to practice. Werewolves lived several human lifetimes, but they were close lipped regarding exactly how many. Shifters were the same. Both aged like norms until they hit thirty and then they faced a slow road to geriatrics. Seventy-nine by the norm count and I still looked in my late twenties—a baby in the world of Weres and Shifters.

I took a moment to assess the damage. Some excessive sweating, a few scratches and an aching shin that threatened to bloom into one hell of a bruise, but nothing serious, and nothing worse than the injuries I'd had walking into the match. Ryan had pulled his punches. He needed to. Full force, a Were's strike, even in human form, would knock me out. I was supposed to be mending.

Shifters did not benefit from the fast healing Weres were privy to. The arm with the bullet wound throbbed with pain and my ribs ached, but I was in a lot better shape than I should've been, thanks to Wick's healing. If the Alpha contained enough power, he could heal any supe with a similar form. Wolf Shifters often hung out near Werewolf packs for that reason alone. Despite what the norm tabloids said, the two preternatural groups weren't the same thing. As a part of their genetic makeup, Wolf Shifters bonded to wolf familiars when they hit puberty or shortly after. Werewolves acquired their supernatural abilities, being *made* by another. The lycanthropic virus might not give the Weres feras, but it did make them stronger, larger in their animal form and controlled by the phases of the moon.

Stepping out with my right foot, I faked a body shot before trying to connect my left foot with Ryan's face. He danced out of the way leaving me overextended. I spun around with the momentum, doing a complete three-sixty, before facing Ryan again.

"Nice roundhouse," Ryan conceded.

I dipped my chin to acknowledge the compliment. Then I pounced. We exchanged a fury of blows—most didn't land. I flung up arms and legs, blocking his strikes. It didn't take me long to figure out we both excelled in defensive tactics. I didn't like that I wouldn't be able to take Ryan in a real fight, at least not in human form. My mountain lion might overpower his Werewolf, but not without sustaining considerable damage. Ryan was old and powerful. No wonder he was Wick's second.

Fuck. I probably couldn't take Wick either. Would I even want to? Heat trampled through my body. Oh, I definitely wanted to do *something* with him.

"Karate?" Ryan asked, interrupting my thoughts. We went back to circling each other. He'd been trying to guess my martial arts background since we started.

Nodding, I unleashed a few combos to give him a hint. He blocked them all.

"Shotokan?"

I shook my head. "Goju Ryu. Shotokan's a good guess. They're pretty similar."

Ryan grunted and aimed a number of kicks to my legs and midsection, but I blocked them using my legs. My shin protested. "I should've picked up on the snake and crane movements. I thought you might have dabbled in Kung Fu."

"I have. Kempo, too."

I turned, setting up my favourite spinning jump kick. Ryan laughed and stepped to the side, his Werewolf reflexes too good to be taken by surprise by a Shifter. He attacked and I switched styles. Ryan's eyes widened, then he smiled slowly.

Growing up, my parents saw a pretty girl in a rough neighbourhood. They enrolled me in karate classes, hoping to give me a means to protect myself. By twenty, I recognized the limitations of traditional karate and joined a different martial art. This one practiced the theology of incapacitating the opponent as quickly and violently as possible. I loved it.

It also helped in my line of work. I wrote my membership off as a business expense on my yearly taxes.

"Huh." Ryan circled me. "Krav Maga?" I nodded.

With a blur of motion, his body slammed into mine. Air whooshed out of my lungs. I grunted on impact with the floor and tried to find a defensive position.

"You need to work on your ground game." Ryan batted my hands away.

"Clearly." I tried to shift my hips and throw him off. The effort failed, the man an immovable slab of rock. "What style was that? Jujitsu or wrestling?"

The grin on Ryan's face spread. "Rugby." A bubble of laughter escaped my lips.

Ryan blocked the leg I tried to hook around his head. "Nice try."

"Would've worked on a norm."

Ryan smiled and caught my wrists. He pinned them over my head. His legs slipped down as he moved from full mount to a completely different position—missionary. Leaning his face down to mine, he spoke softly. "I'm not a norm."

With his lips close enough to kiss, I stared at Ryan in fascination. My body lay limp beneath his. No heat, no stirring of the loins or quickening heartbeat. No anticipation, nothing. Only perspiration and exhaustion. Why didn't my body react?

Ryan noticed what held my attention, or at least what he thought did, and licked his lips slowly. The spicy coconut scent of arousal flooded my nose. Ryan's body had no problems reacting. How could I break it to him that I wasn't interested?

"What style would you call this?" Ryan asked. His voice deepened.

"X-rated," Wick harsh, loud voice penetrated the silence and echoed off the basement walls. "And one that will get your ass handed to you when you're supposed to be on guard duty."

My muscles tensed and warmth flooded my veins. I swallowed and tried to ignore my racing heartbeat.

Ryan stumbled off me so fast I bit my lip to stop the nervous laughter threatening to escape. Red blotches spread across his face and travelled to the tips of his ears. He nodded to acknowledge Wick's presence. His body posture so rigid, I expected him to salute any minute. He didn't.

With the scent of Wick's anger palpable, I got to my feet and looked around. Nowhere to run. Dammit.

"Sparring?" The word came out clipped, not so much a question as an accusation.

Ryan hesitated. "She's a guest."

"An imprisoned guest. She could have escaped."

"If she managed to take me out. She'd still have to get through the others and the locked doors."

"Do not make the mistake of underestimating her." Ryan frowned.

"Thanks for the vote of confidence," I piped in.

Wick transferred the full force of his hostile gaze to me. The Alpha power emanating from his body so intense, I locked my knees and fought the urge to roll over and whine. Fucking alphas.

"My apologies, Alpha," Ryan interceded.

"You are not to have any further physical contact with Andy unless it is to prevent her escape or protect a pack member," Wick stated with calm, crisp words. His irises flashed bright yellow.

Ryan's head snapped up as the order rolled over him. For an instant, rage shone in his expression but he recovered quickly and slid a mask of indifference over his face. No Were could refuse or ignore their Alpha's command without challenging his place in the pack.

"It won't happen again." Ryan flicked his gaze in my direction before walking away. It looked like he tried to convey something to me—regret, maybe? Gone before I could figure it out, I stared at his back. Despite enjoying our time sparring, his departure didn't stir any internal response. Well, maybe something. But I wanted to ignore the tingling sensation dancing along my skin, the anticipation of being left alone with Wick.

With a lightness in my chest, I turned to Wick to find him watching me. The tingling grew stronger, but I shrugged with my palms out. What did he expect? I was a prisoner and I didn't have to play by his rules.

The yellow in Wick's irises receded to his usual espresso. "So you like to fight?" he asked softly.

"I like to hone my craft," I agreed, brushing off my shoulder as if it was dirty. I saw the action on a rap video a couple weeks ago. It seemed like the right thing to do. Show some attitude.

"Then you should practice against a more versed opponent." He stepped forward in open challenge.

Well, now I had to amp up my game. I'd accept his challenge because I needed to know how he fought. To assess his power. Stronger than Ryan, I knew I couldn't take him in a human fight, but I had to know how much stronger he was, how much faster. I forced my muscles to relax and quirked my mouth. "I thought you said no sparring?"

Wick nodded. "With Ryan." His tone sounded suspiciously close to jealousy. Let him think I liked Ryan that way. I didn't do anything wrong and it wouldn't hurt to put Wick on edge. Make things even.

"Besides." Wick interrupted my thoughts, "this will not be sparring."

"Oh?" My breath bottled up in my chest. Wick shook his head and attacked.

It took all my skills to deflect the blows. He moved half pace and pulled his shots as Ryan had, but he was good. Very good. He hadn't been lying when he said he had more experience.

"This will be play," he said. He might as well have

said foreplay with the way his gaze raked my body. My heart thudded in my ears and my fingers ached to reach out and stroke him instead of strike. I swallowed and willed my body to behave, to focus. But it did no good.

A matter of minutes left me hot, sweaty and pinned against the wall—the cold cement refreshing despite the circumstances. It took every ounce of self-control not to rub my chest along the slab of muscle in front of me. Why'd he have to be so good looking? I needed to escape, not find a bed buddy. I meant to assess his fighting skills, not wonder how skilled he'd be in the bedroom. Focus!

Wick pressed his body to mine and leaned in. "Krav Maga and some sort of karate?" he asked.

"What?" I managed, still reeling from the reaction of my traitorous body.

"Your martial arts training is Krav Maga and... Shotokan?"

My shoulders sagged. Everyone thought that. Just because a style was more popular, didn't mean it was better. "Goju Ryu."

"Close enough."

What was with Werewolves? Were they all martial art connoisseurs?

Good mate, my wolf panted.

Maybe, maybe not. I didn't trust my wolf. She'd been wrong before.

"I have you beat." Wick pressed his knee between my legs and nudged them apart. The move sent a shiver through my body. This man sure knew how to press my buttons. Heat rose from between my legs and my nose flared. Crap. If I could smell my desire, he could, too.

Wick didn't act like a man with a girlfriend or a werewolf with a mate, but John had mentioned a woman named Christine.

"What would Christine say?" I blurted out.

Wick's lips spread out to reveal his even white teeth and kissable dimples. "Christine? She can say whatever she wants. I'm not in a relationship with her."

My tense muscles relaxed a little. "Then why did John say—"

"Shhh." Wick pulled my arms above my head.

"Is this where you ask me to surrender?" I asked.

The pressure on my arms intensified, but not from Wick. From invisible hands. I stood paralyzed against the wall, unable to breathe or move, as memories from the past surged forth.

Dylan's hot breath seared my neck as he pinned my arms over my head and forced my bruised thighs apart with his knee. "Andrea McNeilly, you are mine."

My body tensed at the unexpected memory and my vision stained red. I hated Dylan flashbacks. They reminded me of weakness and humiliation. I promised myself long ago I would never put myself in a situation like that again, where I became less.

Wick frowned and loosened his grip on my wrists. "Where would the fun be in that?" His easy going words didn't match his hard tone, but he stepped back and beckoned me to join him in the middle of the room.

Thankful for the reprieve, I shook out the tightness

of my limbs as my reeling mind recovered. Must not show any weakness. People could use it against me. "How about we even the odds?" I asked.

Wick's white teeth flashed. "How do you propose we do that?"

I slowly moved my hand to the bottom of my shirt, a motion raptly watched by Wick. I pulled the cotton tee over my head and smiled. Inside, I felt twisted. I wanted to go back to the fun sparring, not release the painful memories I worked hard to suppress.

"I thought the purpose was to make this even."

"It is." I let the shirt fall to the floor.

Wick's irises lightened to wolf-gold. He stepped forward and then, looking unsure of my intent, stopped. "You will have the advantage if you fight naked." He eyed my bra as if he wanted to rip it off with his teeth. Part of me wished he would. His mouth flattened into a firm line and his body tensed as if he prepared to pounce.

"I don't plan to fight you naked." I dropped the sweatpants.

Wick's expression gleamed with understanding. He rose to the challenge. He removed his clothes without seduction, ripping them off. His outfit had given me a fair impression of what lay beneath, so seeing his naked body shouldn't have come as a surprise. But it still managed to shock me. His broad shoulders led to large, but not too large, pecs. And his chiseled abs tapered down into a narrow waist and a well-defined V. And following that farther down...

My gaze shot back up to Wick's face. He smirked,

unashamed of his arousal. His expression challenged me to react.

I reacted, all right. On the inside. My core revved like an engine, ready to go, and I tried to shove it back to idle with no success. Gritting my teeth, I forced my face to remain blank, despite the burning inferno in my body, racing heartbeat and the very tangible need to throw myself at him. His erection would go away when he shifted, but the image of his perfect, muscle-toned body wanting me would be imprinted in my memory for life. Not fair.

Shucking off my underwear and bra as fast as possible, I gave him little chance to admire my body. I shifted right away. Mountain lion fur rippled out as human skin folded in. I'd fully changed before Wick had started. From the looks of it, the process for a Were involved a lot more pain...and mess. Clear liquid oozed from Wick's altering form as bones cracked audibly.

Slinking low to the ground, I waited for him to finish before I pounced. Wick's wolf shook off the fluids from shifting. I changed direction mid-flight to avoid the spray. It hit the side of my body. *Gross.* I turned and snarled at him. His yellow gaze locked on me and he wagged his tail. I flicked mine in response and lunged again.

We played. No better word for it. We fought as if we were kits or pups in a litter, swatting at each other without extended claws, nipping without drawing blood, tackling without breaking bones.

When the day's activities wore on me, I collapsed on

the mats, panting from exhaustion. Wick joined me. Lying down on his side, his tongue rolled onto the mat as if he lacked the energy to correct it. I hacked in amusement and made the mistake of making eye contact.

He leaned over and licked my face. I swatted his head.

The wolf's grin mirrored Wick's human one to perfection. He shifted back and lay face down on the mats, drawing his breath in deep and slow, the faint gleam of sweat covered his body.

Wick turned toward me. "Shift back. You must be exhausted."

He was right, of course. The shift for me involved a lot more pain than it should have. It always did when I had less energy. When it finished, I lay naked and shaking.

Wick ran a jerky hand through his short hair, rubbing it back and forth. He watched me, muscles tense, without saying anything. I kept my attention trained on him, unsure of what to expect, and allowed my body to lay limp against the floor. The shaking stopped and I released a long breath.

"Hungry?" Wick asked, his earlier tension gone. His lazy expression caused me to hesitate. "For food," he clarified. Then he winked at me and shot to his feet in one smooth move.

"Starving," I managed to say without looking at his dick.

I stood up. It must've been a little too fast for my brain to follow because the room tilted. I staggered and started to topple over. A firm hand gripped my upper arm and stabilized me, kiboshing my feeble attempt at a falling tree impersonation.

"Maybe we shouldn't have been so vigorous." Wick grimaced. He eyed me critically, momentarily pausing on my breasts, before wandering back to my face. "This has probably set your healing back a few days. Your right shin's got a killer goose egg. I could play golf with it."

"Yeah. Sparring was a good idea."

"How do you figure?"

"It will postpone my little date with Lucien." And it told me three things about Wick. One, he'd kick my ass in a real fight; two, he had the body of a god and I wanted to lick it all over; and three, the potent attraction between us went both ways and I could potentially use it to escape.

All playfulness seeped out of Wick's face at my answer. His hand dropped to his side. "It delays the inevitable."

I shook my head. "A lot can happen in a few days."

Wick gave me a pained expression. "Please tell me you're not going to do something foolish like attempt to escape."

"If I told you, would you drop the guards?"

Wick shook his head. "I am forced to follow Lucien's orders."

"But I'm not."

"Not yet."

7

I ran. The sound of wolves howling filtered through the trees. The white light of the full moon illuminated the path. Leaves scattered in the wind as my paws sank into the soft soil, propelling me forward through a night smelling of lilacs and sweet jasmine.

Ears back, I ran faster.

The yips and growls grew closer, their hot breath on my feet and their sharp teeth chomping at my legs.

My foot snagged on a fallen log when I attempted to leap over it. Sprawled in the leaves, I twisted around.

A wolf stood over my quivering body. His icy yellow eyes bore holes into mine. Dylan.

"Easy," a deep voice resonated in my head. My eyes snapped open. Dark room. Stale air. "You're safe."

I gasped for breath. Yellow eyes met mine. I flinched, and then attempted to bolt. Sheets weighed me down. I paused and assessed the situation. Wick, not Dylan. Bedroom, not forest. I released a long stuttered breath.

"You were having a nightmare," Wick explained.

No shit. The sheen of sweat clung to my skin, illuminating my arms in the dark. I turned under the sheets, sticking to them a bit, and looked Wick square in the face.

He lay on his side, on the sheets, not under, wearing an old t-shirt and gray sweatpants—a Werewolf paperweight, keeping me prisoner under the bedding. I would have to roll off the side of the bed if I wanted to escape.

His hand rested on my hip. Heavy and large, it made me aware of the heat emanating from his body through the sheets.

He'd shaken me awake.

I eyed him suspiciously. What was he doing in my bed?

"Why Grandma, what big hands you have." When fear clung to me, like it did now, I found it best to bluff nonchalance. *Fake it till you make it.* I'd heard the slogan once on a reality show with models.

"Better to hold you with, my dear," he said, surprising me. I didn't think he would get the reference. Then again, the wolf story was based on a true Werewolf. He should know it.

The nightmare still clung to me like a silk bath robe after a shower. Those eyes haunted my sleep. If I closed my eyes again, I'd see them, crystal clear, as if they were real. Even after all these years, I hadn't truly escaped Dylan. He still lingered in my mind. Transported back to the hell I tried to forget, I looked into Wick's deep brown safe eyes, dark portals in the dim light, and relaxed.

Tension flowed from my body. Wick's white teeth flashed in the dark in response.

"What big teeth you have." I chuckled.

Wick's grin grew. "I'm not sure you're ready for me to respond to that."

I didn't think I was ready, either. I needed to get this conversation on a different path before it rolled completely in the gutter. "Taking your guard duty a little far, don't you think?" I waved a finger at his body next to mine.

"I don't trust you alone in the room."

Truth, but it seemed like a pretty lame reason to me. "The windows are locked," I pointed out. "And Were-proof."

"Ah, but you're not a Were. And locks can be broken or picked."

"That hadn't occurred to me," I said.

Wick growled.

"Aren't you afraid I'll smother you with a pillow?"

"You could try."

Sighing, I flipped onto my back.

"I would wake before you had a chance to do anything," Wick continued. He was right.

"I think I prefer dumb guards."

He chuckled, but then turned serious. "What was your nightmare about?" I didn't need to see his face to sense his frown. I heard the concern in his voice and smelled his confusion in the air.

"None of your business."

"If it keeps me awake, it will become my business."

"It's nothing."

"It didn't sound like *nothing*." Was he mocking me? My voice couldn't sound as bitchy or clipped as he just made out.

"It's in the past."

"Our past can come back to bite us."

Surprised at the irony, a laugh escaped my lips. "Interesting choice of words."

"Why don't you tell me about it?"

"You're my captor, not my therapist," I said, although his offer tempted a part of me.

Wick snorted. "Have it your way. It's an open invitation."

The silence stretched. "Good night." I wished my voice sounded more final.

"Good night." His soft reply kissed my skin.

8

"Fifteen two, fifteen four, fifteen six, fifteen eight, straight twelve and the jack make it thirteen." I laid the cards down for all to see. Not the best hand, but not the worst either.

Ryan groaned and leaned back in disgust. "Every time."

"One might think you cheated." John glared.

"Who me?" Batting my eyelashes, I moved my peg fourteen notches instead of twelve. They didn't notice.

John put his hand down. "Eight," he bit out.

I hated when people didn't count their points out. I watched him move the measly eight notches and suppressed a grin.

"It's ten," I said when he finished. A growl escaped John's throat as I moved my peg two more notches. In crib, if an opponent missed points in his or her own hand, another player could take them. Normally I didn't steal points, but John brought out the worst in me.

"Where?" John demanded.

I took his hand, counted out the points and tried not to look smug.

"Bitch," John grumbled and sat back. I half expected him to throw his cards. He exploded into tantrums when he didn't win. While healing, I'd come to know Wick's inner circle quite well, and planned to sleuth information from them. My devious plot failed. Nobody would tell me a thing. Not why Lucien wanted me, or how the Werewolves connected to him or my hit on Clint. Nothing. Nada. Zilch.

"Mutt," I replied. He snarled at me, but I ignored it. He knew his place.

"Calm down," Ryan said to John. "At least you win some of the games." He spoke the truth. John and I split the wins pretty much fifty-fifty, leaving poor Ryan out. He had the worst luck at cards, but luckily, he wasn't a sore loser. This last week in captivity would've been unbearable if I had to deal with two Werewolves having snits.

"Purge you," John said, but it lacked heat.

Biting back a laugh, I shuffled the cards. John and Ryan were good friends and bickered like an old married couple.

I dealt the next hand and ignored John's brooding look as he picked his cards up. Lousy poker face. Guess he blamed my dealing for his bad hand.

The slamming of the front door startled the cards out of my grasp. They sprayed out in all directions. Turning in unison, the three of us watched Wick stalk around the corner. Ryan and John stood up, while I remained in my seat. I sank into its plush cushions of the oversized armchair and waited.

Wick stopped in front of me. I tried not to be impressed by his dominant, attractive appearance, and failed.

Wick looked me up and down. His brow furrowed.

"What?" I asked.

"Try to look pathetic," he said. "And…"

The sound of the front door opening and closing cut him off.

"What the hell?" I asked.

Wick waved me off. Biting down a terse response, I looked at the other Weres. Their muscles tensed and their weight shifted to their toes. If they'd been in wolf form, their hackles would be raised.

The unmistakable scent of dried blood and dead meat hit my nose before a solid Asian man walked into the room.

"Vampire," I breathed.

"Lovely welcome," the Vampire's smooth voice rolled over my skin and raised goosebumps. He walked farther into the room, his graceful movements making him look like he almost glided. "I don't know what I was thinking, expecting house manners from dogs."

John's chest rumbled. One look from Wick stopped his growling. The Vampire wiped his hands off, as if touching the doorknob had soiled him. He looked around the room with obvious distaste and sneered at

John. "It appears you still need to house train some of your pack."

I frowned. The Vampire stole lines from my insult book, though it didn't sound so witty coming from him. But that wasn't what bothered me. I wanted to defend the Weres, and I shouldn't.

They're not pack.

Eyeing the Vampire, I decided he wasn't Lucien, but probably high up in the horde hierarchy. He was also one of the biggest East Asian men I'd ever seen. Not sumo wrestler big, either. His muscles strained under his well-tailored suit. Black hair cut short and chiseled features made him more handsome than he deserved.

The Vampire moved to stand in front of me, beside Wick. "Are you going to introduce us?" he asked.

I stood after he spoke; not out of respect, but necessity. Sitting down wasn't a good defensive position.

"Allan, this is our prisoner, Andrea."

Wick used my full name, thankfully. I didn't want to be on familiar terms with Allan.

"Allan?" I asked.

He dipped his head in acknowledgement. His gaze travelled up and down my body, assessing me.

"Doesn't exactly inspire a lot of fear," I stated.

Allan flashed his fangs. A Vampire smile unnerved me no matter how many times I saw one. "Is that what you would like, little girl?" His voice offered promises I didn't want.

I shrugged and refused to look away.

"Do you have a Chinese name?" I asked, purposely

making a mistake. I wanted to see how he'd react. The vampire's high cheekbones, strong jaw and large eyes made his country of origin difficult to place, but it was the slight accent that gave his ethnicity away.

"I'm Japanese," he said with a flat voice.

"Oh? I'm sorry. I didn't realize."

All three Weres snapped their heads to me, scenting both lies. Wick wasn't pleased. He stepped forward, like he wanted to throttle me.

Allan's hand on Wick's chest stopped him. "Easy, Wick."

Wick glanced down at Allan's fingers like he wanted to bite them. He must've thought better of it because he rested his weight on his heels.

Assured of Wick's compliance, Allan turned back to me. "You're not and you did," he said.

"Excuse me?" I asked.

"You're not sorry and you knew I had Japanese ancestry," Allan stated.

I crossed my arms. "Vampires can't scent lies."

"True. But we've had years and years to read humans."

"And masters gain powers as they age," Wick added, his voice warning.

"I like to think we're like fine wine. We get better with age." Allan examined his nails.

Oh shit. Please don't be a mind reader.

Allan flashed his fangs again.

"Ah fuck," I breathed, visualizing a forest with birds chirping away.

Allan laughed. "At least you're not an idiot. What a delight. Keep thinking of your sanctuary, Shifter. While you checked out my muscles and thought about my handsome face..." He lifted his eyebrows, daring me to contradict him. My cheeks flamed. Someone growled. "I got what I needed," Allan finished.

"And what was that?" I asked.

Allan ignored me and turned to Wick. "She deliberately antagonized me in hope I would harm her. It would delay her meeting with Lucien and give her more time to escape."

He'd read well past my surface bitchiness. Allan glanced in my direction and smiled. His fangs descended a little more—the Vampire equivalent of a hard on. *Gross.* He kept his gaze locked on mine while they grew longer.

Wick's chest rumbled, sending vibrations across the room. Or was that me?

"And if I accidentally killed her, at least it would be fast and not the slow, tortured, drawn out death like the one Lucien has planned."

I shuddered. Allan went deeper than I knew possible. What else had he seen?

"Don't suppose you'd like to clue me in on why I'm here? When did Lucien concern himself with hits on mere norms?"

He shook his head.

Jerk.

Allan's fanged smile broadened before he nodded at me and turned to Wick.

"What piques my interest, wolf, is why you shield so tightly." He leaned in. "What is it you don't want me to see?"

Wick directed an unfriendly smile at Allan. "You've groped enough nerve endings here. I think it's time you ruined someone else's night."

"The night is still young," Allan agreed. "One week," he said, glancing at me before gliding toward the exit. "Then we'll see how deep I can go."

The door clicked shut and released whatever hold Allan had on us.

"Ugh," I said, brushing off my shoulders. "Vampires."

"For once, we agree," John said. "I feel dirty being near them."

Ryan grabbed his sweater from the couch and put it on. The room wasn't cold.

"Handsome?" Wick asked, still standing in front of me. He hadn't moved.

"Seriously?" I asked. I put my hands on my hips and waited for Wick to move out of my way. He didn't. "Out of everything he said that's what you comment on?"

Wick shrugged. "The rest is expected."

"Yeah." Ryan nodded. "Pain, death, torture, suffering...yada, yada, yada. Vamp threats are all the same."

If that was true, why did Wick and Ryan look worried?

9

The hairpin snapped. I grimaced and looked down at the traitorous half that fell from the lock. I bit my tongue to stop the curse threatening to burst from my mouth. Those dogs could hear anything. I'd been in Wick's house for another week now, healing faster than I'd like and waiting for an opportunity to escape. My days filled with watching paternity tests on daytime television, kicking some ass playing cards and sparring with Wick. My nights filled with restless sleep while I tried to ignore the beefy paperweight sleeping next to me.

No opportunity to escape presented itself, the guard duty impeccable. Never left alone, not one window cracked open, not one door unlocked. My little date with Lucien became more of an impending reality. Allan's visit made everything more real. I didn't get to stay and play at the Wick Wonderland forever. My introduction to the Master Vampire would be any day now. I was royally screwed.

I picked up the piece of my hairpin and worked on the other half still jammed in the window lock. I didn't possess any lock picking skills, but when Wick told me to "sit and stay" like a good little puppy in his room, I decided it couldn't hurt to try. At least it felt like a more productive way to pass the time than counting threads in the sheets or looking through Wick's drawers. He wore boxer briefs. My mind drifted to the first time we'd sparred. He hadn't been wearing anything then.

Focus. I bit my lip while I concentrated on the jagged end of the pin. I wanted out of this locked room. *Sit and stay.* Wick used those exact words. The audacity! His cheeky smile made me want to punch him in the face. I wasn't his to command.

Keeping my rage close to the surface, I continued to wiggle the pin. It helped distract me from what else I would like to do with that man's face. Talk about Stockholm syndrome. I needed out of here.

The end of the pin snapped off when I pulled it to the side. I flailed backward. My head snapped back against the floor and pretty little stars danced in my vision. I took a deep breath to find some inner calm and failed. Sitting up anyway, I assessed my progress. A jagged end of the pin protruded out of the lock, barely enough to pinch between my finger and thumb. If I didn't get it out, Wick would notice and I knew how he'd punish me.

I enjoyed our daily sparring. Wick kept trying to goad me

to shift to my wolf form. That would be a mistake. I avoided shifting altogether, much to his disappointment. The stripping down process with him watching felt like a mistake. Too much heat in his gaze and too much energy between us.

Time to escape.

I made a promise years ago. Never get trapped again. Never be *owned*. I shut my eyes against the memories and the images of Dylan's face. At least I no longer had panic attacks.

"Shame on you," a deep voice startled me.

I cursed and scrambled to my feet. My muscles protested the quick movement. Wick leaned against the door frame with his arms crossed. His lips quirked up at one side and his eyes crinkled. Wrapped up in my attempt to escape out the window, I failed to hear him approach the room or open the door. Andrea McNeilly, badass assassin.

"Those anti-picking locks are expensive." He squinted in my direction. "You better make sure you get that pin out."

Fuck that. I'd leave the broken pin jammed in the lock now to spite him. I made a show of brushing off my sweats. They weren't dirty.

"I wonder why your room is equipped as a prison." I crossed my arms to match Wick's stance. "Keeping a lady friend too difficult?"

A growl escaped Wick's throat, sending shivers down my spine. "All the rooms are set up this way. The meeting is over, by the way. You can come downstairs now." He turned to leave. "And for the record—I never have to force a *lady friend* to do anything." He shut the door firmly as he left.

Probably not a good idea to piss off the Alpha, which was apparently what I just did. That didn't worry me too much. But why keep me in his room if any of the bedrooms would suffice as a prison? I didn't like the answer my brain gave me. I paced around the room. Maybe there were other prisoners.

Eavesdropping on the pack meeting might've answered some questions, but when I'd placed my ear against the cold and lifeless wood door, solid oak from the smell, not even my superior Shifter hearing could pick up anything. They'd all be leaving now.

I wouldn't race downstairs on Wick's heels like a lovesick puppy. Even if he did have a nice ass. I flopped onto the bed, spilling throw pillows onto the floor. The ceiling had been recently painted. The crisp white glared back, illuminated by a pendant styled light fixture. The home décor in this place so tasteful and precise it drove me nuts. Things needed imperfections.

I glanced over at the lock with my pin lodged in it and smiled. I made my mark and it was better than having to pee on something.

I EXPECTED TO SEE THE USUAL BRAT PACK

lounging in Wick's living room for lunch, but the room appeared empty. "Where is everyone?"

Ryan looked up from the newspaper in the dining room and smiled. Every day he tackled the *Preternatural Times* crossword and failed. Even on the easy Monday ones. I couldn't judge. I sucked at them too—not that I would let on. Four letter word for *'it's usually a drag'*? Bunt? Seriously? What sane person would know that?

Three days ago when Wick sent Ryan away on some chore for the pack, I hid the newspaper and switched it with the paper on the next day. Ever since, Ryan worked a day old crossword. He never checked the dates and hadn't caught on. I kept the newest paper with the answers for the previous day's crossword well hidden.

I might not be a crossword genius, but a genius in my own rights. The Weres thought I was a human encyclopedia.

"They went with Wick on an errand."

"Does he need that much backup?"

"Yes." Ryan focused on the crossword. His brow furrowed.

"Why?" I slid into the seat across from him. Ryan glanced up. "Lucien."

That stopped me from assessing Ryan's lack of progress on the puzzle. I looked up and briefly met Ryan's piercing blue eyes before his gaze slid away.

"Did he send for Wick?" I asked.

Ryan sighed. "If you think Wick would go to him willingly, you haven't been paying attention."

Sinking back in my seat, I looked around. And bit

back a gasp. The windows behind Ryan in the dining room were open.

Open!

I hadn't noticed when I came downstairs. *How could I miss that?*

"They should be back soon." Ryan glanced up from the paper.

Huh? Oh. Wick and the other Werewolves. They'd be back soon. I'd have to act fast. I glanced over at Ryan. He was quick. Too quick for me to make a run for it. I'd have to distract or incapacitate him to escape. And I needed to make my move before the others returned.

"What's a five letter word for wolf?" Ryan asked, oblivious to my conundrum.

I gave him a flat stare. "Seriously?"

"What?" He looked up, confused. Even I wasn't that bad. "Lupus?"

His white teeth flashed as he scribbled in the letters. I got up and looked around. Maybe I could find a baseball bat and knock him out. Too risky. Weres were difficult to sneak up on and if he caught me skulking around with a beater stick, my chance to escape would be gone. Let my cat maul him? He didn't deserve that. I couldn't shift to a falcon in my clothes. My wings would get caught in the bulky material. If I shifted in a different room, he'd smell the change and be waiting to intercept me. I had to shift close to the window. Naked.

It would be difficult to explain why I stripped. Unless...

Thinking it over, I walked into the kitchen and looked for my hidden paper.

"Okay, Andropedia," Ryan said. The nickname made me smile and my stomach twist.

"What's ten letters for 'horsewoman who barely made it through town'? Two words and starts with an L."

"Hmm. Let me think," I stalled.

I'd hid today's newspaper with the cleaning supplies under the kitchen sink. I made a show of cleaning up on a regular basis so it would explain why I kept going into the cupboard. Maybe I spent too much effort on something as trivial as crossword superiority. It wouldn't help me escape. It did, however, provide me with a form of entertainment.

Rummaging around the various bottles, I pulled out the all-purpose cleaner and today's newspaper. I knocked over a white bottle and reached to pick it up. When I realized what I held, I smiled. Bitter Apple—the dog repellent that discouraged chewing and used for helping new Weres gain control. Perfect.

"Well?" Ryan asked.

"I'm still thinking," I called out. "Go to the next one."

"I already have," Ryan grumbled. I don't think he meant for me to hear.

"Lady Godiva?" I said, reading off the crossword. "Does that fit?"

"Of course!" Ryan exclaimed. "That makes sense.

She rode through town naked. Whoever writes these crosswords has a great sense of humour."

I coughed to hide my groan.

"I would never have thought of that," Ryan said.

Me neither. Walking over to the living room, I hid the bottle of Bitter Apple under the couch. "Have you seen the remote?" I asked.

"No. Isn't it on the coffee table?"

Pretending to look surprised, I picked up the remote. "So it is. I must be blind." I flicked on the television. "Want to find out if you ARE the father?"

Ryan chuckled. "Normally I like to refrain from watching trash TV before noon, but okay. I need a break from this one anyway." He threw down the pen and pushed away from the table. I waited until he walked away from the open windows and over to me before I made my move.

"What are you doing?" Ryan asked as I removed my shirt.

"I thought that might be obvious." I slunk up to him. He flinched when I reached out.

"I can't touch you," he said. "Wick's orders."

"Wick said nothing about me touching you." I slid my hands up Ryan's chest and over his shoulders. My body pressed against his. I reached back and popped my bra off. The friction against his body made my nipples hard.

"Seems unfair." His voice roughened.

"That's the thing about Alpha orders. There will

come a point where your own basic needs will break the command."

I would know. Survival instincts and desire were the two emotions powerful enough to break the will of an Alpha.

Ryan raised his brow. "He'll find out."

Running my hand down his hard chest, I smiled. "Tell him I took advantage of you. It will be the truth."

Ryan laughed and opened his mouth to speak when I pressed my finger against his lips.

"No more talking." I used my favourite line. It worked every time.

I leaned up, rubbing my breasts against his chest again, and nipped his jaw. He growled in response. He tried to reach out, but Wick's compulsion held him back. I kissed him gently. He tried to say something, but I slipped my tongue between his parted lips.

My wolf stayed silent. She didn't want Ryan. And if I was honest with myself, I didn't want him either. Ryan would figure it out, too. I had to act fast.

I pushed him onto the couch and let him lie there while I slowly removed my sweatpants and undies. I crawled on top of him. One part of his body had no difficulty reacting to me. My one hand pinned both of his over his head—a pitiful hold, but he couldn't move against it. Not yet. Not unless he knew I planned to escape.

I ground against his hard erection. He growled again, but this time it originated somewhere deeper and more primal, close to breaking Wick's control. While I kissed him again, I groped the side of the couch for the bottle. My fingers brushed along the smooth surface and I grasped the container.

Giving no warning or apology, I leaned back and sprayed him in the face.

Ryan howled in pain. He swung out blindly. Out of his reach and running toward the window, I spread my arms out and willed the change. My shift quick, I soared out the window and into the fresh spring air. Free. At last.

10

The wind pressed the underside of my wings—the familiar pressure a gentle caress. Ever present, the bird's predator instincts weren't as aggressive as the wolf or mountain lion; instead, it soothed and brought a sense of peace to whatever inner turmoil raged inside me.

Ryan would be calling Wick right now. Something pinged in my little bird chest—because I betrayed Ryan's trust or Wick's? Ryan didn't deserve what I did to him, but it was gentler than a bat to the head or a mountain lion mauling. I lacked options.

No. No point in regretting my escape. Seducing Ryan and leaving Wick were a small price to pay for freedom. They might be great guys and Wick might be...well, something, but they'd both give me up to the Vampire Master in the end.

I angled toward the park where I left my car and

shook away any further thoughts of the werewolves like a player shaking off women with attachment issues.

Circling the parking lot a couple of times gave me the confidence that the area remained wolf free. Midday on a work week, no norms or other supes milled around either.

As soon as I touched down beside my car, I shifted back. Automatically my cat and wolf pushed forward, fighting to dominate my senses. A strong need to analyze the area emerged—to sniff out information like a hound dog or prowl around as an angry cat. Both tempting.

I'd learned the hard way not to think of the wolf or mountain lion in falcon form. Being much smaller and different in nature, I struggled to keep focused. I didn't want to shift into a hundred and twenty pound mountain lion mid-flight. Luckily, when I'd first learned this lesson, I'd been close to the ground and walked away from the learning opportunity with only a broken arm and splitting headache.

I straightened and eyed my car in dismay. The dilapidated rusty-red Ford Contour. I purchased it solely for its ability to get from A to B without drawing attention.

Good luck with that now.

It reeked of wolves and bums—not the Gluteus Maximus kind of bum, the homeless kind. They'd smashed all the windows save the front windshield and the trunk hung open at a weird angle. Multiple tickets caked the wipers and the one intact piece of glass. They flapped in the wind in greeting. Smells of urine, garbage and dirty sex radiated from the interior. A miracle my A to B car hadn't been towed.

The metal emitted a loud, nail-grating sound as I pried the trunk open farther. I peered inside and groaned.

Tipping my head back to look at the sky, I tried to calm down. Everything was gone, including my emergency clothes. They were probably outfitting one of downtown's homeless right now. The instinctive predatory urge to track them down hit me. My cat hissed, clawing to get out.

Settle down. They're just clothes.

Mine, she said.

Ignoring the cat and her territorial issues, I ran through my options. I'd have to drive out of here naked as the day I entered life. When I opened the front door, I saw shards of glass scattered on the driver seat. *Fuck.*

After brushing the majority of the glass off, I sat down. Despite being tempered, the curdled pieces dug into my ass, promising an extremely uncomfortable drive.

I reached under the wheel and ripped the panel off. My spare set of keys fell out. If someone was motivated enough to get the panel off and hotwire my car, they may as well have the keys, because they were going to drive off with it anyway. At least this way there'd be less damage to the car if I ever recovered it. I looked around the interior of my molested car and sighed.

A to B started right away, which surprised me. I patted the dash and thanked her, before reaching over to close the empty glove box. I didn't want to listen to the door bouncing around.

As soon as I drove over the first speed bump, the glove box flopped open. It swung back and forth, held in place by one hinge. I went over another speed bump. *Swish, swish, swish*. I ripped the glove box door off and flung it into the backseat.

Too risky to go to my house. My insurance papers had the address on them and I assumed the wolves knew it. Too bad. I loved that place. Instead, I would drive as far as the gas in my tank would take me toward my safe house before I shifted to my falcon.

I would have gone straight there after escaping from Wick's stronghold, but my wing started to ache. I desperately hoped they'd missed my car, but Wick's pack was thorough.

The light turned red and I slowed to a stop. Maybe a thief had my insurance papers. My fingers drummed on the steering wheel while the wheels in my head turned over and over. I eyed the wires that stuck out from the centre console where my radio had once been. No music on this road trip.

By now, Wick knew I escaped and would search for me with the rest of his pack. They'd check the parking lot.

I made a decision and flicked on my left turn signal. Some of the cars behind me honked in outrage. It pissed me off when people signalled late as well. Instead of flipping them off, I owned it and waved. *Sorry.*

My house was too good to not try first. A drive by with the window down would be all I needed to sniff the air and figure out if the wolves had been there. I glanced at my broken windows and smirked. No need to roll them down.

II

Attachment to anything or anyone was a professional error. I would leave this place if I had to, but it didn't mean I had to like it.

The block my house sat on was deserted. The work day had yet to end. Living in a neighbourhood full of professionals certainly had its advantages. Only a few had kids and I was thankful for that. I didn't dislike children, but they were too curious for their own good. I would move before I took out a child for seeing something not fit for young eyes. And I hated moving.

My home was a two bedroom, two bathroom condo. Well, one and a half bathrooms if you're a realtor. The dark blue siding contrasted with the crisp white trim. Inside, the open concept made a bright spacious area. The main selling feature was the master bedroom, with a walk-in closet and a gorgeous ensuite featuring a deep soaker tub. But I liked the bay windows with seating the best. There'd been countless mornings where I dragged my sorry ass out of bed to sit wrapped up in a warm blanket against the windows. I'd sip my coffee and watch other people battle the elements for their morning exercise. I didn't need to run in the rain. My Shifter metabolism and martial arts training kept me svelte enough.

I made two laps around the block—once in each direction. Time and daylight slipped away with each full roll of my tires. Once night fell I'd have to contend with a horde of Vampires as well as the pack. A faint smell of wolf lingered in certain nooks, but nothing fresh. They'd been here.

Wick had been here. Though faint, his telltale sugar aroma blended with the signature Werewolf scent of rosemary and rushed into my body as if my wolf sucked it in.

The idea of nipping in and out to grab some clothes before they got here flashed in and out of my mind. A risk. Too much of a risk.

"For fuck's sake. I can't catch a break."

I navigated my car from the curb and made my way to the highway. In the rear-view mirror, I said goodbye to my home. My stomach dropped at the thought of losing yet another place, one that started to feel like a home. My handler would have to sell the condo for me.

My handler.

Time to pay Landen a visit. This wasn't a straightforward hit. First, I got caught. Second, the Master Vampire wanted to see me about it. Third, Clint had been a norm. I needed more information and Landen had it.

But the safe house came first. My handler would take me more seriously as an interrogator if I had clothes on.

There was an odd disconnect to driving on the motorway naked with all the windows smashed. At first, I felt exposed, uncomfortable and cold. Frigid air burst through the open portals of my car and slammed against my exposed flesh, and there was nothing I could do about the open stares, leers and the judgmental frowns of each passerby. I drove faster and focused on my goal.

When the gas light blinked on I took the next off ramp. Part of me gave thanks for being done with the high speed wind tunnel portion of the trip and the other part of me was disappointed I didn't make it farther and would have to cover the rest of the distance by wing. I would be sore—very sore.

If I made it.

A cramped wing over the Strait of Georgia wasn't something I needed. I couldn't shift into a fish.

The sun had set half an hour ago. The air, when not blasting against my skin during the drive, felt mild, not bad for a long flight. The odds danced in my favour for once—the air currents moved in the right direction.

With the last of my gas, I rolled the car into a Supe-Mart parking lot, and got out. My arm ached when I stretched, still fatigued from my initial flight. An angry red spot marked the bullet hole. The skin strained thin over the wound, feeling raw with a shiny look, but more healed than it should've been. Wick's pack magic somehow sped up the healing process through my wolf. I didn't want to think about the implications or the possibility of belonging to another pack.

The wind swirled around me and I froze mid-stretch. Wolf.

I looked up to see two SUVs barrelling toward me. With no time to think, I willed the shift. The sting was fast and gripping. My arms condensed into solid wings and a sharp pain radiated from my injury.

My wings beat frantically to take off. I got a few feet in the air when a heavy weight slammed me back to the ground.

Shaking my head cleared some of the stars. I hopped around underneath what I now realized was a net. Someone's hand grabbed my wings through the net and flipped me onto my back—a submissive position in any form.

Men surrounded me, appearing larger because of my size and vantage point; their wolf-yellow glares an unwelcome sight. Their wolves were close. The flight or fight instinct of my falcon kicked in and I flapped and twisted uncontrollably under the net trying to get away. I couldn't turn over. My screech of frustration echoed off the pavement and the walls of the surrounding mall. My head snapped from side to side searching for a way out. I'd been so close. The taste of freedom still lingered in my mouth.

Another SUV pulled up and a large man stepped out. Anger vibrated off him. Wick.

He stepped up to the other men and joined them in

their group glare—his big frame more imposing as he loomed over my petite form.

"Shift," he said. His Alpha power rolled over my feathers.

I flapped my wings against the net in defiance.

Wick squatted down beside me. "Do not mistake my past congeniality as weakness. I will pluck every feather from that bird body of yours until you shift."

A shiver rippled through me. Pluck my feathers?

No, thank you.

"Shift." The power in his voice called to my wolf, demanding obedience. Fucking alphas.

I used the momentum of his power to change, not out of submission, but because I was partial to my feathers. My mountain lion rippled out.

"Christ!" One of the men holding down the net leapt back. He hadn't been briefed.

"Hold her down."

The men standing back joined their pack mates as they held the net down on my rage. I railed against the barrier. My claws snagged in the mesh. Too strong to rip apart, the skin at the base of my nails tore instead, releasing the coppery scent of blood into the night. Abandoning the effort with my paws, I lurched forward with a snarl and tried to bite my way through—until my gums started bleeding, too. These Weres had arrived well prepared. My ears pinned to the back of my head as a hiss ripped from my throat.

The pack smelled of triumph, confidence and pride. One smelled of fear. I turned to him and yowled.

The sound hung in the air. The young wolf averted his gaze, but held strong.

My thoughts of freedom vanished.

I huffed again and lay my heavy head down on my front paws.

"If you're done with your temper tantrum, it's time to shift back," Wick said.

I turned my feline gaze to him and hissed again.

He held up sweat pants and a t-shirt. "If you shift now, I'll let you ride back fully clothed."

I licked the blood off my front paw.

"Just because you have no feathers to pluck, doesn't mean we're at an impasse."

I shifted my attention to my other paw.

"Don't make this harder on yourself, Andy. We have tranq guns."

His statement froze my tongue. I hated tranquilizers. The recovery from one shot meant days of feeling like the sludge from the bottom of a stale beer barrel.

"Shift."

I hacked, knowing he was right. They could tranq me and haul my cat ass into a cage. My body shook from exhaustion as soon as my cat form shifted to human. Cold air hit my naked flesh. I shoved my shaking hands under my armpits.

The net lifted. Wick flung the clothes, smacking me in the face, and adding insult to injury. I clutched the soft material in my hands and slowly stood up. The blood I missed caked to the base of my nails. Ignoring the full body ache as best I could, I clambered into the sweatpants and t-shirt. As soon as I pulled the shirt over my head a hand with an iron grip clamped onto my arm. Wick ignored my glare and hauled me to the nearest SUV. John sat in the driver's seat and adjusted the rearview mirror to give me a smug look. I flipped him off. He chuckled and put the vehicle in gear and drove without saying a word. Wick sat in the back beside me, gripping my arm hard. Obviously, he didn't want to take any chances that I'd get away. Like I'd manage that in an SUV. His anger stunk up the whole vehicle, tickling my nose. I sneezed. The silence was heavy and oppressing.

"Did you think I wouldn't try to escape?" I asked.

Wick shook his head and refused to speak or look at me.

"You would do the same thing," I said. Why did I feel defensive?

Wick continued to stare straight ahead. The tightening pressure on my arm, the only indication that he'd heard. I let out a big sigh and slumped back in my seat.

After a long, quiet drive back to the house, John pulled up and parked. After taking the keys out of the ignition, he dropped his hands to his lap and waited. No one moved or spoke.

Wick's soft voice broke the silence. "I will meet you inside, John."

The other wolf nodded and hopped out of the SUV. I leaned over to get out of the vehicle. A deep sense of apprehension covered me like a blanket and I suddenly had no desire to be alone with Wick.

Wick yanked my arm and I flailed in his direction.

"Nice try," he said. He opened his door and pulled me out after him. He turned to me midway up the drive. "Ryan despises you."

"Because of the crossword thing?" I feigned ignorance.

"Crossword thing?" Wick sputtered, clearly not expecting my response. "No." He glared. "The seducing and then spraying dog repellant in his face thing."

I shrugged.

"You have made an enemy."

I shrugged again. "Not on purpose."

He gave me a flat look. "In a time where you need all the allies you can get, you made a stupid move."

"Oh? Are you saying you or anyone else in your pack will run to my defence when I meet Lucien? Or that if I play nice, you'll stow me away instead of shipping me off to Lucien?"

Wick looked away.

Got him there.

We stood awkwardly in the driveway. I had a feeling Wick waited for me to say something.

"I wasn't planning to use him," I said. Without further words, we walked toward the house. This was the longest driveway ever and this conversation got more uncomfortable by the minute.

"He will see it that way."

"He shouldn't. I saw an opportunity and I took it."

"To seduce him?" His voice raw.

"Of course not. The opportunity was the open window. I could incapacitated Ryan a number of ways. I chose the way I would enjoy the most." Not completely true. I chose the way that would do the least physical damage. I didn't want to hurt Ryan.

Wick stopped walking. "What?"

"I like him." Not *exactly* a lie. I didn't specify *how* I liked him.

Wick must've heard the truth in my statement because he pursed his lips and his shoulders sagged a little. "Maybe it's a good thing he hates you."

"Maybe he won't after I have a chance to explain."

"You will not pursue him."

The command hit my wolf and made her want to roll over. My vision narrowed and turned red. My hands flew to my hips. "You do not have the right to dictate who I do or do not like or choose to pursue."

Wick stepped in. I refused to give ground to him, so we stood an inch apart. Wick's espresso eyes sparkled as yellow specks appeared. They turned golden. I watched in fascination as his wolf rose close to the surface. I should play submissive and not antagonize the big Alpha wolf.

"You are mistaken. I have every right."

"And why is that?"

He grabbed my wrists and pulled me closer. My body pressed into his. The growling vibrated through his chest.

"You are my mate," he rumbled.

A shiver tore through my body. My wolf howled and acknowledged the truth in his words. She'd known all along. Heat spread through my body and pooled between my legs. The scent of my desire mingled with Wick's. My shocked gaze flashed to his, the yellow in my irises reflecting back to me. My wolf surged forward, demanding control. I couldn't hold her back. *Ah fuck.*

His mouth crushed mine.

Hunger spiralled up and my mouth melted into his lips. The smouldering warmth inside built to a boil, threatening to explode.

"Mine," Wick growled against my mouth.

Dylan's powerful frame built for intimidation smothered me. He savoured the air, my scent laced with trepidation and terror, his aphrodisiac. "Andrea McNeilly, you are mine."

A cold shiver sliced through me more sharply than the memory. I pushed against Wick's solid chest and broke contact.

"No," I breathed, stemming the panic attack.

"No?" Wick released me in surprise.

"No," I said more firmly, shaking my head.

His nose flared. "You have nothing to fear." He gripped my arms as if he wanted to shake some sense into me, but I couldn't look at his face.

My wolf leapt up again, seeking control. I squashed her down and shook my head again. "I'll not be controlled again," I said. My cat's awareness answered my call. Her dominance smashed my wolf away and broke the connection with Wick's wolf. He shuddered.

His hands dropped to his side, limp. After a moment, he seemed to regain his composure. "What do you mean *again*?"

I shook my head. Dylan's words raced around, bouncing off the inside of my skull. *You are mine.*

Wick pursed his lips. For the first time since I met him, uncertainty blanketed his face. He opened his mouth to say something else, so I jumped in to change the topic and the mood.

"You have a job to do." Keeping all emotion from my voice, I let my familiar stony expression slide over my face. I nodded toward the house, knowing full well my behaviour was mean and unfair. "Lead on, Captor."

A bead of sweat pebbled on my nose as I fought to remain still and not squirm under Wick's hard gaze. It threatened to crack my cold resolve, break the barriers I erected between anyone and myself. My walls did the job for years. But one penetrating look from Wick and they weakened under the force.

I crossed my arms and stared back.

"As you wish." His voice steel. Wick pulled me forward and we walked to the house in silence.

12

Apprehension shimmied down my spine as my four car entourage pulled up the long manicured driveway to a huge mansion. Lucien lived on South Marine drive. What did I expect? The house looked like one off a Hollywood reality show, with multiple levels, palm trees, a pool and some serious landscaping. Palm trees? In Vancouver?

Normally I would have felt like a princess...or the president, but the bound hands, cold stares and silent treatment ruined the fantasy. They didn't gag me or put a bag over my head. That surprised me. Then again, everyone knew where Lucien's lair was and nothing I said or did would prevent this meeting.

Since the situation with Wick in the driveway, I'd kept my cat close and my panting, hormonal wolf deeply suppressed. Wick wasn't pleased. He only spoke to me if required. *"Change the channel. I will not watch that."* Frustration and anger embedded in every word.

The rest of the pack, sensing his mood, behaved as if on edge. Without having to say anything, I knew they blamed me. Plenty of death stares and cold shoulders were sent in my direction.

Wick didn't bat an eyelash when I asked for a separate room. I guess we silently agreed we needed space and detachment. He had a sick sense of humour. Ryan was my personal guard. Awkward didn't cover it.

Learning from his mistake, he treated me as a true prisoner. The perfect professional.

The solitude gave me too much time to reflect on my life. Since I started working for the SRD, I merely existed. Working on finding my humanity after thirty years of living like an animal. No goals for my life except to survive and get from point A to point B, like my car, moving from one hit to the next. I compartmentalized my trauma—using my body to lure targets but avoiding intimate relationships. Sure, I enjoyed the simple things in life, like chocolate and sleeping in on rainy days, but that wasn't enough. Not anymore.

I'd wanted to find my birth parents, to learn what I was and how to control it, but once the SRD hired me, I never had the opportunity to pursue it. I should've found a way to access the sealed files years ago. Now, I might never have the chance.

Vampires only wanted healthy, fully recovered prisoners for two reasons. One, they lasted longer under torture; and two, they tasted better. Facing what would most likely be my imminent death, had me thinking, wishing, but most of all regretting. I was born with the great gift of shifting, which came with the added bonus of an extended lifetime. And I used it to do what? Capturing and killing supes for the government? The same administration that withheld information from me?

Not all my fault.

No. Dylan had twisted my lifeline and spat me back out on a different path.

Regret was a nasty emotion. It didn't smell good either. During the remaining portion of my captivity, whenever I was allowed out of my room, a number of Weres wrinkled their noses in my presence and kept their distance. They could think what they wanted. I refused to correct them. Not even Wick.

The car pulled up and stopped in front of the solid wood, double door entrance. Two Vampires who looked like they belonged to the goon squad opened the car doors. Both Caucasian with dark hair slicked back and wearing black tailored suites with sunglasses. At night.

Vampires were all about image, but I still made fun of people who wore sunglasses inside or at night. I disliked them on sight. The scent of dead meat wafted off their skin.

"Get out," one of them said.

I shimmied over and exited the vehicle as gracefully as possible with my arms bound. My hands shook, and I clasped them together. Sometimes I didn't like to be the centre of attention. This would be one of those times. I didn't look over at Wick as a matter of pride. His anxiety rolled over the entire pack. I didn't like knowing Wick worried; it didn't help my nerves or my situation.

My chest hurt and I had this insane need to pee, even though I'd gone before we left. The Vampires led me through a grand foyer. It looked like I expected—lavish, expensive and overdone. Lucien had many lifetimes to accumulate wealth and he spent at least some of it on his interior decorating.

When I entered what must've been meant as a grand ballroom, I knew right away which Vampire was Lucien despite the crowd. He looked like an Italian model. Maybe he was at one point in his life. Vampires never gifted immortality to the ugly and probably had a rule in their Vampire Code on the matter.

Lucien emanated power and my heartbeat picked up in response. The other Vampires in the room lined a red carpet that led to his throne-like chair, their bodies leaning slightly toward him. The two cookie-cutter Vampires dragged me down the runway between the rows of minions while Wick followed close behind. The situation oddly reminded me of medieval courtrooms where criminals were hauled in front of their king before he bellowed, "Off with their head!" Not good. Definitely not good.

Surveying the room made things worse. My heart gave up its racing speed and settled into a hard lump in the middle of my chest. No way could I escape a pack of Werewolves and a horde of Vampires. There had to be at least fifty supes in the room. Their dead scents flowed in the air currents.

Most of the guards had handguns strapped to them in holsters, some carried semi-automatic rifles and two of the ones we passed at the main entrance had bows and arrows.

My arm twitched in pain at the thought of being shot again in falcon form. Not a pleasant thought.

My charm and charisma would have to get me through this.

My stomach dropped. *I'm doomed.*

Allan stood directly to Lucien's left. He probably heard my entire inner dialogue. We made eye contact. He winked. Yup, he'd heard it all. After envisioning punching his face in, he rewarded me with a toothy grin.

"Andrea," Lucien's said in a smooth velvet voice, bringing my attention back to him. Every other head in the room turned toward me.

"Lucien." I dipped my head in formality. "Is there a title I should use?"

A dimple appeared on Lucien's porcelain skin when he smiled. No fangs. Good sign. He didn't plan to eat me...yet. "Lucien is fine," he said.

An awkward pause stretched as we considered one another. I still didn't know what he wanted with me. This night would be a long one if someone didn't start talking. "I hear you have some questions for me?" I asked.

"Who do you work for?"

"The SRD," I said. When everyone in the room stiffened, including the wolves, I frowned. "Surely you knew that?" I looked over at Wick. He had his head down, but his brow furrowed. He hadn't known. He must've thought I worked as a mercenary.

"I did," Lucien agreed. I looked up to see a thoughtful look on his face. The knowing smile on Allan's told me how he'd found out.

"You really dug around in here." I tapped my head.

Allan grinned.

"You would have me believe the SRD sanctioned a hit on a human?" Lucien asked.

I shrugged. "It's not my job to question. I received the order from my handler. It seemed odd, but I carried it out."

Lucien leaned forward in interest. "And who would that be?"

"Who?" Nice. Play dumb. *Maybe he'll be lenient on me if he thinks I'm an idiot.*

Allan chuckled and shook his head.

"Your handler," Lucien sighed.

He could torture it out of me, of course. But he probably already had that on the agenda. I tried not to think about what else Lucien planned. "Why are you so interested in a norm anyway?"

"An excellent question." Lucien snapped his fingers. A figure who'd been standing behind him moved.

Clint stepped into the light.

13

If it weren't for the vise-like grip on my arms from the Weres beside me, I would've toppled over when I staggered. I squinted at Clint. It didn't make sense. He stood perfectly healthy and unaided, his neck unblemished.

"Ah fuck," I said.

Lucien's slow smile spread across his face. It didn't make me feel warm or fuzzy. "I believe you are acquainted with my human servant?"

"How?" I asked.

"Human servant," John hissed into my ear. He may as well have tacked on "you idiot," because that's what his tone implied.

I shook my head, ignoring John. My attention remained glued on Clint. "I tore your neck out, human servant or not, that's hard to survive."

"It was." Clint's voice was raspier than I remembered. "Thanks for that."

"Nothing personal." I offered a smile, only to be met with a blank stare.

"When I recall your behaviour in my hotel room, I'd have to disagree with you," Clint said. "That was very... *personal*."

No amount of forceful thinking could stop the warmth spreading through my cheeks, and Allan's knowing grin only made it worse. I could smell Wick's outrage behind me. My brain clamped down on any thoughts of him before Allan could pick more from my brain.

"I'm inclined to agree with Clint." Lucien's brows bunched together and his lips puckered out in a classic "angry model" look. Reading emotion on a master's face never meant anything good. It meant they'd lost their tight grip of control. "Attacking my human servant when he didn't break any of the SRD's pitiful human laws is a personal attack on me."

"I was following orders." My voice was firm.

"Ah, but whose?"

I frowned. He had a point. I worked off the assumption Landen relayed the SRD's orders. He could've gone rogue, taking orders from someone other than the SRD. The muscles in my body tensed as I came to a conclusion. I'd been played.

My vision stained dark red. I wanted to smash something. My brain tingled while my animals within howled. I felt the stirring of the beast and quickly squashed it down in order to become detached. I looked at Lucien.

He must've seen my fury, because a slow, mean smile spread across his face.

"I'm not sure, but I plan to find out."

Lucien looked over at Allan, the Vampire lie detector, who gave a slight nod.

"Yes, you will." Lucien walked the few steps down from his throne to stand in front of me, before running a finger down my face. His touch was cold, like ice, and despite the gentleness of his motion, I had to squash the instinct to bite his hand.

Not prey, my cat hissed. A prickly sensation radiated down my spine. My feras screamed to attack and get away. The need to flee kicked at my instincts and it took all my willpower to keep two feet planted firmly on the ground.

"Let me be perfectly clear, *Andy*, you owe me a debt for this insult," Lucien said. As a Vampire, Lucien would've detected the spike in my heart rate and the smell of fear emanating from my skin, but he continued talking as if oblivious to my internal struggle to flee. "And if you don't provide me with answers in a week, you will be Clint's new toy. Do you understand?"

I nodded.

"Say it," he hissed.

"Yes. I understand."

Lucien transferred his gaze to Wick. "Have her chipped and keep her close."

Wick nodded and grasped my upper arm, giving it a little tug. *Time to go.*

Clint stepped in before I had a chance to turn away.

"You're mine." A promise of what he planned glinted in his expression.

A painful memory from my past echoed Clint's words. *Dylan's voice rasped against my soul, "Andrea McNeilly, you are mine."*

I shivered.

14

In any other district, the old brick multi-storied warehouse would've been a heritage building, but this was Gastown, the rundown part. The inhabitants were a homeless mix of drug addicts, criminals and the mentally ill with a population of unhealthy-looking sex trade workers that could've fit into any of the previous categories. The government had cut funding to social services, including the local hospital that treated mental illnesses, and it showed—the streets more over-crowded than before.

I stood on the sidewalk and looked up. The windows of the building had long been broken, likely from addicts looking for a place to squat. The last owner had boarded the windows before they gave up and abandoned it. Multi-coloured graffiti added character to all the exposed surfaces within reach. The layers of tags upon tags bright-ened the otherwise drab colour of the old, washed out and neglected bricks. There was a faint smell of fetid urine, and I knew from experience it grew stronger in the summer months.

This building had been the perfect location when I met with my handler. I didn't know where Landen lived, what his surname was, or hell, if Landen was his real name. After becoming an SRD employee, I was given Landen as my primary contact so I could go off the grid.

I couldn't shake the feeling my current plan would essentially peg me in the ass with a homing beacon and expose me to anyone who wanted to find me. Did it matter now? There was already a giant target on my back. All Lucien had to do was say the word and I was done. Nothing scared me more than being controlled by someone again—trapped, *owned*.

Focus on one thing at a time.

Right now, I needed to find Landen. When we were first assigned to each other, we'd gotten shamelessly drunk and fooled around. Well, in truth I got him drunk to learn more about him and to find out where he lived. With a performance worthy of an Oscar, I'd insisted we go back to his place.

When I returned to the townhome a week later, he was gone. His scent erased and left with no other clues, I couldn't track him. He ditched and cleaned the place as a professional precaution, which shouldn't have come as a surprise, but it did. I'd thought my charms were invincible. My plan to learn more about my only point of contact failed, but it served as a bitter reminder of the world I lived in. Trust no one and no one trusts you.

All I knew about Landen was his physical appearance, his slightly floral scent, his preference for boobs over booty and where we met. Here. Since he conveniently left all my recent calls unanswered, my plan was to back-track his scent using my wolf—she was an excellent tracker. If Landen covered his tracks like he did years ago, my sole lead would be gone.

I ducked under the police caution tape—like that stopped anyone—for some crime committed in the past. The police had given up long ago on the case, without bothering to remove the tape. The metal double doors for the main entrance hung off their hinges.

Squatters had made this building their home until unusual sounds and animal sightings, a.k.a. me, scared them away.

When I got to the room where I'd met Landen previously, I stripped down and neatly folded my clothes. I placed them in a pile on top of my shoes so they would touch as little of this place as possible.

The wolf form came easily—muscles stretched and bones snapped into place. I instinctively inhaled my surroundings and instantly regretted it. This building might smell bad as a human, but it intensified to something far worse with the heightened senses of the wolf. My fur shook as I exhaled the vile air.

There were so many different scents. I picked up the one unique to Landen and huffed in relief. He'd grown complacent. I sniffed the air again, targeted Landen's trail, and followed it out of the building.

A wolf loping around the downtown core didn't raise any alarms. For one thing, I wasn't beastly huge like

Werewolves and two, this city was riddled with coyotes and I looked pretty similar. Besides, the inhabitants of this area knew to look the other way and not ask questions if they valued their health. Most saw what they wanted to see—a slightly oversized coyote looking for food.

There had been an unfortunate incident years ago where an elderly lady thought I was a stray, rabid husky and called the SPCA on me. I was locked behind bars with a horny malamute and fed no-name dog chow for three days straight before I managed to escape.

Suppressing the memory, I followed the stale scent of Landen across the downtown core. He'd not been here in weeks, maybe not since we last spoke. I didn't know if he handled any other agents. One time, he'd slipped and said I was "more than a handful." Not sure if he referred to me as an agent, or my breasts. If he did have other agents, he'd have different meeting places for each of us.

I approached a building in Yaletown. Posh and trendy, with boutiques oozing glamour and the eclectic vintage look that cost a fortune, or in other words, not where I'd normally hang out.

Maybe I should quit and become a handler. My nails scraped against hard asphalt. If Landen could afford to live here...he likely had gone rogue. A government paycheque couldn't pay for this.

I huffed and pawed the pavement to stir up the scents, confirming this was Landen's place. The front entrance had layers of his scent. None were newer than the one I'd followed. My hackles rose with apprehension.

Either Landen had run or he'd holed up soon after our meeting. Neither could be for a good reason, but it did explain why he hadn't cleaned his scent trail.

I circled the building and my sense of unease built. No new trails. Landen was in the building or gone. Sitting back on my haunches, I scanned the building for what I needed—an open window. The night, not particularly cold or wet for once, meant there were several.

Behind a dumpster, I willed the change and stretched my wings out wide. It felt good. My falcon had been neglected since my ill-fated escape attempt. I soared, letting the wind push me up, and relishing the freedom, I hovered a little longer than needed before maneuvering through the open window.

My falcon shifted away before my feet hit the plush carpet. I looked around the room. An elderly couple slept soundly beside each other in bed holding hands above the covers. *How sweet.* The faint odour of pharmaceuticals surrounded them. Most likely, they were drugged up on a cocktail of prescription medication to get through the night with as little pain as possible. They slept on their backs with their mouths open. Spittle blew in and out with each breath before pooling at the corners of their mouths.

They both snored loudly.

I wondered why they left their window open. Old people were cold all the time. My grandmother used to complain about it. "It seeps into my bones," she would say.

Smiling at the memory, I slunk out of the room and

walked through their cluttered apartment decorated by a nation's worth of doilies. The view from their front door peephole didn't reveal anyone loitering in the hallway. I snuck out and sprinted to the staircase, like the road-runner on crack. Although it would've been easier and less physical to ride the elevator to each floor to look for Landen, it contained too much risk. I was butt naked and it would take one person to hit the up or down button to ruin my night. Talk about an awkward elevator conversation.

Hi, how are you? Naked and yourself?

The door to the hallway staircase wouldn't open. I cursed. I needed a key fob, but that didn't stop me from jiggling the doorknob a couple more times just in case I could open it with sheer strength and will power.

Admitting temporary defeat, I jogged back to the old folk's home. It didn't take long to find their keys because they were in a dish by the door, next to some candies.

I made my way back to the stairs and used their key fob to get in. Landen seemed like the type to enjoy looking down on others, so I headed up the stairs. Luck-ily, the doors were not locked from inside the stairwell. I opened the door on each level to see if I could smell my handler. Five floors up, I found his scent.

And something else unpleasant. Death.

It would be strong enough in a couple more days for the norms to detect, which meant old death. My wolf howled in my head and the back of my neck tingled as the tiny hairs rose. This didn't bode well. I walked to the doorway suffused with the smell of Landen and the stench of decay. There was no need to knock. The door was unlocked.

I pushed open the solid door, and bracing for what was on the other side, walked in and pulled the door closed behind me. I didn't want the smell to get out any more than it already had and alert the norms before I had a chance to investigate.

If there was a way to turn off my nose, I would've gladly used it.

Landen lay splayed in the middle of his living room —his body eviscerated, with bloody entrails strewn across the hardwood flooring. A quick death, but pain stamped Landen's once handsome face. And surprise. I reached out to check his body and hesitated.

Death surrounded me every day, but it had been awhile since it visited someone I knew, much less someone I'd fooled around with. I didn't particularly like Landen, and I was pissed that from all appearances, he's gone rogue and used me, but his glazed over eyes made something inside me hurt a little.

Odd.

My stay at the Wick Wonderland had made me soft. I shouldn't feel bad for this guy. I might be spending eternity as Clint's sexy-time play-toy because of him. Hell, if he hadn't already been killed, I might've done it myself.

I stole a quick breath and picked up his hands to examine them. There didn't appear to be any defensive wounds; his arms and hands one of the only unblemished parts left.

What remained of his clothes told me when he'd

died. He wore the same thing the night he gave me my assignment, which meant he'd turned cadaverous soon after. This whole thing reeked of a set-up. Someone was tying up loose ends, and unfortunately for Landen, that meant him. What had he dragged me into?

His place gave nothing away. It reminded me of a luxury hotel room or a staged home in a realty show. Few personal belongings. I hadn't pegged Landen as a minimalist, but then again, this might not have been his only home and his job required him to pick up and disappear at a moment's notice. People could say the same thing about my place.

I opened a window to let some of the stagnant air out and shifted into my wolf. I sniffed the dead meat.

Wait a minute. I shook my head. *The body. Landen's body*. The last thing I needed was my wolf's instincts to kick in fully. Yeah, I might've disliked Landen, but I didn't want to get snout deep into his bloody corpse because my wolf mistook it for a free meal.

My perfume still clung to Landen's clothes. It confirmed his time of death. But underneath the putrid smell of decay was something else.

Cat. Big cat.

My hackles rose. Padding around the room, I looked for other clues. The cat scent clung to a chair in the corner of the room and mingled with the subtle fragrance of male cologne. There was something enticing about the smell, but when I focused, the faint appeal escaped, like water slipping through fingers.

A growl escaped before I could stop it. Either a

Shifter or a feline Were sat and waited for Landen to return home before killing him. Landen knew his attacker, or he would've put up more of a fight. *Another SRD agent, maybe?* His death had to be related to my current situation.

Shifting into my falcon, I flew out the window into the cool night air. The wind refreshed my body, cleaning the repugnant smell of death that clung to it, but the wind couldn't wipe away the look on Landen's face, nor the sinking feeling I was screwed.

15

My arm looked like a well-loved chew toy, burning and angry red as my nails dug in, scratching back and forth. Wick had injected the microchip under my skin after returning from Lucien's and instead of feeling better with time, it managed to feel worse. Now I knew how micro-chipped pets felt. I sent a heartfelt apology to Spanky, the affectionate American Staffordshire we had when I was a kid. Easily excitable, Spanky'd practically vibrate before jumping up and freaking out our guests. Having a seventy pound "vicious pitbull" lunging at them meant many family friends avoided us at first. But once they got to know him, they realized their fear was baseless. A few tummy rubs and free range licking and Spanky's heart would be theirs. God, I loved that dog.

"No amount of scratching will get that tracker out." I turned around to see Wick leaning against the door frame. There was no point in locking me in now that I had a tracker injected *under my skin*. Gross. It felt foreign and wrong. Worse, no amount of shapeshifting had dislodged it from its home.

Hesitating, I considered taking a knife to it. *They could always inject another one.*

"It itches."

"That will go away eventually." He sounded confident. My face scrunched up with doubt and he turned his forearm out so I could see a similar small lump under his skin.

"*Eventually* is too far away for my liking," I grumbled and turned back to the laptop on the floor I lay in front of. "Has Lucien ever removed a chip from one of his tagged supes?" I asked, dreading the answer.

"No."

"What if I deliver on my promise?"

Wick cast his gaze up to the ceiling before walking into the room. "He has claimed you. Even ordered you to remain in my house, under my watch despite the tracking chip so we can *observe you better*. You tried to kill his human servant. As far as he is concerned, you are in his debt."

I huffed. The air blew my bangs off my face. "Great. Not much incentive to make good on my promise."

"Besides your life?"

I closed the laptop and banged my head on it repeatedly—not hard enough to damage anything important, but enough that I felt better. I wanted to go home.

Lucien's orders gave me a new goal in life—find the

person behind my hit on Clint, but it also gave me something to drive toward—freedom. Once I lost it, I realized how much I wanted it back. After I paid my debt to Lucien, I planned to get the hell out of here and find something more productive to do with my life, something more than being an SRD agent. Find a real home. No more A to B.

What would I do, exactly?

No fucking clue.

Maybe track down my birth parents, if they lived, and ask some pointed questions, maybe learn more about what the heck I was, maybe find a new job, or maybe work on being a better person, healing all the hurt I buried deep inside.

Whoa. Where'd that come from? Back up.

"Did you find anything?" Wick asked.

Glad he interrupted my mental life planning before I cried and called the SRD shrink, I rolled over on to my side and stared up at him. "Besides my handler being dead? No."

"Dead? Why didn't you say something sooner? Like an hour ago when you came back."

"Do you know who killed him?"

Wick exhaled slowly and perched on the corner of my bed. He shook his head.

"Then telling you didn't help, did it?"

"Andy." Wick's tone was a reprimand. "You should let me help you."

"No offence, but you're Lucien's lapdog. Conflict of interest."

"My *interest* is to help you." His voice sounded calm, but emotion flashed across his face, too quick to catch.

"You smelled happy when Lucien claimed me. I don't trust you." I got up and stalked out of the room.

A firm grip on my arm stopped me. Before I could break free, Wick reached over and grabbed my other arm. Pulling me back into his body, he breathed into my ear. "I was upset Lucien claimed you. I do not like the idea of any man's mark on or in you. But, you are right, I was also happy, because it meant you are staying." His lips brushed my ear, sending a tingle down my body. "Here. With me."

Any thoughts about my current predicament flew from my mind. I was thinking about something else entirely now.

I shook my head to clear the pornographic images— Wick tearing off my clothes, me raking my nails down his back, his hips pumping.

"Tracker or no tracker. I will not be trapped like a caged animal." I pulled my arms out of Wick's grip and walked away.

And stopped abruptly when I walked into the living room.

"Andy!" A familiar woman's voice bounced off the walls. Looking over, I met Mel's piercing blue eyes.

The painful memory that haunted me every night slammed into my brain and froze me on the spot.

Sweat and fear mixed with the acrid scent of blood, rolled off the pack women huddled in the corner of the room. Naked. Hair plastered to their heads. Waiting for their turn. They avoided eye contact to save me further humiliation, except one. My friend Mel mouthed our mantra, "Survive."

Dylan's hot breath seared my neck as he pinned my arms over my head and forced my bruised thighs apart with his knee. "Andrea McNeilly, you are mine."

Anger. Hot, searing, molten rage. And hatred. Long repressed, it rose fast and furious, twisting and tangling with something else inside me. Something feral. Something fierce.

Power rippled through my skin. My eyes snapped open, burning with dark energy. My face turned to the side. I met the desperation and fear in Mel's gaze.

The final trigger.

My body shifted. Transitioning into a monster caged deep within me.

And then all hell broke loose.

"Andy?" Melissa cocked her head.

Paralyzed as the memory faded, I stared at the blonde beauty. I'd not seen Mel since I escaped Dylan's pack. Not since I broke his Alpha control and destroyed half the males in the process. Mel had been in a forced union as well—with David. I'd torn his guts out.

My eyelids squeezed shut on the bloody images the memories brought up. That night, something more than my mountain lion, wolf and falcon combined—a beast— had risen from within, answering my desperate call and it went wild—uncontrollable.

It took years of surviving as a mountain lion in the

wilderness before a sane woman could walk out of the forest.

Two arms wrapped around my body as Mel enveloped me in a hug, her blonde hair fluttering in my face. She smelled of apple blossoms, her favourite shampoo. "I can't believe it's you. I've missed you so much." She squeezed me hard before pulling back. "I owe you so much."

A wave of hot and cold pinpricks surged against my spine, ran up my neck, crashed against my brain and settled behind my eyes. I blinked. And realized Mel waited for a response.

"Um..." came my intelligent response. Mel's lips trembled and I tried to ignore the tears streaming down her face. Too much of a possibility they'd start running down mine any minute.

"Mel?" a low baritone spoke behind her. "Do you know her?"

Mel turned around to reveal a nice looking Hispanic man. "Dan, this is Andy." She turned her megawatt smile on me. "Andy, this is my mate, Dan." She leaned in. "My true mate."

Still unable to find my words, I nodded at the man. I recognized him as one of the Weres who held the net over me when I was captured the second time. He gave me a brief nod before he went back to frowning. "I know her name, Mel. She's the one Wick captured and had to bring before Lucien. Are you saying this Andy is the same as..."

"...as my Andy. From my last pack. Yes." Mel squeezed my arms again. "We looked for you after, you know. The girls. When we couldn't find you, we split up and went our own way."

"Oh," I said.

"Your last pack?" Wick interrupted whatever Mel would say next. She turned and nodded at him.

Looking around, I realized every Were had stiffened at the mention of Dylan's pack. Mel must've told them about it—the forced unions, the rapes, and the humiliation. My heart thumped against my breastbone. I smelled the burnt cinnamon of their anger and the salty, sickly sweet tang of my fear.

I squeezed my eyelids shut, and whispered my new mantra, *Dylan's dead.*

Wick turned to me. "You were in the same pack as Mel?" he asked. His sweet rosemary scent, overpowered by burnt cinnamon rolled off his skin in storm waves that hit my face, one after the other. I wrinkled my nose at the smell and looked away, unsure of what to say.

Mel reached over and rubbed Wick's arm, comforting him. He removed her hand, but squeezed it before letting it go.

"You were in Dylan's pack?" Wick asked me again, spitting the other Alpha's name. He waited for a response making it clear he wouldn't let this go.

Stay cold. Stay untouchable. I couldn't feel right now, or I'd break down. This wasn't my home, not my pack, not my people. I couldn't trust them. Not even Wick. *Stay strong.* Squaring my shoulders, I turned to face him. "I was his mate."

If the room was quiet before, it was deathly silent

now. The scent of Wick's anger rose and spread through the room, setting everyone on edge. Every head turned to me. Every eye locked on my face. No one dared move.

"That explains a lot," Wick said quietly. "It's a good thing he's dead." He balled his hands into fists. "I wish I could have done the honours myself."

"Now that we have that out of the way." I bristled. "I have some more investigating to do." Flashing Mel the biggest smile I could muster so she'd know it wasn't personal, I stalked out of the room.

16

"Welcome to the Supernatural Regulatory Division Employee Hotline. My name is Amy and I will assist you with your call." The computerized female voice droned on, "For workplace injury including the loss of limb or accidental death, please say, 'injury'. To request supplies, such as spell ingredients, weaponry and silver ammunition, please say, 'supplies'. To report a crime involving a Supe, please say, 'crime', or hang up and call the Supernatural Disaster Hotline at 1-800-555-2424..."

My nails tapped out the tune for the Star Wars anthem, the one they play for Darth Vader, while I waited for the option I wanted. If Amy was a real person, I could at least visualize punching her in the face. The idea of slamming the computer operated voicemail machine repeatedly against the floor, however, provided some therapy.

"For all other queries, please say, 'other' and wait for the next available SRD representative," Amy finished.

"Other," I sighed.

"Did you say injury? If yes, say 'yes', if no, say 'no'."

"No," I growled.

"My mistake. For workplace injury including the loss of limb or accidental death, please say, 'injury'. To request supplies…"

"Other," I spat into the receiver. There was no way I would sit through her listing off all the options again.

"Did you say office? If yes, say 'yes', if no, say 'no'."

"No."

"My mistake. For workplace injury including the loss of limb…"

"OTHER!" I held the handset back and shouted into it.

"I'm sorry, I didn't catch that. Please hold, while I transfer you to the next available representative." For a computer, Amy sounded a little put out.

"Oh for the love of God," I cursed and sat back in my chair, well, Wick's chair. Despite the high level of comfort it provided, I wanted to rest in my own lounger, in my own home. Then I could wander around in my underwear and drink milk straight from the container without judgment.

The phone blasted out some classical electric fusion music some musician on speed composed back before the Purge. It did nothing to soothe my nerves. My fist needed to sink into something.

"Supernatural Regulatory Division. My name is

Patty. How may I direct your call?" A woman's real voice cut off the music.

"Hi, Patty," I said as calmly as possible. "This is Agent McNeilly. I am a contractor under Handler Landen. Last name unknown. He's dead and I've encountered difficulties with my last assignment..."

"Agent *Andrea* McNeilly?" the woman's sharp voice cut me off.

"Yes," I stated. How many Agent McNeillys were there?

"Please hold."

This time the music was pop from my adolescent years. Normally I would have hummed along, but this time a string of curses escaped instead. It didn't help my current mood. Sparring would relieve some of my pent up stress and other frustrations, but playing fisticuffs with Wick was no longer an option. I didn't trust either of us to behave in close proximity.

"This is Agent Booth." The woman's husky voice scratched my ear through the receiver. Too many cigarettes. That or she'd gone clubbing with her girls the night before and had no voice left. "Is this Andrea McNeilly?"

"Yes," I said.

"I need you to answer a few security questions to confirm your identity before we can proceed." Her fingers tapped away at her computer.

"Okay..." This wasn't standard procedure. What was going on?

"Please tell me your employee number, month and

day of birth, your mother's maiden name and your safe word."

"16113, May 15th, Anderson and Serendipity," I listed the answers quickly. When I was a child, I'd read a book with a purple dinosaur named Serendipity. I didn't know what it meant until I looked it up years later. Serendipity—by chance. Regardless, it had always been one of my favourite words and became my safe word for the SRD when I joined fifteen years ago.

"Thank you, McNeilly. I'm relieved you contacted us voluntarily. Turning yourself in is the right thing to do."

"Turn myself in!"

"Well...yes. Isn't that why you contacted us?"

"No." I clutched the phone tightly. "What is it you think I did?"

There was a long pause. "McNeilly, where is Landen?"

"He's dead."

"I see." Booth's tone was flat. More clicking sounds came from her end of the line while she vigorously typed something on her computer.

"I tracked him down after the last assignment he gave me went bad."

"I see." There was another long pause. More clicking.

"What the hell is going on?" I asked after I realized Booth still stewed on what I'd said. Taking a deep breath, I focused on relaxing my grasp on the phone before continuing. "I've followed every order given to me since the start of my employment. I've submitted debriefing statements to my handler and I've maintained a low profile, just like I was hired to do."

"McNeilly, we haven't given you orders for two years."

The synapses in my brain stopped firing. I sat in silence while a weird fuzzy sensation moved up my back.

"You can play dumb all you want, but you and Landen have been wanted by the SRD for the last two years for going rogue."

The handset fell into my lap. I stared straight ahead but couldn't see a thing. How the hell did this happen? If that son of a bitch Landen wasn't already dead, I'd track him down and peck out his eyes.

"Agent McNeilly?" the receiver croaked. I picked it back up. "Agent McNeilly? Are you still there?"

"Yeah, I'm still here..." I wiped away the sweat forming on the bridge of my nose. "I'm not sure what to say. I'm shocked. I swear I had no idea."

"What do you mean?"

"I mean, when Landen gave me an assignment, I assumed it came from the SRD."

"Are you honestly trying to tell me you weren't aware the orders Landen issued you were outside SRD initiatives?"

"Yes! Of course, I wasn't." Something cracked. I paused and looked at the phone and realized I'd gripped it too hard again. "How would I know otherwise? My contact with the SRD is through my handler. The only reason I'm contacting you now is because he's dead."

More clicking. "Hmm. Yes. I can see how this could

happen. We might need to amend our Handler-Contractor protocol. Could you please hold?" Without waiting for a response, music from my parents' generation came on.

I can tell you what to do with your protocol. This woman was either an absolute pain in the ass, or a much needed ally. And I couldn't tell which.

The music snapped off, but before Agent Booth's voice could scratch my ears off, I spoke. "What do I do now?" I took a deep breath. "I'm innocent."

"You need to come in so we can sort this out. Will you consent to a lie detector test to prove your innocence?"

"Absolutely." I sounded more sure than I felt. This could be a trap. Or did Agent Booth believe me? I'd prefer to do almost anything else than place myself on a platter for the SRD, but I had no choice—I needed to go through with it to get answers. At least a lie detector test would work to my advantage, if Booth spoke the truth and they actually administered one.

Agent Booth tapped away at her computer again. "Tomorrow at two o'clock in the afternoon at our Vancouver branch. The building is downtown. Will you come in voluntarily?"

"Yes." There was something with the way she phrased the question that had my warning bells going off. My chest constricted. My wolf snarled. *Danger! Danger!*

"Do you need directions?"

"No."

"Then I look forward to seeing you tomorrow. Please

wear something comfortable. It will be a long inter...
view." Weak save. She had started to say interrogation.
"Please be prepared to list all your actions for the last two
years."

Click.

If the music had come back on, it would've been
playing the anthem for the *Twilight Zone*.

17

Pacing back and forth, I tramped a path into Wick's perfect carpet while my brain fried cell after cell trying to think of alternatives. No way around it—I'd have to ask Wick for a favour. My heart did a weird flip thing at the admission. Crap.

My plans to avoid Wick and whatever existed between us would have to be put on hold. Oh, I knew what manifested with our wolves. But blatant denial made it easier to cope. I couldn't give in to my wolf—she'd led me wrong before. Bringing my mountain lion so close that my claws and teeth ached to elongate, I mustered the courage to confront the Alpha Werewolf.

I found him in the living room, lounging on the sofa, flicking through the TV channels, pausing barely long enough to recognize the show or commercial before moving on, telling me he channel surfed more out of habit than an intent to find something. It contradicted his dominant personality. Most alphas picked something and stuck to it. Maybe he had a lot on his mind as well. I walked around to face him.

Hands on hips, I stated, "I need a favour."

Wick's eyebrows rose. Then a slow smile spread across his face. "Oh?"

He wasn't going to make this easy for me. I closed my eyes, held my cat close and pushed on, trying not to notice how great he looked sprawled on the sofa. "I need to borrow a vehicle."

"What for?" he asked.

"None of your business." I wanted the car to retrieve some decent clothes from my place and to go to the SRD headquarters. The last thing I wanted was to show up bedraggled and disarrayed from taking the fifty-two window sports coupe, the loser-cruiser, the city bus. *Ugh.* I spent more than twenty years using the bus to get around. Without fail, I ended up sitting beside a nut job every time—the drunk who'd pissed his pants or the man who hadn't bathed in weeks. The idea of stepping onto public transportation, even one more time, set my teeth grinding.

"That attitude will get you nowhere." Wick's deep voice jumped my thoughts away from the local transit. He undressed me with one look. I tried not to envision what it would be like to throw myself on top of him, rip his clothes off and rub against his hard muscles. I failed.

"You can borrow a car..." Wick said. His smile grew and I waited nervously for the condition that would make me say, 'oh shit, why did I bother asking?' From the sparkle in his eyes, I knew it was coming.

"But it will come at a cost," he said. Bingo.

"What do you want?" My heart took a bulldozer to my chest and the little devil on my shoulder nudged me knowingly—I knew what Wick wanted, because it mirrored my own desires.

Wick straightened up in his seat. His deep brown irises flecked with gold. "A kiss," he said.

I groaned, knowing I was doomed the moment he named his price. "Fine," I bit out. Leaning in, I gave him a chaste peck on the lips.

Wick laughed. "I should have specified."

"But you didn't. Too late now." I held out my hand expectantly, trying to get him to hand over the keys by sheer force of will. Now would be the time to develop Jedi mind tricks.

Wick stood, unfolding to his full height. Like a thrall, my fascination and desire held me in place as he stepped closer. My wolf panted as his fingers caressed the side of my face and brushed a stray tendril of hair back.

"A kiss from me," he said, his voice a soft whisper. "That is the price I demand for your favour."

I hesitated.

"You have to let me kiss you, Andy."

Wringing my hands together, I jerked my gaze up and focused on the ceiling. "Some ground rules." My voice came out strong despite my crumbling will power.

Wick shook his head. "No. I get to kiss you. No other rules."

"On the lips?" I pointed to them in case Wick needed further clarification.

Amusement danced across Wick's face along with something else. He nodded.

My teeth sank into my bottom lip and my gaze travelled down his muscular frame to where I wanted to place my hands...and my mouth. Although tempted to give in—to let him lead where my body wanted to go—I couldn't. "And if I decline?"

Wick shrugged. "Better get ready for a long flight." Exasperated, I shut my eyes and let my head fall back. There was no way I could fly that distance. My arm was still too weak and I hated breaking into my own place naked. "You're impossible," I groaned.

"Your call." His voice wrapped around me and my eyes snapped back open. Wick's attention fixated on my exposed throat. But he held back and waited. His wolf had risen and with a musky coconut scent floating across the room, I smelled exactly what he wanted—me.

My body responded instantly. Heat moved like molten lava through my veins. I was on fire. And he hadn't touched me yet.

Want. My wolf panted. *Good mate.*

Wick's knowing smile caused another heat to spread across my cheeks. "Red is a nice colour on you," he said. His hands moved up to cradle my face. He leaned down so our lips almost touched. His peppermint breath brushed against my mouth. "Do we have a deal?" he asked. His deep voice rumbled, sending shivers of pleasure rippling down my body.

No longer capable of speech, I nodded. His lips quirked up in a smile before he brought them down to meet mine. *Son of a bitch*. I'd expected a hard demanding kiss, but what I got was gentle. His lips were soft and smooth on mine, searching, and inviting me to respond. One of his hands moved to the back of my head to curl up in my hair. The other slid down my body. Grazing over my breast, he brought his hand up to cup the weight. His thumb ran over my nipple. The simple touch through the fabric sent sensual sensations through my body, making it throb with desire.

My arms wrapped around his muscled frame and splayed across his back. Our bodies pressed together, forming an unbearable searing intensity. Lost in the sensation of feeling him everywhere on me, I was vaguely aware of being lowered on the sofa.

Instinctively, my body arched under his caress. My head dropped back. "Wick," I breathed. His face rose up to meet mine again. His lips crushing the protest I was about to voice. Lost in his touch, I melted into him. Pinning me back, there was a ripping sound and a brief sensation of cool air on my skin before Wick's body covered me.

Dylan slammed me against the wall, shredding my clothes with one swipe of his claws. Paralyzing fear trembled over my body, raising goosebumps on my arms and the tiny hairs on the back of my neck. My heart pumped fast and hard against my chest.

Just kill me. Please.

Wick dropped his head to trail kisses down my body, but I remained immobile, consumed by the fear leaking out of the hole in my soul. Wick looked up from my navel. His nose flared and the line between his eyebrows deepened. He froze into a rigid mass of muscle, hovering above me.

"What's wrong?" His eyebrows pinched together. "Why do I smell fear?" He kept his body poised above mine and looked down at me with concern. "I would never hurt you."

I shook my head. "We can't do this." I scrambled out from underneath him.

Wick let me go before collapsing on the couch. "Please don't run from me, Andy. We need to talk about this."

My stomach rolled. I knew to what he referred— what I needed to talk about. But no amount of talking could heal the scars Dylan left. My nightmares would still haunt me. Holding the fragments of my shirt together, I turned to face him. "Where are the keys?" I asked.

Wick didn't answer; instead, he sprang up from the couch. There was hurt in his expression, and he smelled frustrated, but he stalked silently out of the room, only to return a few minutes later to hold out his hand and jingle the car keys on his finger.

When I reached out, he snapped the keys away from me. When I flinched at the quick movement, Wick's face softened. "Mel told me about Dylan's pack, Andy. About the forced unions."

I stiffened and dropped my gaze to the floor.

"I would never do that to you. To anyone."

My head shook back and forth in denial. Wick wasn't the problem. It was me. He would never understand that. I could use my body for jobs because I was in control. But I could never trust my heart to a man.

Reading my reaction the wrong way, Wick stroked my face. "You can trust me, Andy. Our wolves have chosen each other. This will be a true mating."

My body relaxed as Wick's Alpha power smoothed over me like a calming balm. Reaching up, I clasped Wick's hand and removed it from my face. "It's not that simple," I said, and released his hand.

"Yes, it is." He stepped forward.

"You're forgetting something."

"What's that?" He smoothed my hair away from my face.

"I'm not a wolf. Not all of me, at least."

Wick frowned. "That doesn't bother me."

"It should."

"Why?"

"My wolf has chosen you, I won't deny that. But my mountain lion hasn't. What if she chooses another? What if my falcon does?"

Wick stiffened.

"Would you want to share me?"

His hands dropped to his side.

"That's what I thought." I took advantage of his shock, snatched the keys from his hand, and stalked out of the house.

I had no idea if having multiple forms complicated a true wolf mating, but Wick didn't know that. I had to get out of here and away from him. The longer I spent in his presence, the less I was able to think, and remember the reasons why I shouldn't be with him. And there were plenty. Wick belonged to Lucien. He might want to help me, or be with me, but ultimately he had to obey his master. His choices were not his own.

Wick called after me, but I didn't hesitate. He could've caught up if he'd wanted, but he let me go. For both our sakes, I hoped he left me alone. We'd get hurt otherwise.

18

The gray building resembling an oversized children's building block stared down at me. More oppressive than impressive, it possessed too many windows for an organization publicly priding itself on being supernaturally unbiased. It couldn't be a comfortable destination for any Vampire. No supe liked feeling vulnerable. Although the SRD probably had sun-safe rooms inside, the impression given by the windows, or the 'glass portals to the death star,' made me want to turn around and go back to Wick's house. Screw the SRD. But I couldn't. I had to face them and clear my name.

The air smelled crisp and clouds moved in, dark and angry. A typical Vancouver Spring day. Tugging at the charcoal blazer I'd retrieved from my house, I gave my outfit a once over before walking into SRD headquarters. Agent Booth had said to dress comfortable, but I wasn't showing up in sweats. I wanted to come across professional. The two piece business suit fit in with the downtown corporate vibe. I could've been a lawyer walking into a business meeting.

I pulled open the glass doors and took long strides to the security desk. No need to draw this out. My heels clicked loudly against the hard slate tile. The sound ricocheted off the walls. Crossing the large sterile expanse of the main lobby, I focused on the guards like they were two chocolate bars at the end of a diet.

They tensed before giving me a hard look. There was no mistaking the vanilla and honey scent. I tried not to lick my lips as I smelled the sweet air. *Mmmm, Witches.* They smelled good. Then again, so did demons. An unpleasant shiver travelled through my body. I would be ecstatic to never deal with a demon ever again.

Shaking my head of dark memories, I plastered on a fake smile before I reached the desk.

"Agent Andrea McNeilly to see Agent Booth. She's expecting me."

The security guard with the sandy-brown hair and green eyes, tapped away on the keyboard in front of him. The other guard with limp blond hair and a plain face didn't turn toward me; instead, he surveyed the lobby room for possible threats, while watching me out of the corner of his eye.

"Your visitor pass." Guard number one jutted his hand out too far and jabbed my arm with a plastic card.

"Thanks." I snatched it away from him before he

could do more damage. After clipping the pass to the lapel of my jacket, I looked at the guards expectantly and cleared my throat.

They returned my probing look with blank stares.

"Directions?"

"Through the metal detector, take the elevator on the right, tenth floor," guard number two said with clipped tones. Clearly, he was annoyed.

"Thank you." Hopefully my sarcastic tone came across so they'd know I meant the exact opposite. They nodded and went back to staring at the entrance. By far, the most boring Witches I'd ever come across.

Next time, I would ask for a later appointment so I could take the time to case the place. If there was a next time. The metal detector remained silent as I walked through. There were no weapons for it to detect, because I didn't need them. I *was* a weapon. It amazed me the SRD had no idea what I was. They asked for disclosure during the interview and training process, but I declined to answer. According to our country's laws, supes still had the right to refuse to identify themselves as anything that could be used to discriminate against them. *Ahhh politics.*

If the SRD ever found out, my name would be quickly added to the top of their next hit list or worse, their retrieval list. Shuddering, I stepped into the elevator when the doors dinged opened. The last place I wanted to end up was in the government lab as a specimen. *No thank you.*

The SRD would know from the autopsy reports of

my targets that I could change into an animal. They'd assume I was a Shifter or Were. And apparently, that was enough for them. Results spoke, and as long as I was in the good graces of the SRD, there was no need for them to push the issue. Well, I was no longer on Santa's 'Nice' list. They could call it an interview all they wanted—I *knew* I walked into my own interrogation.

When the elevator reached the tenth floor, I squared my shoulders and walked out with as much confidence as Superman around kryptonite. The receptionist with boobs too perky to be natural sported a rock solid updo that must've taken hours in the morning to create and half a container of hair gel. I never had that much patience. One shift and it would be a mess anyway. On a regular day, my hair was tied back in a ponytail and if I felt like making it fancy, I'd add some twists or braids. The only time my hair came down was when I acted as slutty bait for a target, or when I slept.

The receptionist looked me up and down, and her lips curled in a nasty smile. One minute of visual analysis and she'd determined who the more attractive woman was. Too bad she got it wrong.

"Andy McNeilly to see Agent Booth." I cut right to the point. This woman looked mean. When her citrus and sunlight scent reached me, I tensed. Wereleopard. As if she could sense my discomfort, her smile grew. She probably thought she'd take me in a fight. She probably could if she finished her shift before I gutted her. But I was quick on the draw, and I didn't hesitate.

"One moment," she purred. She pressed a button on

her desk and spoke into it. Sniffing the air again, I analyzed her scent. Not the same as the one from Landen's apartment, but similar, familiar. Relative, maybe? Same prowl? This couldn't be a coincidence. I eyed the receptionist, wondering about her connection to Landen's killer. She was too busy checking out her reflection in the computer screen to notice.

"Put her in room two," a familiar raspy voice croaked over the intercom.

The receptionist nodded despite the other woman not being able to see her. She looked up. "Please follow me," she said as she pushed away from her desk and stood up. She was a small thing. *Petite*. That was what her online profile would say. She seemed like the type that would hunt men on dating sites only to chew them up like a gazelle femur and toss them aside.

I followed her swinging hips to ominous room two, all the while wondering who she wiggled for. She didn't strike me as a lesbian, so there was no need to saunter around like a sex kitten when no one else accompanied us. Unless she couldn't help it. Or was she trying to make me feel inferior? My lip curled up in a scowl. I hated her type.

"Please have a seat. Agent Booth will be with you shortly."

I nodded and tried to ignore the satisfied smile she flashed me before closing the door. Her scent lingered in the room and I made a mental note to track her after I finished up here. Something wasn't quite right with her —other than her double D's.

A lie detector machine, sprouting wires and straps like a forgotten potato in the pantry growing roots. It sat in the corner of the interrogation room, looking archaic and out of place. This thing probably dated back to sometime before the Purge. *Why would they bother with a machine when they could use supes to scent out lies?* Did the norms not trust us?

The air in the room stirred as the door swung open to admit a middle-aged woman with graying black hair. A large hooked nose jutted out beneath trendy purple-rimmed glasses. Her lips pursed into a straight line. Not a good sign. I stood when she entered the room. Not out of respect, but as a defensive maneuver.

"Agent McNeilly?" she asked. When I nodded, she held her hand out.

I reached over and clasped it. *Ouch!* The woman had a vise-like grip. At least she didn't do the soft noodle hand shake a lot of women seemed to prefer. I hated weak handshakers—didn't trust them. But it would take more than a firm handshake for me to invite this woman to my confessional booth.

"I'm Agent Booth." She gestured for me to have a seat. We sat down in the plastic chairs facing each other. They never had comfortable seats in an interrogation room. Agent Booth stared at me. She'd lined her cement gray eyes with green eye make-up. She wouldn't get the satisfaction of seeing me squirm.

Then I noticed Agent Booth had no scent. She didn't smell like a norm, didn't smell like a Were or Shifter, didn't smell like a Witch—didn't smell like *anything*. I bit down to prevent a growl from escaping. She hid her scent. Now I really didn't trust her.

"Thank you for volunteering to come in," she said, opening a faded folder, ringed with coffee stains. Some loose papers fell out and she quickly tucked them in, but not before I saw my picture. The file they had on me was thick—thicker than I'd expected, thicker than I liked—and from the state of the disarrayed pages, someone had obviously been studying it. Maybe they didn't need to ask me about my supernatural status because they already knew. Had I been ignorant to think I got away with not fully disclosing?

Booth trained her attention on me as she waited for my response. I dragged my gaze away from the file and brought it back to her face. "Like I said on the phone—I didn't know Landen went rogue and because he was my only contact to the SRD, there was no way for me to find out."

"So you say." Her tone was clipped.

I was about to launch into another defence when a knock on the door interrupted us. Booth's expression darkened.

"Wait here," Booth said before turning away from me. When she stepped out of the room, I got a glimpse of a young man in a dark gray business suit. His attire looked expensive and well above my pay grade. The low murmur of their voices leaked into the room. Good sound proofing. Normally I would have been able to catch their entire conversation. Booth's voice raised a bit, edged in anger.

The door swung open and Agent Booth stalked back in. She put her hands on her hips and glared at me as if all her problems in the world were my fault. The man who'd interrupted us walked in after her. He looked excited and eager. Not good.

"Agent McNeilly, this is my associate Agent Tucker. He will conduct the rest of your interview." She waved her hand absently at the man behind her and after giving me another dark look, marched out of the room. Tucker. The name sounded familiar.

"Ms. McNeilly." The man addressed me and held out his hand. I stared at it, distrusting him immediately. Tucker was a norm. His frail human scent coiled around me, stirring the predatory instincts of my animals. My falcon wanted to peck out his eyes, which startled me. She was the most passive of my feras. His expensive cologne tickled the inside of my nose.

"Have I been stripped of my position without due process?" I asked. His hand dropped and he frowned in confusion. "Am I no longer an agent?" I asked.

"Oh," he said and sat down. He tugged at his tie and cleared his throat. "As far as the SRD is concerned you were stripped of your position two years ago when you went rogue."

"I didn't go rogue," I seethed. "Landen did."

Tucker shrugged. "You got proof?"

My falcon might have her way if the man continued like this. "Your stupid protocols put me in a vulnerable position. It's not my fault you saddled me with a bad handler and he took advantage of the situation."

"If you had stopped to think and question your targets, you might not be in this situation."

Struck dumb by shock, I stared at him. A sudden coldness hit my core. After a moment, I collected my thoughts. "You're joking, right? Part of my job description is to *not* ask questions."

Agent Tucker blinked in response. I took his silence as an opportunity to examine him further. Nothing remarkable about his appearance. Everything average—dull hazel eyes, not too tall, not too short, boring brown hair, and clear skin. His shiny Rolex watch glinted in the harsh lighting.

"Did Daddy not make you go through regular training when he handed you this job?" I asked, taking a guess. It would explain Booth's agitation. She looked like a woman who clawed her way to the top. This man didn't have the same look. His posturing reeked of entitlement and he looked...soft.

A red blush travelled up his cheeks. "Just because my father is the director of the SRD, doesn't mean I didn't earn my position."

Bingo. I relaxed back in my seat, savouring the scent of his lie. "Of course not."

A knock interrupted whatever he planned to say next and saved him from further embarrassment.

What is this? A fucking tea party?

Tucker got up and opened the door to let in another man. For some reason, I liked this one on sight. He was old. Wrinkles creased his face, showing he smiled more than he frowned. He nodded at me before taking a seat beside the lie detector contraption.

"Agent O'Donnell will set up the test and then we'll see whether you're telling the truth." Tucker jutted his chin out and puffed up his chest before stalking out of the room.

"Don't let him get to you," the old man said. His voice was crisp and clear, sounding like it belonged to a much younger man. When the scent of a coyote reached me, I smiled. O'Donnell was a Shifter.

"I never let spoiled brats get to me," I said. O'Donnell chuckled and pulled out tangled cords.

He motioned me to come forward. I struggled to sit still while the agent strapped various things to my body that would look more appropriate in a sci-fi movie.

"Why do they bother with this machine when you can scent a lie from the truth?" I asked.

"The SRD trust a Shifter over technology?" His tone was incredulous, like he couldn't believe I'd ask such a question.

Tucker flung the door open and glared at the old man. A coyote slipped in the room after Tucker. The younger agent turned his sour look on the animal familiar. The coyote spared me a quick glance and curled up at O'Donnell's feet. The old man leaned back in his chair, smiling.

"Is she ready?" Tucker spat. O'Donnell nodded instead of speaking.

Tucker grabbed a chair, flipped it around and sat backward on it, placing his face a mere foot from mine.

He'd probably seen the move on a cop television show and thought it looked tough. I was unimpressed.

"Let's get started shall we." His expression was entirely too eager for my liking.

ABOUT AN HOUR INTO THE INTERVIEW, I regretted my decision to look professional. I would give anything to trade my high heels for flip flops and the skirt for jogging pants. The chair made my butt sweat. As for the questions, they weren't difficult. I kept excellent records and provided Tucker with a printout of all my contracts for my entire career—not just the last two years. Tucker looked like he swallowed something foul tasting. He'd given up on his tough guy act forty minutes ago.

"Are there any kills you have made in the last two years that are not on this list?"

Thankful that he had specified the last two years, I smiled and leaned in. "For the third time, no."

Tucker bowed his head down into his folded arms and sighed.

"Agent Tucker, are we done here? I've more accounted for my past activities, and unless I'm mistaken, I've passed your lie detector test with flying colours."

O'Donnell smiled.

"We're done when I say we're done," Tucker grumbled.

Great.

"What are you?" he whispered.

"Excuse me?"

Tucker looked up, a determined sparkle in his eyes. "You heard me. What are you?"

"I hardly see what that..."

"It has everything to do with this and will affect whether you are prosecuted or whether you'll be reinstated as an agent with the SRD."

Well damn. "Human," I said.

Tucker laughed. It sounded hollow and forced. "You're pressing your luck, *Andrea*."

This man was not winning any personality awards. "A Shifter," I breathed.

O'Donnell's head snapped up at the same time as Tucker's. The old man's nose flared as he scented the air. A deep ridge formed between his eyebrows as he frowned.

Tucker turned to O'Donnell and stared, his mouth forming a hard straight line.

Without checking the machine, O'Donnell spoke. "She speaks the truth." His voice expressed his disbelief.

Tucker's face scrunched up. "That makes no sense. There were different animal wounds on your kills."

I shrugged, going for nonchalance when all I felt inside was twisted panic.

"You smell of the forest," O'Donnell whispered. He said it to himself as if it made sense.

"What was that, old man?" Tucker asked.

"Nothing," O'Donnell mumbled.

When Tucker turned back to me, I struggled to keep my face blank. It must've worked because the young agent scowled.

"Where's your fera?"

My knees banged against the table as I leapt across the desk—the injury a mere flea bites in comparison to what raged inside my head. There was no chance to consider the ramifications of my actions. I strained forward and ignored the pain from the machine straps and chords ripping off my skin. I slammed into Agent Tucker and we crashed to the floor.

Tucker's soft neck squished between my hands. I increased the pressure. No norm asked about feras nowadays. None. Not if they valued their lives. Shifters had been the hardest hit after the Purge. Every dumbass redneck who owned a gun ran out and used feras for target practice. So many died in the first years of the purge that they nicknamed the time the Shifter Shankings. I'd been born in the middle of those turbulent years and always assumed my birth parents had been two of the casualties. Why else would I be put up for adoption?

I squeezed harder, enjoying how Tucker's eyes bulged.

The door banged open and Agent Booth stepped in. "Agent McNeilly stand down," she commanded.

"Release Agent Tucker."

After a moment of staring into Tucker's frightened gaze, where I considered disobeying orders and made sure he knew it, I released my grip. Red skin marked where my fingers had dug in. Tucker looked away, no longer able to meet the fury I knew danced in my eyes.

I wiped off my clothes after I stood up and turned to Agent Booth. The skirt was ripped from the hem to the waistband. Anyone looking would see all of my leg and a bit of my hot pink undies. Lifting my chin, I tried to look dignified. If they tried to take me out, I planned to take down as many of them as possible, starting with Tucker.

Booth ignored me and turned to Tucker, who still gasped for breath on the floor. "I told you not to ask her that," her flat tone echoed in the room. Her gaze flickered to me. "If you'll give me a few minutes, Agent McNeilly, I will be right with you."

I flopped back into a chair and tried to ignore the numbness in my ass cheeks. These contraptions were not meant for long term use.

"Will you require any more of my services?" O'Donnell asked from the corner of the room. He hadn't budged since my attack on Tucker. At all. He hadn't run to aid his co-worker. Would he have sat there while I killed him? Probably. Who knows, he might've helped if I needed it.

"No, that's all, Donny. Thank you." Booth's expression softened when she looked at the old man. She liked him. And that made me like her. A little.

O'Donnell unfolded and walked over to me. His coyote followed.

"A pleasure to meet you, *Carus*." He leaned in and

kissed my cheek. His whiskers scratched my face. "I've waited a long time to meet you."

He smiled at my shocked expression and walked out of the room.

"Carus?" Booth asked.

"It's a term of endearment amongst Shifters." I shrugged it off. My heart beat rapidly and I was thankful to no longer be hooked up to the machine. It would have beeped and flashed like a Christmas display, and I'd be doomed to the government laboratories.

Rumpled and visibly shaken, Tucker picked himself off the ground and made a show of straightening his suit. Would he challenge me? Tell me I would regret what I'd done? Part of me hoped he would.

Good prey, my mountain lion hissed.

"Agent McNeilly," he mumbled as he walked out of the room with his head down.

I turned to the other person in the room. She observed me, watching my reactions. Once again I tried to catch her scent.

"You have no scent," I stated.

"Everyone has a scent," she said, flipping her hand in the air as if to say it was no big deal.

I shook my head. "How are you masking it?"

Agent Booth examined her nails, smiling at her little secret. "I don't know what you're talking about," she lied. "And we're not here to discuss me."

I pinched the bridge of my nose and sighed. "What now?"

Agent Booth picked a chair off the ground and sat in it. "Now, we get you a reliable handler."

"So I'm not fired?" I perked up.

"As you pointed out, you did everything right and you passed the lie detector test." She paused to examine her manicure. "The fault and blame lies with Landen."

"No repercussions for my assault on Tucker?"

Agent Booth snorted. "Not even his daddy dearest can defend his actions."

A slow smile spread across my face. "Do I get to choose my next handler?"

Booth's features appeared to pinch inward, the neurons in her brain probably making a zillion calculations. "Do you know any other handlers in the agency?" she asked. "Who would you pick?"

"I don't know any other handlers, but if I can pick, I want O'Donnell," I said.

Agent Booth laughed, the rich sound didn't match her raspy voice. "I will give you O'Donnell on one condition."

"What's that?"

"You find out who Landen worked for and report back to me. Directly." Her probing eye contact let me know how serious she was. Why did she want me to report to her? Was the SRD not the big happy family their public image implied? There was definitely more going on and without having any knowledge, it left me in a vulnerable position.

I pulled back from the table and held my hand out. "Deal. I planned to do that anyway."

Agent Booth stood and shook my hand. Her smile made me wonder whether I'd made a mistake asking for O'Donnell. She looked too pleased.

"Leave your number with Angie and I'll have O'Donnell contact you."

"Angie?"

"The tart of a receptionist they saddled me with." Despite my better judgment, I started to like Agent Booth.

19

I took a sip of my coffee and gagged. They called this *gourmet?* More like Gut Rot Blend, perfectly in sync with the café. Not much of a surprise given its location in the rough downtown Vancouver sector. But this place provided a perfect cover for observing the SRD headquarters.

Outside, the weather offered little to help brighten the coffee shop. Sporadic rays of light filtered through the dense gray cloud cover. An onslaught of rain slicked the sidewalk and a bone-numbing wind chilled the air. A perfect day to stay in bed and read a book.

But I'm here.

Suzy's Gourmet Café provided a warmer and slightly better smelling environment than the convenience store beside it, the only other option where I could stand out of the downpour and wait for Angie. Staring out the window wouldn't raise any suspicions here.

The anti-government, anti-shower, anti-everything

patrons were too busy discussing their obscure views on philosophy to notice anything as insignificant as me. I'd just appear as another coffee enthusiast, chugging back the gut rot like it provided sustenance. If someone asked me to debate Chomsky though, I was screwed.

Angie, or Angelica as I found out earlier, was working late. I planned to follow the Wereleopard to see if she would lead me to the owner of the scent I discovered at Landen's apartment.

Angelica? I snorted into my cup. She totally looked like an Angelica. When I addressed her as Angie, she'd been quick to correct me—her lips curling into a sneer told me she didn't like the nickname. I ignored her request, kept using the abbreviation and enjoyed watching her left eye twitch.

I grabbed the nearest newspaper and flipped it open with a sigh. The first article on the page fumed about humans stealing cucumbers. What next?

The paper crinkled when I folded it up and chucked it on the counter as far away from me as possible. I went back to staring at the front doors of the SRD headquarters. Maybe if I glared hard enough, I'd develop some psionic mind control and force Angie to come out to play. Personally, I'd rather watch amateur ball hockey.

"You're drinking the coffee from here?"

The familiar voice made me jump. Coffee leaked out of the lid and splashed on my hands and shoes. I turned to glare at Clint, Mr. Un-killable.

"What are you doing here?" I demanded.

Clint's massive shoulders straightened. Without a

word, he held up a metallic device. After squinting at the blinking red dot on the screen of his smart phone, I realized he used a tracking app. My arm itched.

"Checking up on me?"

Clint's slow smile spread wider. "I like to keep tabs on my pets." He reached out to stroke my face, but I dodged his hand, hearing my old sensei bark out instructions, slip and counter. Could I get away with punching Clint in the gut? Hmmm.

"I'm not your pet," I said.

"Not yet."

"Look, I'm sorry about tearing out your throat, but I thought I was following orders. I'll find out who set me up and you can find your next pet elsewhere."

A couple of café patrons turned and stared. Maybe I should drop the volume a bit. The sleazy man who huddled in the corner of the café looked at me in disgust.

"What a shame. You would look delicious in a collar." Clint leaned in and wriggled his eyebrows.

The laugh was out before I could stop it. "I would make a terrible pet. I'd be the kind to pee on your carpet and rake my claws down your face."

Clint chuckled. "Your defiance is enticing."

Ugh. Remembering his preference, I said, "I don't do rough."

"I can be gentle."

"Really?" My tone came out skeptical, which I intended, but why did I feel relieved? I still had five days. "Not buying it."

Clint frowned and took a moment to think about it. "Well, no. Not really. But I could try."

"How long has it been since you last tried?" The front of the SRD building started to blur, telling me I'd been staring at it too long.

"About fifty years."

"And how'd that go?"

"Not so well."

"Figures."

Instead of leaving me to the job I had to do, Clint pulled out a chair and sat down beside me. He stared out the window with a pensive look on his face as if trying to figure out what I'd glared at.

In an almost amicable silence, we watched the outside world go by before curiosity got the best of me. "How'd you become a human servant to a male Vampire anyway? You like blonde airheads."

"You're so judgemental. Being blonde doesn't make someone stupid."

"Of course not." I scoffed. "It's being with you that gives away their intelligence. Or lack thereof."

He squinted at me.

"You were explaining your relationship with Lucien..." I prodded. "Are you together?"

He kept his eyes narrowed a second longer before speaking. "Together? Hardly. Being a human servant doesn't have to be a sexual relationship."

"It usually is."

Clint nodded in agreement. "Usually, but Lucien is not one to make an eternal commitment for love or lust."

"What does he make it for?"

"Power."

Grunting, I went back to staring out the window. How would Clint make Lucien more powerful? He was a norm. It had been relatively easy for me to attack him— he was more of a weakness to Lucien. I eyed the large man again. *Unless there was more to Clint*. After all, he hadn't died.

"You've been stagnant for hours. I expected to find your body. What are you up to?"

"Surveillance."

"On who?"

"Shhh... You're bugging me."

Clint sighed. "The one building of interest in the area is the SRD headquarters. This leads me to question why you're scouting out your own employer. We've already concluded they weren't behind your orders. What have you found out, my little pet?"

Exhaling deeply, I turned to him, and hoping my death stare would give him the hint, I paused before speaking. "You will get your full report when I'm ready to give it. Until then, shove off and leave me to do the job your Vampire-dearest assigned to me."

Clint laughed and pushed away from the table. "You have five more days."

"I'm optimistic," I said.

Clint leaned in and spoke to the top of my head. "So am I."

If I didn't know how twisted he was inside, I might've enjoyed the view as he sauntered out of the coffee shop, but I was just glad to see him leave. The man had confidence, power and style, but he creeped me out. He also had a secret, and one I wanted to know. If I failed in my mission, I planned to kill him. And then run, hard as hell.

Caught up contemplating what Clint could possibly bring to the table power-wise and how to off him now that I knew throat-ripping was out, I almost missed the movement of Angie's full hips booming back and forth. When I leapt from my seat, I spilled what remained of my coffee all over my suit.

I cursed, grabbed my purse and ran out of the café into the rain. A norm would follow on foot. A Shifter or Were would've remained downwind and hoped the target didn't notice. Either way, I had an advantage. I jogged to the alley and stripped, flinging off my already torn clothes as fast as I could. My skirt was ruined anyway. A homeless man living in a cardboard box whistled.

Grinning at the man covered in filth, I shifted, letting the falcon form take over. The man cowered in his box and looked away. Norms found it disconcerting to see a shift—even a fast and fluid one like my own.

Stretching my wings out wide, I took to the air and circled the block until I found my target. Her bold red, skin-tight dress underneath a clear umbrella stood out among the blacks, grays and blues of the business world surrounding her. My falcon focused on the moving red body like a mouse in a field.

She slipped with feline grace into a sleek black car and led me in a large house to the prominent, up and coming neighbourhood of Port Moody. With only so much space in the Lower Mainland, and the population spreading like a cancer to the outer regions, new money invested in this location, making it grow exponentially. People liked the proximity to the water and mountains and the direct route downtown to the heart of Vancouver. The area filled with professional couples with fluffy lap dogs instead of children. The pets probably had a more versatile wardrobe than I did.

Perching on the roof of a neighbouring building, I tried to glean as much information as possible. Multiple people went in and out of the house. Good looking people. Big men. Sexy women. All in great shape. I didn't need my wolf nose to tell me this must be the prowl of the Wereleopards.

The rain eased up and I shook the excess water off my feathers. My body vibrated, itching to shift and take in the scents. If I found the one from Landen's apartment, I was a step closer to solving this mystery and saving my ass from Clint's clutches and the death certain to follow when he grew tired of me.

This was not a safe time to be on the ground, sniffing about. The house was full of Weres. They were probably holding a meeting. My cat would be no match for one of them. My falcon screeched into the night, the bird equivalent of cursing. Could I afford to wait? I only had five more days.

My wings hunched up and I dropped my head down between them, hoping to avoid some of the wind. Puffing my feathers out provided little insulation. I would wait until most of the Weres left. If they left. Then I'd go down.

IT TURNED OUT WERELEOPARDS LIKED TO CHAT. Their meeting lasted hours. Honestly, what could they possibly have to discuss? Never having belonged to a prowl, I couldn't imagine what day to day business would entail. How different could it be from a pack? Why didn't they just e-mail each other?

The meeting ended and droves of Weres vacated the building. There were still some inside, including Angie, but this would be my best chance. I couldn't wait for another day. Swooping down to the pavement, I changed to my wolf in one fluid motion, and four paws hit the cement instead of talons. The smell of citrus and sunshine overwhelmed my nose and I struggled to discern one Wereleopard scent from another. I loped around the block a number of times. Each time I caught a whiff of Landen's killer, the scent slipped away—either old and fading, or I'd lost my mind and tried to find something that didn't exist. Landen's scent was absent. Not worn out, fleeting, fading. *Absent*. Landen had never been to this prowl's headquarters.

Angie's scent branched off in two main directions, one toward work and one in the opposite direction. Maybe her plastic surgeon? More like her Witch. I grunted and kept walking. Plastic surgery didn't last on Weres. The body would revert back to its original form on the next shift. The Were virus went right down to the genetic level, and until they were able to splice genes and alter genetic codes, there would be no lasting nose jobs for Weres. There was, on the other hand, Witch enhancements, and I suspected Angie had a standing appointment.

Tired of failure, I made it back to the front of the house and chanced a closer sniff. The stench of dead meat and dried blood stopped me in my tracks. My senses sharpened. It took every ounce of self-control to stop the growl that rumbled its way up my throat. Vampire.

A door inside the house slammed shut and a murmur of voices grew louder, heading toward me. I didn't want to get caught. My wolf scent would be all over the yard and they'd know someone sniffed them out, but not who. Angie didn't know my wolf scent, only my human one, which meant the intrusion couldn't be tracked back to me. Shifting to my falcon, I flew into the night. Safe, for now.

20

Wick stooped over his computer muttering, too engrossed in what he was reading to notice I arrived back at the wolf lair. He looked up and smiled when I cleared my throat. The sight of those shining pearly whites caused something to constrict in my chest.

"What are you up to?" I cocked my hip against the counter and crossed my arms.

"Doing some research." His smile grew. "Andy-style."

"On what?"

"Cats."

"Excuse me?"

"Big cats," he explained. "Like you."

"Oh, that makes a lot of sense." My tone made it clear it didn't.

"Well I have been thinking about what you said," he paused. "About us not being together."

"You listened?" Alphas had a way of ignoring what

other people said if they didn't like it—stubborn to the bone.

"I did. And guess what I found out?" His expression riddled with excitement.

I flopped down on the chair across from him, exhaling the air in my lungs in a big whoosh. "What?"

"Big cats are not monogamous. We don't have to worry about your cat mating with another."

"Wick…" I started.

"No. Listen to this. According to Preter-Pedia, cougars are solitary and adults meet for the sole purpose of reproduction." Wick referred to the online encyclopedia that specialized in information relevant to preternatural groups.

"Wick…" I tried again.

"If we mated, your cat wouldn't interfere with it, because she wouldn't try to life bond with another."

"Wick, being a mountain lion *Shifter*…" I stressed the name. "Is not exactly like being a mountain lion. Like being a Werewolf isn't like being a wolf."

Wick frowned, taking a moment before renewing his attack. "Has your cat ever tried to mate with anyone or given the inclination she wanted to?"

That made me pause. My cat definitely let me know when a man appealed to her, but that differed from what happened between my wolf and Wick's. "Well, no."

"Have you met any feline Weres or Shifters?"

"Yes." It came out slowly, like a hiss. I'd killed a few. Did that count?

"Do they have a mating bond like Werewolves?"

"Not that I know of. They're more serial monogamists," I explained. How the hell would I know? Just because supes limped out of the closet eighty years ago, didn't mean they openly discussed their business. The Shifter Shankings had given everyone else fair warning of the ramifications for such actions. All preternatural groups kept a tight lid on their secrets.

"Did your cat like any of them?" He asked in a matter-of-fact way, as if the answer wouldn't upset him.

Maybe it wouldn't. Personally, I hated hearing about a boyfriend's past relationships. Though I knew the women were in the past, I'd still feel a twinge of jealousy. Okay. More than a twinge. Wolf's don't typically share, and I knew Wick's wolf must be growling in his head, but nothing showed on his face or scent besides optimism and hope.

I shifted in my seat. "A couple."

"Like your wolf likes mine?"

I had to look toward the ceiling and away from Wick's intensity. "No," I breathed.

"Well?"

Wick's attention weighed on me, causing my wolf to pace and whine to be let out. "Well what?" I said to the light fixture.

"Well, am I right?"

Exasperated, I flung my hands up in the air and glared at him. "Wick, stop it! My cat potentially bonding with another isn't the only thing that makes this a bad idea." I waved my hand between me and him in case he misunderstood what 'this' was.

"Like what?"

"Like when I fail to find out who hired Landen in five days and Lucien orders you to deliver me to Clint. Or when Clint tires of me as his new pet and Lucien orders you to *dispose of me*. Are you strong enough to break his hold on you?" I jabbed a sharp finger into his chest. "Are you?"

"He might spare you if we were mated," he said, not answering my question. His avoidance was answer enough.

"Really?" I sounded doubtful.

Wick looked away, giving another silent answer before a low growl escaped his lips. I stared at his mouth, mesmerized by the sound. Wick took advantage of my distraction to step in and envelope me in his arms before I had a chance to escape.

"We will be together," he whispered into my ear. His breath blew my hair out of the way and sent tingles down my neck. "You will not scare me away so easily. When this situation with Lucien and Landen is done, you will have no more excuses. We will be together."

Wick pulled back. His espresso eyes, flecked with gold told me more about how he felt than his words—he cared for me and he wanted me. The air tinged with the scent of his determination. I liked the woody undertones.

Before I had a chance to shake my head and utter more objections, he pressed his lips to mine. Soft as silk, and pliable. He moved them over my mouth as if savouring the taste, flicking his tongue out to stroke my own. Without meaning to, I leaned into his body in answer.

In response, Wick transitioned from a gentle and almost hesitant kiss, to devouring me. His lips demanded a reaction and his tongue forced my mouth to open more, give more. Slipping a hand around my ass, he hoisted me up and pushed me against the wall. I wrapped one leg around him. His hard erection pressed against my core, sending shivers of pleasure racing up my body, flooding my mind. I couldn't think. His other hand roamed up my body and whatever objections I had, fled with each stroke of Wick's thumb against my nipple.

"Mine," he said. A demand, statement and request all at once. Wick pulled back to search my face. Pleased with what he saw, he dipped back down and renewed his plight to make all my nerve endings sing. He hoisted me up farther. Wrapping my other leg around him, I straddled him with my back against the wall. His hands cupped my ass and he dropped his head down to rain kisses on my breasts. The skin on skin contact surprised me. What happened to my shirt? And my bra?

His mouth enclosed around my right nipple and any further questions flew from my mind, replaced with an emotion that needed no words, a feeling as primal as our natures. Wick moved us away from the wall and walked toward the stairs.

The decaying scent must've hit our noses at the same time. We flinched in unison. Wick dropped me and whirled around.

"Am I interrupting?" Allan's smile spread wider.

"This brings a whole new meaning to screwing the pooch."

"How long have you been there?" Wick demanded. He turned to offer me a hand up, but I'd already clambered to my feet, knowing without Allan's smug expression that he'd been there for a while and in our heads. My nails bit into my flesh as I clenched my hands, not liking the idea at all that Allan had been privy to my thoughts at such an intimate and vulnerable time. I scanned the room, located my shirt and threw it on without a bra.

Allan chuckled and shoved off the wall to approach Wick. "Long enough to enjoy the show and know why you shielded so strongly before." He paused to slide a slow evaluating look my way. "An interesting development, to say the least."

Wick growled at Allan's approach and positioned his body in front of mine. I pushed him aside and stood beside him. I was capable of defending myself. Wick shot an annoyed look in my direction, but didn't go all Alpha on me. Points for him.

"It makes me wonder what else you've been able to hide." Allan stopped a few feet in front of us. "Is there anything more we need to know about our dear little Andrea?"

"No," Wick bit out. His lie wrinkled my nose.

Allan examined his fingernails as if they were more important than the conversation. "I was curious how Andrea managed to rip out Clint's throat *and* escape out of the top floor." He looked up and gave me a piercing stare. "Not a Were. A Shifter. Not a normal Shifter.

Something else. Something different. Something..." He paused to tilt his head, probably listening to our thoughts. "Special."

Sweat trickled down the side of Wick's face. Whatever he was doing to shield Allan took a lot of effort.

Allan made a gasping sound that whipped my attention back to him. "Interesting indeed." He reached into his jacket pocket and retrieved a handkerchief. He handed it to Wick. "Wick, your shielding skills won't stop me." The Vampire's lips curled up as he turned to me. "And you have no idea what you are."

"Do you?" I crossed my arms.

Allan dipped his chin, conceding my point. "No, but I may know someone who does."

"Whatever," I huffed. "Does it change anything?" It didn't and I knew it.

Allan grinned, his fangs were out. "No, it doesn't."

"Why are you here?" Wick vibrated with rage.

"Ah, yes," Allan snapped his fingers. "My apologies. I got distracted by the little show you put on." He winked at me.

My lip curled up into a snarl.

Allan continued to observe me, long past the socially acceptable amount of time. "I'm here to remind you, Shifter, that you have five days." He ran his tongue along his teeth. "Less than that. Closer to four now."

Hopefully I conveyed my annoyance with the glare I cast his way. Surely Allan would know Lucien's human servant had already passed along the reminder, unless... Unless his presence here had another purpose—to check up on me and spy on my thoughts, maybe? "Clint's already been around to remind me. I can count to seven, you know."

Allan laughed. "Well isn't he an eager beaver? He must be impatient for his new toy."

"Pet," I spat. "He thinks I will be his pet."

Allan shrugged, as if there was little difference. "Semantics. You will belong to him until he bores of you."

"And then?"

Allan smiled, his teeth grew longer. "Then maybe I'll claim you. Or maybe no one will. Then we will have no more use for you and you will be disposed of." He paused to tap his cheek with his forefinger. "I might volunteer for the task. Disposals can be so fun... and filling." He didn't mean fulfilling either. Allan shifted his attention to Wick, who vibrated with anger. "Or maybe Lucien will command his dog to carry it out."

Wick stepped forward, his gaze a mutinous yellow.

"Down boy," Allan said. "I'm just having a little fun. You animals react in the most delicious ways."

"Well, you've had *your fun* and you've delivered your message." Wick crossed his arms and stared the Vampire down. "You can leave now."

"Remember, Andy, you're supposed to be out there doing the job Lucien gave you...not screwing the master's dog." Allan gave a mocking little bow and sauntered out of the room, taking his stench with him.

"Kind of ruins the mood, doesn't he?" Wick asked

when he turned to me. His control returning, espresso brown replacing the yellow.

I nodded and went to the living room. Good thing we got interrupted. Wick's hot kisses seduced away my resolve to stay far, far away from him, but I couldn't get involved now. Too complicated. And really, how well did I know him?

Remembering the feel of Wick, hot and hard, pressed against me, I closed my eyes. The warmth of him on my skin, the smell of his desire mingling in the air with my own and the taste of his tongue lingering in my mouth. I sat down in the nearest chair and crossed my legs. *No, no, no, no, no.* I squashed down the feelings threatening to boil over and reached for the remote control instead of the hot piece of ass sitting down beside me.

"What's this about Clint?" Wick's tone might've been calm, but his body remained tense.

"He paid me a visit while I was out running surveillance." I flicked through the channels, not really paying attention to what was on, but it kept my hands busy and off of something, someone, else. My skin prickled under Wick's glare, and after a few minutes of pretending not to notice, I gave in and turned to him.

"What?" I asked.

"Could you elaborate?"

"On what?"

"Maybe on Clint's visit with you? What did he want? What did he say? Or maybe elaborate on what surveillance you were running?"

"Apparently, I stayed in one place for too long and

Clint worried he'd lost his toy before he had a chance to play with me."

"He monitors your tracker that closely?"

"It would appear so."

Wick grunted and looked away. "That's not good."

"I didn't think so either."

Wick stared.

"What?"

"And?" he asked.

"And what?" I stopped channel surfing, settling on a rerun of a cop drama I'd already seen more than once and hoped my fixed attention on the television screen would give Wick the hint the discussion was over.

"And the surveillance?" Annoyance seeped into his voice and his agitation filled the room, prickling my nose.

"None of your business."

"Andy," Wick exhaled a long breath. "I could help you."

"No."

"Why not?"

I turned the television off and turned to face him fully. "No offence, but I still don't trust you. You're under Lucien's control." I held up my hand to stop him from speaking. "I'm glad Allan interrupted us, because to be perfectly honest, I don't trust myself around you."

My voice was final. That was all I would say on the matter.

Wick's frown deepened as if my comments disappointed him—they probably did—but instead of pursuing the matter further, he leaned back into the couch and snatched the remote control from my hands. He searched the channels much like I had earlier, giving me a chance to study his profile. He was a beautiful man, and I needed to get far away from him fast. Every day, I struggled to keep myself distant. Without saying good-night, I stood up and scurried up the stairs before I lost my resolve.

"You will," Wick whispered. I don't think he meant for me to hear him.

21

There has to be a joke in here somewhere. I had been stalking the Wereleopard's scent all morning. One trail led to the SRD headquarters, while the other led me on a wild goose chase all over town, branching off in many directions. The bitch backtracked multiple times. Good thing I wasn't only a great tracker, but also determined. Failure wasn't an option and as Clint and Allan had so eloquently reminded me, time was running out.

Angie had been careful. She didn't want her scent followed, which meant I was at least on the right track.

With my wolf nose to the ground, I followed her trail all the way to downtown Vancouver where it abruptly ended. Sitting back on my haunches, I howled in frustration. How did Angie get on the SeaBus in Leopard form? Or did she shift and go naked?

Someone brought her clothes. That had to be it. But who?

Sniffing around the on-ramp, I ignored the stares and gasps of norms waiting for the next vessel to arrive, clad in their business attire, ready for another day in the office. There was no other scent I recognized aside from Angie's. Other supes—Weres, Shifters, Vampires, a few Witches—had been here. But the area had a lot of traffic, so it meant little.

A snotty-looking middle-aged woman with perfectly applied make-up and an expensive haircut eyed me with apprehension. She pulled out her phone.

"Hello, Information? I would like the number for the SPCA." Her crisp and curt voice screamed, *I'm a business woman, don't mess with me*.

The SPCA, great. For norms the acronym stood for Society for the Prevention of Cruelty to Animals. For Supes, Weres and Shifters specifically, it meant confinement, trouble and too much time spent explaining why we ended up naked in one of their cages. Time to get out of here.

The woman ended her call with a terse goodbye and something resembling a thank you before rapidly punching in whatever number they gave her, all the while eyeing me with an equal dose of disgust and fear. Obviously a cat person.

I loped out of the SeaBus terminal and ambled down to the water. Hidden by a walkway, where people walked along the bay on their breaks. Garbage and human waste littered the shoreline and filled my nose, which wrinkled at the assault. Homeless took shelter underneath the walkway, invisible to the general public, forgotten or avoided.

Today, the area was vacant. I shifted to my falcon and flew the short distance between downtown Vancouver and the North Shore.

Finding a similar location on the other side, I shifted back to my wolf and found Angie's scent immediately. Circling the area repeatedly, I sniffed the ground like a cocaine addict over spilt powder. There was no mistaking the mingling of Angie's citrus scent with decaying matter.

This can't be right.

Angie had been picked up in a car from this location by Vampires and the thickness of it told me it happened on more than one occasion. I didn't recognize this particular stench of decaying bloodsucker. They weren't Lucien's as far as I could tell and if they were, they hadn't been in attendance to my little debut at his court. My nose had an excellent memory.

A car wasn't just hard to track on a road; on the number 1 Trans-Canada Highway it was impossible. Why hadn't Angie driven the whole distance? *Because that would make it too easy to follow her in a car.* Why couldn't Angie be stupid? Good looks should come at a cost.

I huffed and sat down, unsure of how to proceed. The idea of becoming Highway 1's next road kill victim was not pleasant or motivating and I still didn't know if Angie and the Wereleopards were connected to Landen's death or my orders, meaning I might be wasting my dwindling time and risking my life needlessly for a dead end.

Wick might know if another Vampire horde stayed in town. I just had to ask him, but that meant trusting him as well. *Nope. Not happening.* I'd have to find out on my own.

The sun, a little past its zenith, meant a few more hours of daylight, and one less day to figure out what The Purge was going on.

Out of sight from the norms, I changed to my falcon again and flew over the honking, bumper-to-bumper vehicles filled with cursing, road-raging drivers, before making my way back to the wolf den. Maybe I'd be lucky to make it to my room without running into Wick. I practically fled the house this morning in an attempt to avoid him.

Maybe he'd still be at work.

What did he do all day?

Careening sharply to the left, I narrowly avoided hitting a telephone pole. I couldn't believe I didn't know what Wick did for a living. I'd assumed he did Lucien's bidding, but that wouldn't pay the bills or explain why he was away during the day, every day. He had a job. He worked. And I had no idea where.

Why didn't I realize this sooner?

In my defence, I did have other, more pressing things on my mind—like escaping Wick's house, then surviving Lucien and now finding Landen's real employer to escape Clint. All the escaping in my life consumed a lot of energy and apparently my attention to detail.

Approaching the house I decided asking Wick about his career path would have to wait, because I needed to avoid him more than I needed to get to know him. He wouldn't approve of my plan to go information digging in a Vampire bar—if he saw me in a vamp-tramp outfit, there was no way his possessive Alpha instincts would let me out of the house.

THE IMAGE REFLECTING FROM THE MIRROR made me smile and come to the conclusion I'd missed my true calling in life. If I could ignore my heightened sense of smell and the stench of Vampires, I could've been arm candy for one. The style of their 'lady friends' suited me. The tight leather pants, corset and knee high-boots screamed working professional, or at least skank, in the norm world, but I didn't plan to go to a norm bar.

One of my biggest guilty pleasures was to dress up like this, and no woman could truly deny her inner vixen when she had a chance to let her out—what else explained why sweet reserved girls dressed up in slutty attires every Halloween? Any opportunity to scout a target in a Vampire bar, I'd take it. I couldn't bring myself to wear this kind of crap on a regular basis—it screamed trying too hard. Besides, leather was difficult to get off in a rush, especially with sweat involved. And who didn't sweat in head-to-toe leather?

Demons, my brain answered. Demons didn't sweat.

The clothes I usually wore allowed movement and ripped easily. Not tonight. I banked on getting through the evening without the need to shift. I had to be on my best behaviour.

My muscles quivered as my stomach rolled. Best behaviour? Unlikely. I seldom prayed to the beast Goddess, Feradea, but I took a moment to do so. I needed all the help I could get.

Opening the doorway a crack, I made sure the hallway was clear. Wick paced and mumbled in his room and I sensed no one downstairs.

This is your chance.

I slunk down the stairs and picked my purse up on the way to the door.

"Where do you think you're going?" Wick's voice boomed behind me.

I stopped in my tracks.

"Well?" he said. I imagined him crossing his arms.

Slowly turning to face him, I discovered I was right. "Last time I checked, it was no business of yours."

His eyebrows rose as he took in my outfit. Then his muscles tensed. With flushed cheeks and twitching fists, he looked torn between being turned on and angry. I had that effect on him.

"If you start bringing customers to my house, it will be." His mouth quirked.

"Are you implying that I look like a sex worker?"

"Are you arguing you don't?"

Opening my purse, I dug around for the car keys as

an excuse to break eye contact. "There's a fine line between a high class escort..." I paused and dared him to suggest I could look like another kind of working class woman. "And a vamp-tramp."

"Vamp-tramp!" He sputtered the label a little and then glared. "You're flouncing off to a vamp bar?"

"Reconnaissance," I explained.

"No," Wick stated.

"No?" My eyebrow rose.

"That's what I said."

When I remained silent, he put his arms on his hips and his lips flattened into a hard line. "You will not go out looking like that."

"You're not my father." I turned and walked out the door, desperately trying to reassure myself I wasn't acting like a pubescent teenager pushing boundaries. Okay. Maybe I tried to push Wick a little, but not in the same way.

I didn't make it far down the driveway before an iron hand gripped my upper arm and spun me around. His fingers dug into my skin, but not to the point of causing pain. *He grabs my arms a lot.* When I looked up, I faced the glowing yellow eyes of Wick's wolf. Feradea obviously ignored my plea. Best behaviour ran off into the sunset. I was about to be bad. Very bad.

His mouth crushed down on mine. All thoughts flew from my mind as his arms reached around and pressed me against his hard body. His mouth demanded a response and boy did he get it.

This man could kiss.

"You should get a room for that," John's sarcastic voice pierced the night.

Untangling my body from Wick, I stepped away and glared at John, wanting nothing more than to shove my fist into the Werewolf's solar plexus, to hell with him being in Wick's inner circle. In truth, I should've thanked him for the interruption. With so much electricity pent up between me and Wick, it took little to unleash it.

"John," Wick growled. It came out slowly through clenched teeth.

"Alpha," John nodded, looking pleased.

Wick turned to me, arms held taunt to his side. "I'm going with you." Statement. Fact. Not a request. *Fucking alphas.* I should be hella pissed at his dominance act, but adrenaline ran through my traitorous body and my mind started flying through *all* the possibilities.

John cleared his throat. The door to the black sedan behind John slammed and Jess walked up to stand beside her mate and took his hand. The simple, sweet gesture caused something to churn in my gut. They both turned to Wick, expectation evident on their faces.

Wick cursed. "The meeting."

"Did you forget?" Jess asked.

"He had other things on his mind, love," John spoke into her hair. His voice muffled with the proximity, but being supes we all heard.

"Did I miss something?" Jess asked. Her eyes ping-ponged between the three of us. Her gaze took in my outfit before settling on my face. "Going out?"

"Yes, I have something important to get to," I said.

Turning to Wick, I gave a megawatt smile. "Enjoy your meeting."

"Andy," Wick hissed through his teeth.

I did a model spin while I pranced away to give him an innocent smile. "Don't wait up." The toodaloo wave was probably over the top, gauging Wick's expression.

"This isn't over, Andy," Wick warned.

His glare could have burned a hole in my back, but I had somewhere I needed to go, information I needed to glean. I couldn't do it with a hot Alpha breathing down my neck, distracting me and intimidating others.

THE VAMP BAR, SITUATED IN THE HEART OF Gastown, didn't resemble the warehouse where I'd met my handler in any way. With an immortal existence, the vamp owner of this establishment should've had a better imagination, but no. He called it Hell. The ground level entrance on the corner of an all-window building consisted of double doors, a foyer where two intimidating Vampire bouncers stood and a spiral case that led down into the basement. Music could be heard when the door at the base of the stairs opened to admit more people. One exit—textbook fire hazard.

By walking through the doors at the bottom of the staircase, patrons accepted responsibility for their own stupidity and if any emergency happened, they waived the proprietor's liability for any injury or damage. No one in their right mind would try to make a claim against Vampires, but just in case, they had a vamp lawyer escort all non-vamps down the stairs and explain the rules, spewing out all the legalities.

The rest of the building sitting above the club conducted daytime business. Mostly lawyers. Go figure.

The norms ahead of me in line reeked of crayons and sickly sweet sweat, making my eyes twitch. Unlike vamps, that particular mix of excitement and fear did not entice me. It didn't turn me on and make me want to bite. I would've been a terrible vamp.

Tapping my foot, I glanced at my watch. I'd been in line for ten minutes, and I hated lines. If this had been a norm bar, I would've gone to the front and used my charm to skip the line. Vamp bars were no different in that respect, but these bouncers likely required more than some harmless flirtation and the vague promise of getting more later. They'd want blood.

I had no intention of giving any. Thomas Leroy had been my first boyfriend in high school. Both fifteen, the relationship lasted all of four days. He slobbered all over my face and stuck his tongue down my throat. The final straw had been when he left a giant hickey the size of a baseball on my neck. Since then, there'd been no interest of my part to ever have anything or anyone suck on my neck.

I checked my watch again. Eleven minutes. Eyeing the door guards, I wondered if there could be another way to get in that didn't involve exchanging fluids of any kind. I checked behind me. Not many had joined the line, so it wouldn't be a huge loss if I got turned away, but it would be humiliating. Everyone, including myself, laughed at girls who thought they were hot enough to skip the line only to get rejected.

The two male bouncers at the door didn't look like they had any personality. Still, worth a try. I tucked my purse under my arm, tilted my chin up and walked to the front of the line. When I passed the women in line, they wore pissy looks, and I could tell without asking what they thought of me:

Who does she think she is? She's not that hot.

I bet she gets turned away.

"Hello, gentlemen," I said. Planting both my feet firmly, I squared off. My body posture indicated this wasn't an attempt at seduction or blood offer.

Both men turned their vacant expressions on me. "Can we help you?" the one on the right asked. His name tag said Justin. He was a large black man. His teeth were pearly white and a sharp contrast to his dark skin. He had a French accent. I loved accents.

"I'm here on business," I stated.

"Business with whom?" the vamp on the left asked. He had some sort of eastern European accent and looked the part with Slavic good looks. His name tag said Dmitri. How fitting.

"Not with, but for," I said. They looked confused. "I'm here on business for Lucien," I clarified.

Dmitri laughed. "Nice try," he said.

"Anyone can throw the master vamp's name around," Justin said. "You're not the first to try."

"Ah, but I *am* on business for Lucien."

Both Vampires shook their heads.

Sighing, I crossed my arms. I was not willing to admit defeat yet. "Did you hear what happened to Clint?" I asked.

The bouncers straightened up. Lucien's name might be common knowledge, but his human servant's was not. Justin gave an imperceptible nod.

"You are a part of Lucien's horde, are you not?"

Another nod. This time from Dmitri.

"So you know the contractor was caught and brought before the horde two nights ago?"

"Yes," Dmitri hissed.

"But neither of you were there," I said.

Justin frowned. "How would you know that?"

"Because you would have recognized me."

Their stances changed from relaxed and slightly bored to attentive. Being the unwavering focus of two large Vampires was unsettling. Not new or unexpected, but it still caused my feras to pace in my head.

Kill. My cat hissed.

Let me out. My wolf demanded.

My falcon gave an indignant squawk. She wanted to spread her wings and fly free.

Sometimes I had to tune them out or I'd go crazy.

Crazy with a side of fries.

"You?" Justin eyed me.

"Me," I said. "And if you know what happened the

other night, you'll know that I was set on a task by Lucien. One that I don't have time to wait for in line." I indicated with my chin to the line behind me. The norms had no idea what was going on or the words we exchanged. We spoke softly, too low for their non-supe ears to hear.

The bouncers exchanged a look and as one, stood back to allow me admittance down the stairs. I smiled, happy that I didn't have to take the next step of threatening them with Lucien's discipline.

"Do you know the rules?" Justin asked.

"Yes," I said and stalked down the spiral stairs to enter Hell.

22

The rules were simple. No prolonged eye contact, no exposed necks, no going into the private enclaves or down to the dungeons, and no agreeing to anything proposed by a Vampire, no matter how innocent it sounded. Of course, these weren't the rules the lawyer told the awestruck norm patrons as he led them down the stairs. He made them verbally acknowledge the establishment would not and could not be held liable or accountable for anything that transpired within its grounds and the surrounding area up to a kilometre away. He also warned if they agreed to something, they had to follow through with it. The SRD and local police had no jurisdiction in a Vampire establishment when the food entered willingly. Come down here and you're on your own.

When the cookie-cutter bouncers at the bottom of the stairwell opened the doors, I stepped into the dark and dank realm of the Vampires. With the lighting low and red, the bass of the music thumped heavy in my chest like a second heart beat. Vamps had no qualms about playing to their stereotype and cashed in on it instead. The place smelled of burnt sugar, sour air, musky coconut, crayons and fear—the last overpowering the rest.

Norms packed the place and milled around, looking for an experience to brag about: *Look how brave I am. Look how bold and daring.*

Idiots. In way over their heads, most of them would be caught in a promise they wouldn't want to follow through on. In addition to the newbie spectators, an odd mix of S&M porn star wannabes and emo rejects—black eye liner, a whole lot of pleather, spiked hair coloured with unnatural hues, and piercings that I could and couldn't see—wore their fang scars as badges. The spectator norms admired or gawked at these regular patrons of Hell like specimens at the zoo.

To Vampires, they were all willing food, nothing more. To me, they were morons—whittling down their self-worth to something less than a walking blood just to feel special and wanted.

Tonight, I'd try to blend in with them, minus the scabs and scars on my neck. Vampires took blood from more places than the carotid and I'd let a lesser mind run with that assumption.

Five minutes into the night, I knew I'd fail. One, not a lot of vamps patrolled for food; two, the ones present reeked of Lucien; and three, one of them was Allan.

He tapped me on my shoulder where I stood at the

bar. I spun around, anticipating a fight. My drink splashed out of my cup, but Allan dodged the flying fluid, narrowing his eyes.

"You." I gave the mind reading Vampire my best death stare before casting my gaze down on my wet shirt.

Allan grinned and used a bar napkin to blot the remnants of my drink from my corset. "Me."

Sighing, I leaned against the bar. "You're cramping my style."

Allan's eyebrow rose while he looked me up and down. "And what exactly is your style?" he asked, dropping his voice into a seductive purr.

My skin crawled in response.

He laughed. "I have no interest in you at the moment kitten, but if Clint were to see you..." He left the rest of his sentence for me to fill, but I didn't like anything I came up with.

"I'm not his type."

Allan shook his head. "Clint likes the thrill of the fight, of the hunt and conquest. Nothing turns his crank more than dominating and breaking down someone's will. To him, you're a wet dream."

"I'm not blonde."

"He's booked an appointment for you at Lola's next week. I believe he mentioned a dye job on the phone."

Screw that. Lola's was an expensive and exclusive hair salon in the West End where only the trendy and the wealthy went. Should I be impressed? Instead, the back of my throat ached and I tried to ignore the heavy weight in my chest. The idea of being a toy to the sick fuck, well, it freaked me out a little. Or maybe a lot. I pretended to gag, but Allan's smile only broadened to reveal his fangs. They lengthened as I stared.

Gross.

"I thought you had no interest?" I snarled.

Allan shrugged. "I'm not Clint." He twirled the amber liquid in his cup. "I like feeding off fear. You don't have enough of that..." He eyed me. "Yet."

"Never." I snorted, and then knocked my drink back. He'd been following my thoughts. I'd have to clamp down on those.

"You might say differently after Clint is done with you. After you've been broken, he'll grow bored and pass you to me. He often does with his women. And by then, you will be perfect for me." He licked his fangs. "The anticipation is riveting."

"Surely you can find some willing little things to frighten?"

"The willing are less fun. Their fear is thin, not authentic, with a...tainted taste to it. I prefer the air laden in terror."

"So you take Clint's sloppy seconds?"

Allan laughed. "Trying to antagonize me?"

"I want you to stop talking about what gives you and Clint hard-ons. It's not my topic of choice."

Allan shrugged again. "Piece of advice. If you want Clint to lose interest in you as a toy, act obedient and complacent."

I frowned into my empty glass. "That's a bit of a stretch."

Allan laughed before I spoke, having plucked the thoughts from my head. "I know." He nodded at the bartender and two new drinks arrived faster than humanly possible. "So, why are you here, kitten? What brings you to Hell?" His lip quirked at the line, but I couldn't tell if in amusement or disgust.

"Reconnaissance," I said.

"Here? You think one of Lucien's was behind the attack?" His tone relayed his doubt.

I debated not telling him anything. Obviously, I couldn't trust him, but I needed answers so I settled on a little snippet. "Not one of Lucien's."

"Only Lucien's horde is permitted to enter any of the vamp bars unless escorted."

Well damn. I wish I had known that.

"You think it was a rogue Vampire?" he asked.

"I don't know," I said, honestly. "Is there a horde visiting from out of town?"

Allan frowned. "There are Vampires visiting all the time."

"Any with reason to harm Lucien or Clint?"

"They all want *harm* to come to those two. Vampires are territorial and competitive in nature. We want what another one has. It's in our blood, if you pardon the expression. Lucien squashes attempts for his territory on a regular basis." His eyes met mine. "Is that what you think is happening?"

"When I know for certain what's going on and have the proof to back it up, I'll report everything to Lucien."

Quick! Think of rivers and chirping birds in the forest.
Need to shield my thoughts from Allan.

He laughed. "I could help you, you know."

"This coming from the man who told me he looks forward to when I've been broken so he can scare the bejeezus out of me and get off on it?"

Allan smirked. "I can separate my personal life from professional."

"Riiight."

He shrugged. "Have it your way."

I don't know what I would've said next, because the sight of a man with a predatory gleam in his eyes approaching us had me cursing instead. Allan quirked a brow and looked over his shoulder.

"Clint!" He welcomed the norm and made room for him to stand with us. "What a surprise."

Clint nodded at the bartender and a drink was promptly placed in his hand. Looked like scotch or whiskey. He turned and looked me over. "Andrea." He smiled. "There was no need for you to dress up for me."

I rolled my eyes.

He continued to stare, running his eyes over my body. "I prefer you naked."

My glass made a loud thunk as I slammed it on the bar. "And I'm done."

Both men laughed.

"Good night, *gentlemen*," I said.

"Four more days, Andy," Clint called out to me. "Four more days."

I flipped him the bird and stalked out of the club.

23

Four *days left.* And tonight was a total bust. My throat constricted. I rubbed the base of my neck and tried to get the troubled feeling to ease up. I didn't want to be Clint's. I didn't want to be anyone's possession. *Never again.*

When I stalked into Wick's house, I threw my purse on the floor, and let a growl escape my lips in frustration. Braced with both hands on the edge of the nearest counter, I dropped my head and took several deep breaths in. And froze. The entranceway reeked of Werewolf. An Alpha's house acted as a constant revolving door for his pack, so smells of others always lingered, but this was different. Fresh. I walked around the corner and into the living room to find it occupied.

Wick and Ryan sat opposite of each other on the couches with numerous empty beer bottles on the coffee table between them. My nose crinkled at the sharp smell of alcohol in the air. Shifters and Weres had fast metabolisms, but if motivated enough, a supe could get drunk. Clearly, Wick and Ryan were very, very motivated.

Wick leaned back into the cushions and grinned at my entrance, but Ryan had the opposite reaction. His whole body tensed and his easy smile stiffened into a grimace. Despite his earlier guard duty, we hadn't spoken since the day I seduced him to escape. He'd avoided any eye contact and attempts at conversation since. I couldn't really blame him, either.

"Hi boys." I went for casual, but the words came out high pitched and nervous. "Trying to get drunk?"

Wick's smile spread across his gorgeous face. He took a slow sip from his bottle and eyed me over the rim as if he drank me instead of the cool amber fluid. A tingle ran up my thigh.

"Not anymore." Ryan put his bottle down on the counter a little too hard. It made a loud thunk, spraying beer out onto his hand and the table. I would've laughed, but I'd done the exact same thing in the bar earlier, and Ryan hated my guts. Rightfully so.

Ryan stood up with an annoyed expression on his face. "See you later, Wick."

"Good night." Wick looked torn, his expression somewhere between sympathetic and amused, like he couldn't decide how to feel or whose side to take.

Ryan brushed past me and headed to the door without saying another word. I glanced back to find Wick watching me closely, waiting for me to act. When it became clear I wasn't moving, he patted the cushion beside him. Not so drunk after all. As much as I would've loved to sink into the couch and those arms, there was something I had to do first. I turned and ran after the other Werewolf.

"Ryan!" I called out.

He froze with his hand on the doorknob, but didn't turn around. "What?"

"I want to apologize." That came out whinier than I wanted.

Ryan spun toward me, but his face gave nothing away. "Why?"

"I'm sorry I used you to escape. It wasn't…" At a loss for words, I looked down at my hands to discover them fidgeting. "Right."

"Why apologize for that? It's what you do, right? Seduce targets and eliminate them." He continued before I could utter any semblance of a defence. If I had any. "At least you didn't slit my throat."

He had a point. I was a government contractor. A ruthless killer. "I think it's a testament to how much I like you that I didn't."

Ryan choked on a bitter laugh. "Like me? You have a funny way of showing it."

Sighing, I leaned against the wall. "I like you as a friend. I like that you can kick my ass in martial arts, that you lose at cards, and you couldn't solve a crossword on your own to save your life. You can't hold it against me that I wanted to escape. I needed you incapacitated to give me time to shift and escape, but I didn't want to hurt you."

He continued to glare at me.

"At least not physically."

Silence.

"You liked me," I pointed out. "Yet even if I hadn't tried to escape, you would've brought me to Lucien trussed up like some stuck pig."

Ryan glared at his feet while he clenched and unclenched his hands.

"And I would've understood. I do understand. I'm not sorry for trying to escape, but I apologize for how I did it. If there'd been another way to leave us both unscathed, I would've used it."

That surprised Ryan into looking up. His eyes focused on me and narrowed.

I continued. "I'm sorry I hurt your feelings and you now think everything was an act. It wasn't."

"It wasn't?" he said, his voice rough as gravel.

"No. It wasn't."

"So when you kissed me and rubbed your tits against my chest like a rabid bitch in heat that wasn't an act?" His gaze burned.

I looked away. "Ok, well that part was."

Ryan's laugh was hollow. "Whatever." He walked out of the house and slammed the door behind him.

I let a long breath out.

"I wasn't joking when I said you made an enemy in Ryan." Wick's voice directly behind me didn't come as a surprise. I'd sensed him approach during my pathetic attempt at an apology.

"If you say I told you so, I'll kick your ass."

"No." Warm arms wrapped around me. Wick pulled me back to rest against his strong body. "That's not what I'm doing. You offered him a nice apology."

Another sigh escaped my lips as I allowed myself to enjoy the moment of comfort in Wick's arms. "Not enough."

"No," Wick agreed. "But he might come around in time."

"Sure." I pushed Wick's arms away before I could get too comfortable and walked around to the living room. "But I'll be gone before he finds forgiveness."

Though I couldn't see him, I knew the second Wick tensed. The air crackled with his anger.

"Don't say that," he growled.

I spun around to find Wick fighting with his wolf. His whole body vibrated, his fists shook and his eyes, when he didn't have them squeezed shut, were bright yellow. I started to speak, but he cut me off.

"Don't," he said. "Don't antagonize my wolf like that. It's hard enough holding him back when you're around as it is." Sweat trickled down his face. When a Were's animal wanted something, it pushed and pushed, forcing a change. Despite being a facet of the Were's individuality and not a separate entity, the animal inside believed it could get what it wanted if it had control.

"Wick." I wanted to tell him to be reasonable, but the wolf was beyond reason. Animals were instinctual, not practical. It wouldn't help Wick to hear how there was no way I could stay and risk Lucien's control over me strengthening, that I planned to clear my name, cut out the tracker and run away to lick my wounds. To hell with what my wolf or Wick's wolf wanted.

Wick shook his head while I stood prone. I didn't want to make it harder on him, but after the crappy night I had, the last thing I wanted to do was play submissive to placate Wick's wolf. It would give him more power over me and make it more difficult for my wolf to keep detached. Maybe I could distract him.

"What's your name?" The question poured out of my mouth before I had a chance to filter. "Your full name."

Wick's vibrating stopped, his internal struggle momentarily side-lined, and his head popped up. "Brandon," he said. "Brandon James Wickard."

"And you go by Wick?"

He snorted. "Well I couldn't exactly use BJ as a nickname, now could I?"

A laughed escaped my lips. "So what do you do?"

"Do you mean for work?"

"Yes, for work."

His eyes crinkled with amusement. "Why so interested?"

"I'm not." Leaning against the wall, I tried to look casual, but doubted I pulled it off—too tense. "Only curious."

"I'm a building developer." He took a couple of steps

toward me. A predatory gleam in his eye marked me as prey.

"You build stuff?"

"Not with my own hands. Not anymore."

My eyes drifted to his hands and my thoughts flew to the gutter. *What else could he do with his hands?* My attention snapped back to Wick's. As if he could read my thoughts, he smiled wide and stepped in. His gaze could melt chocolate. If he kept looking at me like that, my will-power would crumble.

"How much longer are you planning to resist this, Andy?"

Maybe he could read minds. I looked away, desperate to break his power over my body and salvage my fast beating heart. The warmth radiating off Wick pressed against me moments before the hard contours of his body. His hands smoothed the goosebumps on my arms before caressing upward to cradle my face. He tilted my head, urging me to look at him again. What I saw in his eyes melted my last remnants of resolve. My wolf howled in my head and my body shook to respond before my mind had a chance to catch up, to process. I was lost in the golden gaze of Wick and his wolf.

He paused long enough for my brain to send one message to my vocal cords. "I can't give you my wolf," I said and leaned in for his kiss.

Wick pulled away, abrupt and unexpected. I stumbled forward, missing the contact. My lips sucked the air like a baby without a soother. I straightened up and frowned at Wick. *What the hell?*

His eyes searched mine, narrowing. "Why not?"

"I can't give you that, Wick."

He shook his head and his fingers softened their grip on my arm. The smell of uncertainty and disbelief tainted the heady scent of his desire. "When I have you..." He tilted my face up with his finger. "And I will. I want all of you." He walked away and left me gaping at him.

He'd have to wait a long time.

24

Mentally confused and sexually frustrated—an unfortunate mix that might get me dry humped by rabid dogs if I didn't reduce my emission of pheromones—I knew beyond a doubt my day would get a lot worse before it got better. I sat in the SRD library in the downtown headquarters on an old computer, clicking through archaic records. The hope of finding a nugget of information to solve my case kept spurring me on despite the innate knowledge I wasted my dwindling time. I found nothing and my mind kept wandering to last night—to Wick.

In my heart I knew he hadn't rejected me. He wanted me, but he also wanted something I couldn't give. When I was in a forced union with Dylan, my feras saved me. I'd been able to keep part of my wolf from my previous Alpha, despite his concerted efforts to force the mate bond. In the beginning, before I saw him for the evil man he was, he managed to get some sort of hold on me, but not enough of one. When things turned ugly, he kept trying to complete the mating process. But by then, I'd smartened up and held my wolf close. He didn't know about the other feras. My mountain lion and falcon eventually weakened his power and I broke free. When I did bust out of the shackles, I became a monster from an adult horror flick and destroyed the entire pack. At least most of it. The other women survived.

All this time, I'd feared I had consigned them to a fate worse than death, a life without their mates, but Mel not only survived, she thrived. From the sounds of things, the other women did, too. I would never have hurt them willingly. Maybe the death of a mate affected Weres differently when they were from a forced union.

Werewolves mated for life like Shifters. If my wolf mated with Wick's, the bond might be unbreakable. Not being a 'normal' Shifter, I didn't know what rules applied to my life and that freaked me out. If permanent, there'd be no running away if he turned out to be like Dylan. Or if it bound Wick for life and not me, would I resign Wick to a life of unhappiness?

The poignant smell of coyote swirled around and drew me out of my head. It's hard to describe what coyotes smell like. Mischief. Trouble. Yet instead of disliking the smell, it brought a much needed smile to my face. A furry body brushed my leg.

"O'Donnell." I smiled without turning around. His fera familiar huffed and flopped down at my feet. I reached to scratch behind his ears.

"Carus." The old man's voice sounded pleased. I

looked over my shoulder to find the old man smiling, deepening the wrinkles that creviced his face.

"I hope you're not here to give me a new assignment. I'm still in the process of botching the current one." I tapped the computer screen. I'm not sure why. It didn't prove my point, but somehow it made me less frustrated.

The old man lifted both shaggy brows and chuckled. He took the seat beside me and sat down. "No new assignments. I scented you in the lobby and wanted to check in on you."

"Why do you call me that?"

"Call you what?"

"Carus."

"It means 'beloved'."

"I know that. I have mad Google skills. But why call me that?"

O'Donnell tilted his head to the side and frowned. "Because you're beloved to all Shifters." He leaned forward and his expression opened, signalling he was on the verge of launching into dialogue.

"Hold on." I interrupted whatever speech he was about to give. "Are you actually a grumpy old wizard? Here to tell me I must join you, a lethal barbarian and a gallant nobleman on some mysterious quest?"

"No."

"Does this involve some sort of sorcerer's tower, a creepy tall building of any kind, or a magic sword?"

"No."

Was his tone a bit exasperated? I groaned and leaned back into my chair. "Is this where you tell me

I'm the long lost descendent of some fabled Shifter? Or that I, and only I, possess strange and formidable powers and am the only one who can save the Shifters from certain doom. Or ooo..." I sat up. "Only I can vanquish the dark demon lord king and create world peace?"

O'Donnell started to speak.

"Is there a prophesy?" I demanded.

The old man pinched his nose as if to stem an oncoming headache. He sat in that position with his head down for a while. Then his shoulders shook. He was laughing.

"To answer your last bout of questions... No. No. No and not that I know of. God, I hope not. You're not exactly prophesy material."

"Umm. Thanks?"

"Did your parents not explain this to you?" He wore a puzzled expression. It looked like his eyebrows were trying to figure out how to become two separate entities, instead of a bushy monobrow.

I flicked my fingers up to emphasize my points. "One. My parents are dead. Two. They adopted me."

O'Donnell made a silent 'ahhh' face. "That explains a lot. Your file didn't mention any adoption."

"I chose not to disclose that information," I said, after getting over my initial shock of the SRD's ineptitude for background checks. "I assumed the SRD knew anyway."

O'Donnell pursed his lips. "The information regarding your parentage must be in a classified file above my clearance—guaranteed they know. Adoption leaves a large, glaring paper trail."

"So I do have mysterious parentage?"

He shook his head. "A Shifter like you comes around maybe once every five hundred years. You're not one of a kind, but you are unique. You have exceptional skills. And you're cherished amongst our kind because you're the beloved chosen of Feradea." He made some sort of gesture of reverence to the wild beast goddess—touching two fingers to his lips, then his forehead, then above his head in the air. It reminded me of the motion for 'thank you very much' in American Sign Language, except instead of the hand going out in front, it went up.

"So I should stop cursing her?"

The dark look O'Donnell gave provided the answer.

"How was I to know she was real?" I shrugged. "She's never appeared to me."

O'Donnell's expression made it clear he thought I was a colossal idiot. "After all the supe groups exposed over the years, you still doubt Feradea exists?"

I squirmed in my seat. "Well, no."

A long, raspy sigh escaped O'Donnell's mouth. He looked like he aged five years. "Gods exist. They are around us. Every day. Our beliefs lend them sustenance. She probably didn't appear because you're a non-believer." He cut off whatever he was about to say to look away, clearly agitated.

Stop upsetting the old man. The voice in my head didn't belong to me. Or my feras.

"Huh?" I looked around. Sharp teeth sank into my

ankle. My knee slammed into the bottom of the desk as I jumped out of my seat.

"Ow!" I rubbed my ankle and glared at the coyote at my feet. I swear the mangy beast grinned at me.

You have a lot to learn, little Carus. The voice rasped in my head, foreign, but not unpleasant. The coyote nipped me on the ankle again. I managed a smaller jump, and avoided bashing my knee into the desk for a second time.

"Ummm." I looked at O'Donnell. "Is your fera speaking to me?"

The old man smiled. "Why don't you ask him?"

I looked down at the grinning little devil and tried to direct my thoughts at him. *Are you speaking to me?*

Of course, the fera said. *It is one of the gifts Feradea bestowed on you. All feras can speak to you this way and you to them.*

Huh. That was my intellectual response.

My name is Ma'ii. The old man calls me Ma.

Does that have some sort of special meaning? I asked.

It's Navajo for coyote. The fera yawned.

Isn't that a bit redundant?

Ma bit my ankle again as a response. Not enough to draw blood, but it hurt.

Ouch!

Use these direct consequences as a learning opportunity. He looked away and began to lick his hind leg.

I rubbed the tooth marks on my ankle and turned my attention back to O'Donnell. "I'm not sure I appreciate Ma's form of guidance."

The old man laughed. When he finally looked me in the eye, his smile was twice as wide. "I think we have all suffered enough teachings today. Is there anything in particular I can help you with?"

"Do you know much about Lucien's court?"

He shook his head. "The basic hierarchy."

"Do you know of any hordes in town?"

"There's a few. Lucien's court has an endless stream of envoys coming in and out. It's a desirable area for Vampires. Long winters. A large port for easy access and travel." He shrugged. "Is there any horde in particular you're interested in?"

"I'm looking for one with ties to Wereleopards."

O'Donnell frowned. "I don't know of any offhand. I can look into it if you would like."

"I would definitely like." I shoved away from the computer and jabbed the off button with enough force that the contraption would have no excuse for misunderstanding my disappointment and anger with it.

The old man's eyes crinkled as we both stood up. I glanced down at my bite-ridden ankle with dismay. Being fast to heal, it no longer throbbed with pain, but my previously smooth and unblemished skin was now riddled with tiny, itchy scabs.

"I want to know more." I hoped my voice didn't sound as desperate as I felt.

O'Donnell nodded. "In time. First, you must get out of your current predicament. When you are ready, you will need all your attention to focus within."

"In the meantime, start praying and apologizing to the Feradea?"

The old man grunted. "You're learning."

My phone beeped on my drive back. Wick had given me the far-too-advanced-piece-of-technology in the morning. Apparently everyone under Lucien's control possessed one—the Vampire treated his minions well and recently supplied the entire pack the latest contraption on the market with everyone's phone numbers prepro-grammed into it. Mine had been on back order, and now that I had it, I'd been ignoring suggestive texts from Clint all morning. There had to be a way to block someone, but I hadn't figured it out yet. More elaborate than my old paperweight flip phone, it took a while to get used to it.

I waited until the next red light to glance at my phone. Wick. The law prohibiting cell phone use while driving made sense. A lot of people got into accidents because they took their eyes off the road. I risked the fine and read the text message anyway.

Where are you?

I glanced up at the light and saw it was still red. I texted back:

Omw from SRD now. May take a bit.

I wasn't the most text savvy person out there, but I had recently learned that "omw" stood for "on my way." I tried to use it as often as possible to sound more hip—not sure if I fooled anyone.

My phone beeped again, but I ignored it. The horns honking behind me encouraged me to be a safe driver. At the next light, I looked over at my phone and read Wick's text:

Why?

I need caffeine. Going to stop at the gas station.

For the cocaine?

What?

Read your last message.

So I did. Instead of "caffeine" I'd texted "cocaine." Damn autocorrect. I waited until the next stop light to text:

OMG! I meant caffeine, Wick!

Well I hope the SRD isn't tapping your phone.

Laughing alone in my car I took the exit to the nearest gas station, and unfortunately for me, the one with the slowest cashier in the Lower Mainland. Carrying two bags of medium roast random blend coffee in one hand and a bag of strawberry-flavoured liquorice in the other, I made sure my posture indicated how put out I was for waiting. It went unnoticed.

"Would you like to donate one dollar to..." The cashier entered her sales pitch for a fundraiser oblivious to the growing line in front of her till in the tiny store.

"Would you like to buy another one? They're on sale. Two for two ninety nine..." This was the third item of the man's five-item purchase she tried to upsell. I ground my teeth and squashed my mountain lion's desire to shift and claw her face off. *Down, kitty.* The Shifter three people up in the line looked to be having the same struggle and the Witch behind me cracked her knuckles. This area of the Lower Mainland, dense with the paranormal demographic, meant it could get messy if this lady, oblivious to the agitated supes in the line, didn't hurry the fuck up.

"One second." The cashier held up one finger and answered the phone. "Hi, Mom. Uh huh. Uh huh. No. Well, maybe." She glanced up at her customers. "Hey, it's getting a bit busy." Pause. "Well, no." It took another few minutes, a promise to come over for Sunday dinner and to call her mom back in an hour to get off the phone. In that time, the acrid scent of anger in the room doubled. The witch abandoned her purchases on the nearest shelf and stalked off.

I sneezed.

Anger was one of my least favourite smells. Pulling my shirt over my nose, I read the headlines of the magazines in a rack beside me for the third time. One of my guilty pleasures was to read about young Hollywood trash and find out what debacle they managed to get into since the last time I read about them. Money may not buy happiness, but it did buy a whole lot of drama.

The cashier finished processing the now irate customer. Luckily the guy behind him only had a pack of gum and gas to buy. She rang him through in a relatively short time, having little opportunity to upsell or do fundraising pitches in between items. Getting to take two shuffles forward seemed to appease most people in the line and I risked popping my nose out of my shirt to see if it smelled better.

Citrus and sunshine swirled around and forced my spine ramrod straight. I spun around. One smirking Wereleopard stood behind me, clad in a skin-tight red dress with white polka dots. *What was she doing here?* Angie shifted her gaze, somehow managing to make her lips twitch into a more condescending expression while she ran her gaze over my appearance.

What's your problem?

From the minuscule flinch in her expression and the turned heads in my direction, I realized I'd said that out loud. Oops.

She flipped a noncommittal hand in the air. "I don't know what you're talking about." Her words said one thing, but her actions said another. She made sure to look me up and down again and raise an eyebrow. I squashed the urge to pounce on her and have it out girl-on-girl fight style. Obviously, her problem was me. I wore sweats and a t-shirt. They were mine, but they smelled of Wick. For some reason my wash kept getting mixed up with his. I didn't need her pointed looks to know my attire didn't meet her standards. *Good.*

I returned the unimpressed appraising look and eyed her ballooning boobs almost springing out of her dress. At least, I hoped it came across as distaste, not envy. From her smug grin, I wasn't successful.

"You positively reek of dog." Her lip curled up.

I hitched my hip and tried to think of a retort. I couldn't exactly say she smelled of pussy, now could I? That was derogatory to women everywhere and not my style. "I might smell of a dog, but at least I'm not a bitch." *Ha. Take that!*

I was so impressed with my own witty comeback, I didn't notice someone approaching until Angie's attention moved from me to over my right shoulder. I glanced behind me. A Werewolf I'd never seen before strolled up to us. He had his hands in his pockets, but his body language made it appear as if he had my back. He smelled faintly of Wick.

Angie's eyes widened. His scent must have reached her. Not being the idiot I wished she was, Angie put two and two together and realized the Werewolf was from the same pack as the one whose scent I wore.

Angie rolled her eyes and shoved her purchases on the nearest shelf and stalked out of the store. She still managed to swing her hips—boom, boom, boom—and made it look sexy. My dislike for her increased.

I turned to the Werewolf, who openly assessed me.

He was medium height, medium build, brown hair, light brown skin. He wasn't exceptionally attractive or repulsive, but his eyes stood out—a piercing, gem-cutting emerald. And they sparkled with amusement. He held his hand out. "Steve."

"Andy." I clasped his hand firmly and smiled. His scent wasn't familiar. He must've missed out on the Supe-Mart parking lot take down. Probably a good thing. That had been embarrassing. Odd that he'd be here, very coincidental. Or was it? The gas station sat along one of the major commuter routes that led to Wick's place.

"I know," he said. At my puzzled expression he continued, "I told Wick a woman who smelled of the forest and wore his scent was having a showdown with a hot Wereleopard and asked if I should do something."

I didn't recall hearing a phone conversation while I had my stare down with Angie. But then I'd been too distracted to notice him enter the building and approach us. He could've communicated with Wick telepathically through their pack bond. "You think she's hot?"

He gave me a flat stare.

"I would have preferred being the one described as hot and Angie described as slutty..." I shrugged. "But there's no accounting for taste."

Steve chuckled. He looked down at my purchases— at least what I intended to be purchases. At this rate, I wasn't sure if they would be within their three year expiry date before I paid for them. "You are what you eat, you know." His smile flashed.

I'm twisted like liquorice? Somehow that didn't feel

like a compliment. I bit back the immediate 'screw you' response and smiled wide. "That's funny. I don't recall eating sexy beast this morning."

Steve paused while he tried not to laugh. "I take it you're not a health nut like Wick."

"Nope. Speaking of which, what'd he say?" I asked.

"What do you mean?"

"What did Wick say when you asked him what to do?"

Steve's smile broadened. "He told me to protect you at all costs."

The cashier interrupted whatever I would have managed aside from 'huh,' by calling out "Next!" She seemed perturbed at being made to wait. Steve winked at me and walked out of the store before I could ask him anything else.

"Bye!" I called out at him, and he waved without looking. I stared at his retreating back, only noticing now that he hadn't purchased anything.

The cashier took hours to ring up my three purchases, which gave me time to think. *Wick said protect at all costs*. He'd basically announced to a pack member I was his mate. The Alpha's mate.

I chewed through half the liquorice on my way home while I tried to figure out how I felt about that. About Wick. About everything. One thing was for sure—the big boy and I were going to have words.

25

I let the door slam when I walked into Wick's house. Prepared to launch into a tirade, the fresh scent of other Werewolves in the house pissed me off. Well damn. I'd have to wait. With my body overheating, I used my shirt to fan myself before walking down the hall. Though I expected to see a number of people, I froze when I rounded the corner. The place was jammed full of Werewolves. *Packed with pack.*

My scent drifted into the room before me as a silent announcement, and the Weres turned toward me as a collective whole. Some growled their disproval.

Cold invisible hands clamped around my throat, squeezing, as a memory surfaced. Unable to breathe, the panic numbed my body, sinking my feet into the plush carpet. I stood helpless, unable to move, forced to relive the images as they bitch-slapped my mind.

"They're watching," I whispered. *"They're all watching." A familiar humiliation broiled, deep in my gut.*

"They're pack, Andy." Dylan gripped my hair and threw me to the floor. "They'll do what I say."

"Please don't do this." I hated the weakness in my voice, how pathetic I'd become, whittled down to a shadow of my former self.

When confronted by a pack of Werewolves not showing or feeling fear was imperative. I'd just failed that test. My scent gave away my emotions, even if my face didn't. Fuck. The whispers in the room flowed over my body, waking it up and disrupting the vision from going further, to a place I didn't want to go. Never again. I took a deep breath, then another. I could not allow the memory to control me, not in front of a pack. I lifted my chin and threw my purse on the counter. "Wick, I didn't get the memo about a pack meeting."

Wick's smile flashed across the room. He rose out of his seat and the Weres parted for him to approach me. "It was impromptu." He leaned down and kissed me on the cheek, his lips quirking as he withdrew. *Was he daring me?*

"Nice turnout."

Wick nodded and turned toward his pack, giving his back to me as a silent testament of his trust. If anyone had thought to challenge me from my show of weakness, they might rethink it now. Wick's pack observed the exchange in silence—some still growling, some smiling, while others wore unreadable expressions, blank slates. I could only imagine what the internal pack dialogue sounded like. John pinched his nose.

Wick looked over his shoulder. "If you had received the memo?"

Huh? Oh. "I would've avoided your house like a sesquipedalian safe word."

Wick mouthed *sesquipedalian* in confusion before he shook his head in defeat.

"Long, multisyllabic word," I explained.

Wick's eyes narrowed. "I had a feeling you wouldn't show if you knew. That's why I didn't tell you."

My eyes snapped to Steve, who sat among the smilers. "You didn't tell me everything he said, did you?"

Steve had the audacity to wink. That's one thing I hated about Weres and fellow Shifters. We were superb at telling half-truths and lying by omission.

"Is she the reason we've been waiting?" The unfamiliar voice belonged to an attractive woman. A skinny model type dressed in a black lace cocktail dress with four inch heels, she looked a bit out of place amongst the otherwise laid back and casually dressed Weres.

"Shush, Christine. You're being rude." Mel spared the woman a glance before she waved at me. One of the dressiest people I knew, Mel wore jeans and a tank top. Skinny jeans, probably designer, but more casual than Christine's outfit.

John had mentioned Christine. So far, not impressed.

Wick cut in when Christine's look turned venomous. "Yes. She is the reason I wanted you all to wait. Some of you have already met Andy." Wick gestured to me.

"Lucien's newest bitch," Christine grumbled. I gave

her my best death stare to let her know I heard. She smirked and looked back at Wick. There was a fevered regard in her gaze. *Oh crap.* I didn't have to be the sharpest tool in the shed to know what that meant or to figure why she took an instant dislike to me. I needed an obsessed, jealous Werewolf nosing around about as much as a submarine needed a window screen.

"Andy has the protection of the pack," Wick stated. Silence. Shocked silence.

"I claim the right to challenge." Christine's bold words punctured the quiet room. More than one Were gasped.

Wick frowned. "On what grounds?"

"As Alpha female." Christine stomped her foot.

"Christine," Wick's voice turned soft. "Let's go outside to talk."

She shook her head, but Wick walked up to her and gently took hold of her arm to steer her out of the room. Rather pointless, if he'd asked me. As Weres, everyone in the room could hear their conversation.

"I'm the Alpha female."

"Christine, we are not in a committed relationship—"

"Yet."

He sighed. "You were the incumbent Alpha female, if anything."

"Don't you dare. Don't you deny that I would've had the position for good if *she* hadn't come along."

Stabbing sensations spread across my chest as my heart dropped into the pit of my stomach. I didn't need

Dr. Phil around to figure out why. I didn't like that Wick was with Christine before I came along. Looking at the past with present feelings was never a good idea. My body twitched with jealousy.

"We're not mated." Wick interjected Christine's tirade. "We never were and never will be."

"We're mates!" her voice adamant. Several Weres in the room flinched.

"No Christine, we're not." The strength of his Alpha power laced into the words.

"I'm Alpha female."

"Not anymore."

"She's not Were."

"It doesn't matter. She's wolf."

"Let me stay as Alpha female. She couldn't possibly handle the role." Her voice turned plaintive. Whiney. Embarrassment racked my body on her behalf. If she started grovelling or begging, I'd have to break it up. Besides, Wick hadn't technically claimed me as his mate, although that's the general assumption, he only gave me the protection of the pack. If I conquered the current Alpha female in a challenge though, incumbent or not, that changed things. Christine wasn't planning on losing; she wanted to put me in my place. The problem for her was I didn't plan on losing, either.

"That's not for you to decide." Wick's voice took on a new firmness.

"It's not for you to either. You can't fight her battles for her."

Wick stayed silent. As soon as Christine made the

point, I started pulling my clothes off. When I heard the click of her heels against the hardwood heading in my direction, I was ready to shift. The other Weres drew back to the edges of the room. Some of them glanced at me, surprised to find me naked. I knew pack dynamics. Either fight for dominance or be a doormat to some Werebitch—throw down or get thrown down. I wasn't a sub and if I didn't assert my dominance, some primal part of Christine would continuously drive her to pick a fight with me until the hierarchy could be established.

Christine stalked into the room. "I challenge—" Her eyes widened when she turned in my direction. She didn't have time to finish her sentence. I pounced.

Weres took longer to shift. She didn't have time to make the vulnerable transition. I had her pinned on the ground with my jaws clamped around her throat, squeezing hard enough to draw blood. My growl vibrated off the skin on her neck and tickled my mouth, my intentions clear.

"I will not concede." Her voice strangled against my teeth.

I growled again.

"I will not submit! Either kill me or give me a fair fight, you bitch." Her voice sounded less sure than her words. She stank of fear, but her pride held strong.

Killing her outright would be the smart thing to do, but Wick's pack didn't seem like the kind that fought challenges dirty or to the death. And the fair fight dig got to me. I released her throat and backed off. My tail twitched as I waited to see what she would do.

Christine stood up. Her knees wobbled a bit, but she straightened and turned to me. No one helped her. Interesting.

"Fight me as a wolf."

Dammit. A Werewolf versus Shifter wolf had one clear outcome, and it wasn't in my favour. But this was pack business. Not the realm of the SRD. I couldn't fight dirty here and expect any respect. *Did I even want it?* I wanted Wick, but I also wanted to get the fuck out of this situation. Easier to lose respect than earn it. I'd have to fight this dominance battle the hard way.

I shifted into a wolf and waited, watching her every move and looking for weaknesses. Without the advantage of my mountain lion's strength and quickness, I'd have to outsmart her.

Christine frowned. I hoped my quick shift intimidated her. Not enough to stop her though. She stripped off her dress and held it out. When no one took it from her, she looked around with pursed lips. After a few awkward seconds, a nameless woman stepped up and snatched it from her hand. Christine nodded and quickly slipped out of her undergarments before handing them over.

I waited, taking delight in knowing my breasts were larger than hers.

Meeeoow. What a ridiculous thought to have. Apparently, I could shift out of the mountain lion, but I couldn't take the cattiness out of the woman.

She started the process of transforming. I cleaned the fur on my front legs as I waited. Mel walked over to stand behind me. She reached out and scratched behind my ears. I relaxed under her ministrations, taking the time to enjoy the support. She knew this wasn't the first challenge I'd faced. If I'd been in my mountain lion it would probably have been the easiest. I wondered if Mel tried to warn Christine. Maybe that's why Christine insisted I use my wolf form. I glanced up to see Mel smile, a sad twinkle in her eye. She mouthed our mantra to me, "Survive."

No. Mel wouldn't have said a thing.

Christine growled and my attention snapped back to her while she completed the final stages of the transition. *Thank the beast goddess I'm a Shifter and not a Were.* That looked downright painful.

Small for a Werewolf, the force of her mental attitude alone must've been her dominating strength. Bonus, for me. Instead of taking time to orient her body after the shift, Christine lunged. I jumped out of her path, but she must've anticipated the move, changing direction at the last minute and slamming her body into mine. *Oomph.*

We rolled over one another claws and fangs flashing, skin and fur ripping—a chick fight hopped up on methamphetamine. But she was stronger, much stronger than me.

"Be better with mud," someone commented. It sounded like Steve.

Christine aimed low, getting her head and front body under mine. Then she surged up, flinging me a few feet in the air. I smacked into someone's legs.

"Get in there," John said. He pushed me back into

the cleared circle with his foot. Asshole. I saw red. I tried to turn and snap at his foot, but Christine tackled me, trying to pin me down. With a front leg across my back, she bit into my neck, hard. The scent of my blood filled my nose. Pain lanced down my body, leaving it cold and shaky. My breath came in short huffs. I couldn't get enough. Not enough! I couldn't breathe. The room narrowed and my vision shook. With weakened knees, an overpowering urge to just lie down and submit consumed me.

No!

The beast rose up with a surge of adrenaline. My chest fluttered and my lungs relaxed, letting in a large whoosh of air. My muscles tightened in response, ready for action. I pushed with all my strength against the ground and flung myself back. Christine yipped. Her teeth still imbedded in my loose neck fur, I arched over her, bringing her with me. My heart raced, nearly exploding, as I landed hard against her stomach.

Now on her back, Christine released my neck and started thrashing. She kicked me off. We both scrambled to our feet and once again, we stared at each other, face to face, assessing. I knew she'd try to take out my legs again, or throw her body against mine. She'd use her strength. She'd aim low.

As she lunged, I leapt up and twisted, landing on her back. I wound my legs around her in a feline move and clamped my jaws tight against her neck. She tried to buck me off, romping and flailing around the room like a bronco. When she staggered and toppled over onto her side, I quickly freed her neck and flipped her onto her back, using all my weight as leverage. I locked my mouth over her throat again and growled. Christine wiggled and fought against my hold. I clamped down more. Her skin gave way and my teeth sank in. Blood poured into my mouth and out onto the carpet.

Christine whined and stopped struggling.

Warmth radiated through my body. I'd won. And as a wolf. It had been a long time since I'd trusted this form to do anything besides act as a bloodhound. Dominance asserted, I shifted back to human and stood up. I felt ultra-awake, rejuvenated. Pumped.

Mel smiled and punched me in the arm. Her throwing form was horrible and it must've hurt her hand, because she shook it out by her side. A few others, like Jess smiled. The others viewed me with blank expressions, withholding judgment. I'd take that over open hostility.

John had a black eye. When our eyes met, he grimaced. How'd he get that? I'd hit his legs, not his face.

I clambered back into my clothes and then found Wick in the crowd. He smiled, rubbing red knuckles.

"We need to talk," I said to him.

He nodded and turned to the pack. "Meeting's over. Help Christine and clean up."

Wick's feet hit the steps hard as he stalked after me.

Not waiting for Wick to enter his room completely, I spun around and flung my hands up. "I'm not your Alpha female."

Wick took his time shutting the door behind him. Probably hoping I would calm down by the time he turned to face me. "Your success at dominating Christine would suggest otherwise."

"I didn't exactly have a choice."

"You could have submitted."

I gave Wick a flat stare so he'd understand how unlikely that was. "I don't want the position. Christine can go on being the Alpha female for all I care."

"Really?"

"Really."

"Usually the Alpha female and the Alpha male mate, Andy. Are you saying you don't care if that happens? It wouldn't bother you if I took Christine to my bed?"

A sudden pain stabbed my heart and robbed me of breath. I couldn't speak. Wick stepped closer.

"If I put my hands on her like this." He ran his palms up my arms to cradle my face. "Or kissed her, like this?" His lips were soft and supple. Gently he worked his mouth on mine. I moaned and opened to him. His tongue slipped inside. Lost in his kiss, I twined my arms around his neck, clutched his hair and drew him closer.

Sucking my bottom lip, Wick withdrew as gently as he started. "You wouldn't care?"

"Ugh," I managed. "Shut up. More kissing." I drew his head back down to mine.

Silently, Wick went back to his task of kissing me as if he possessed an owner's manual I never knew existed. My lips were already swollen and my skin ached for his touch. Wick hoisted me up and I wrapped my legs around him. His hands grasped my ass as he dragged his teeth across my bottom lip and moved his mouth like a caress down my neck.

My wolf rose up to meet his and I beat her down. I didn't want her to interrupt the wondrous sensations zinging throughout my body. Wick lay me down on his bed and smiled. "This is where I want you," he said. "This is how I see you in my dreams."

Before I could comment or move, he lunged onto the bed and caged me in with his forearms. I wanted to feel the weight of him on me. I pulled him down, or at least tried to. He smiled against my skin, kissed down to my shirt collar and refused to lower his body. He held his weight off me in a super plank and I hated it. I wanted his warmth.

He did something exquisite with his tongue on the sensitive skin at the base of my neck. My head snapped back to revel in the feeling as I gripped his back. A sharp ripping sound marked the end of my shirt—I didn't like it anyway. The scent of musky coconut filled the air, from me, from Wick. Wow. I *wanted* him. Wick flung something out of his way. When his hot mouth enclosed my nipple I realized he'd ripped off my bra. I didn't like that article of clothing either.

Wanting his lips back on mine, I grabbed Wick's head and pulled him up. His eyes were yellow. His wolf was at the surface—the sight intoxicating. A soft moan escaped my lips when Wick lowered his body onto mine and the hard ridge of his erection dug into me through his pants. He readjusted for a better alignment and slowly rubbed against my core. Hang on. Where did my sweats go?

His tongue plunged into my mouth and he drove it in with the same timing as he ground against me. Wait. What was the question? Mmm. Who cares?

"Andrea." Wick's whiskey and cream voice vibrated down my body.

My hand snaked down to unzip his jeans. He went back to the plank position so I could push his pants down using my feet. I shivered at the sudden cold. As soon as his pants were off, he dropped back down on top of me, enveloping me back into his wolf scent. His hands went into my hair and clasped hard. His mouth became more insistent, his wolf driving him.

My lungs closed up. I tried to draw more air in, but couldn't breathe. And then the memory took hold and consumed me.

Yellow eyes tracked every subtle shift of my body. His powerful frame built for intimidation hovered over me. He savoured the air, my scent laced with trepidation and terror, his aphrodisiac. I'd loved this man. I chose him.

Wick's head snapped back and his eyes narrowed.

"Andy." This time my name came out more like a question than a caress. "Come back to me."

Unable to speak, I shook my head. His hands released my hair and he ran a finger down my cheek. "Please?"

My head fell against the pillow. A deep sigh escaped my lips. My crotch throbbed with unfulfilled need.

Wick rolled onto his elbow beside me, still close and hovering half on top of my body, but somehow the move gave me the space to breathe, or flee, if I needed to. His eyes flared with emotion and a war of scents radiated off his skin: affection, sympathy, lust, confusion, anger, frustration, but his pain cut me deepest. I needed to erase that look.

I took a deep breath. "You said you wanted *all of me*. Then you have to accept all of me. You have to accept that I can't give you everything right away. Not yet. Not after you hear why I hold back. Maybe then you'll understand. Maybe then, you'll accept what I offer and not push me too hard, too fast."

"Not after I hear what happened?" Wick growled. "I don't need to hear how that dog forced a union on you. His actions..." Wick squeezed his eyes shut. "If he was alive, I'd tear him apart."

"We can dance on his grave later, but it wasn't forced. Not at first."

Wick frowned. "Explain."

"Umm...maybe we could put some clothes on?"

Wick shook his head. "Tell me now." He held his body rigid, with every muscle taut and contracted. His eyes still blazed yellow as he fought his wolf for control.

He'd never hurt me, but he might rip everything around us to shreds. So I told him, reliving the events as if they occurred all over again.

"I met him when I was twenty. I'd just discovered Krav Maga and went to a convention as any new enthusiast would. Dylan was an instructor and seemed so strong and knowledgeable. My wolf liked him instantly, but looking back, it might've been because Dylan was the first Werewolf I'd met. I was infatuated with him—obsessed. He treated me like a princess, doting on me, buying me lavish gifts, taking me to expensive restaurants, and spending every moment he could with me. He told me we were mates. I didn't notice any of his manipulative comments; the ones that made me doubt my friends or myself. After a year, we moved in together and I started to meet his pack. That's when I realized not everything was rainbows and donuts."

I took a deep breath and continued. "I started asking questions, like why hadn't I met his pack earlier, and why did all the female Werewolves act like deranged Stepford wives." I met Wick's yellow eyes. "He'd been prepping me for the mating bond the whole time, to be his personal minion to do his bidding, and I hadn't seen it. Not right away. I was alone except for him, having alienated my friends and family long before because of his needling advice. My feras saved me. They held back a part of me, the essential part of my essence so even when I thought I was willing something prevented me from completing the bond.

"Dylan still had a hold on my wolf to a certain extent,

and though it prevented me from running, it frustrated him the bond wasn't whole. Near the end, after eleven years of being trapped with him, he became truly desperate in his attempt to break me. I won't go into the details, but it was humiliating, painful and terrifying." I took in a big gulp of air. "But no matter how bad the stuff he did to me was, it couldn't erase the knowledge that my wolf chose him. *I chose him*."

I kept my voice calm using an even and clinical tone. It seemed to calm Wick and his wolf. The yellow of his wolf receded so his soft chocolate eyes gazed at me instead.

"That wasn't your fault, Andy."

"But it was. I fell for his act. I thought I was in love and he was my match. I allowed my wolf to mate with his."

Another growl escaped Wick's lips.

"But I didn't finish it." I blushed, knowing Wick would understand what that meant. Completing the mating bond involved a strategically timed bite—the one wound that would scar instead of heal on a Were or Shifter. The mark of a mate.

"You need to trust your instincts."

"What if I'm wrong again? It *broke* me, Wick. It took me thirty-three years living as an animal in the woods to find my humanity again. Barely. That's why I've been working for the SRD for the last fifteen years. Even now, I'm not whole. I don't know you. I don't care if my wolf wants to hump your leg. I can't go into a mating bond blind. I don't think I have it in me to break a bond like that again and survive it."

Wick's chest rumbled. "When we mate, it will be for life. There'll be no breaking it."

"Exactly my point," I huffed. "Shouldn't we get to know each other a bit better first? It's not too late to walk away."

"Weres don't have a shitload of potential mates running around, Andy. It will not be easy for me to *walk* away. It will be impossible."

"Easier than if we're wrong about this match."

"Not wrong." He leaned down and bit my jaw. "We are meant to be together. How did you react when you first took in my scent? I felt the same overwhelming thing. You are just scared."

He'd felt that, too? "Maybe I am. Why can't you give me time? What's a few months in respect to a lifetime?"

"Months?" His voice made a strangled sound.

I shrugged. "Maybe less if you play your cards right."

Wick's chest rumbled. "So what are you suggesting? You want to *date* me?" He made the word sound dirty.

"Time to wine and dine, baby." I slapped his butt. The hard muscle left my hand stinging, but I couldn't help myself.

Wick pretended to grumble, but his lips twitched. "So wait. You met Dylan when you were twenty, spent eleven years with him, thirty-three years as a mountain lion and then fifteen years with the SRD?" He paused, probably doing the mental math. "That makes you seventy-nine."

"Don't remind me."

"Just a baby." He licked his lips.

I stared at his mouth. "Exactly how much are you robbing the cradle?"

He shook his head and didn't answer. "I hope you don't expect me to keep my hands off you," he said.

"I expect you to have them all over me."

No more encouragement was needed. With a wicked grin, he dropped his head to my breasts.

"But," I said.

Wick froze. "But?"

"I don't think I'm..." I paused. "Ready for..." How should I put it? Sex? Commitment? Vulnerability?

Wick nodded. "I get it, Andy. We'll go slow." He trailed kisses down my body. One of his hands slipped under to clutch my butt. He squeezed it hard and dragged his teeth along my hip bone.

"I love how your skin tastes." Wick's voice vibrated off said skin. Ripples of pleasure travelled up my body. My nipples ached. Every inch of me hummed with deep longing. His actions defied his words. He might be working my body slowly, but this hardly qualified as a PG-rated activity.

"Wick." His name came out as a plea.

His lips curled up and then he dipped his head between my legs. Running the bridge of his nose along the crease between my right leg and crotch, he drew in a deep breath, scenting me. "I want to taste all of you."

I ran my hands through his short blond hair before clasping his head and angling it up to meet my eyes over the length of my body. His irises blazed yellow, his wolf in full control. "Wick," I warned.

Wick swore and dropped his head. He took deep breaths in and out.

"This isn't slow."

"No," came his strangled reply. He rolled off me. "I know. You are going to be the death of me, woman."

I sank into the mattress and pillows, aching with unsatisfied need. *Right back at you.*

26

"Where do you think you're going?" Wick's voice, laced with frustration and anger, hit me like an ice cream brain freeze. Not bothering to lift his head from the bed, he kept his arm draped over his face when he spoke. I tried not to check out his tented boxer briefs, and failed. My mouth watered and I shut it before Wick sensed my weakness.

"To my room." I perched on the edge of the bed and tried to find my various articles of clothing. My shirt was in shreds, same with my bra. "Where are my pants?"

Wick growled.

"That's not very helpful."

The vibrations emitting from his chest deepened along with the scent of burnt cinnamon.

"What's your problem?" Spotting my sweats, I hopped off the bed and padded to the corner of the room, but lifting them revealed they'd been ripped as well. "I'm the one who needs a new outfit. You're getting me new stuff. That was my favourite bra."

Wick sat up and glared. When he tried to speak another growl came out. He closed his eyes, probably counting to ten, and then spoke slowly. "You are not leaving."

"Well not now. I need to borrow some clothes." I crossed my arms. "I'm not running down the hall in my undies." Not with all the vagrant Werewolves frequently in the house, even if they had all seen it.

Wick leapt off the bed, clutched my head with both hands and walked forward to bump me hard against the wall. Despite the caveman dynamics of the move, I didn't feel threatened or in danger; instead, there was a possessiveness in the gesture that made my heart flutter. His mouth was on mine before I could demand an explanation.

"You. Are." He nipped the tip of my nose before drugging me with one of his kisses. "Not. Leaving." He pulled my head back by my hair. "Do you understand?"

"I understand that I'm going to go bald if you keep yanking my head around by my hair like a pubescent girl in a bitch fight."

Wick released me and closed his eyes. He leaned forward until his forehead rested against mine. "You're going to be the death of me."

"You've said that already," I huffed.

"Andy."

"Wick?"

"You cannot leave."

"That's ridiculous. Of course, I can leave. I need to. First, I've got to get dressed and then I'll figure out what the hell is going on."

"Tonight?"

Sighing I looked out the window. Already dark, I'd wasted another day. "No. Tomorrow. I'll get a fresh start."

"You stay."

I rolled my eyes. "I'm not one of your wolves to command, Wick. And I get it. I'm staying. Now give me some clothes so I can go to my room with some dignity."

Wick growled. "I meant you stay here, in my room." *You're mine.* He didn't need to say that part.

"You've a hell of a way of inviting a girl to a sleepover."

Wick leaned down and trailed kisses along my jawline. "Stay...please?"

I pushed him back. "Is that a good idea? Our wolves are too close to the surface as it is."

Wick's body vibrated, his teeth elongated, and then both his arms flew to the wall to cage me in.

"Case in point! Stop growling at me. It's getting old. I need to start Googling Vampire hordes and I can't do that with your hard on giving me the stare down."

Wick snorted and the tension in the room dropped. "A stare down?"

"It's staring." I waved my hand in the direction of his groin.

"You've got it backwards, Andy—you're the one staring." Wick did a little pelvic thrust when my gaze dragged down to the subject at hand.

"Stop that. I can't focus."

Wick's teeth grazed my neck and scraped against my collarbone. A sigh escaped my lips. "Come to bed," Wick whispered. "Let me hold you. That is all I will do. Promise." He ran his hands down my arms, smoothing the goosebumps. "I will even lend you clothes in the morning."

His mouth claimed mine in a gentle, but possessing kiss. His hands cradled my face and despite the dominating manner Wick utilized due to the raging wolf simmering beneath his skin, I felt cherished. My body warmed at his touch and a heady need sprang up again. I squashed it. Wick offered comfort.

"Mrmph," I managed. Giving into the kiss, yielding, I melted into his arms. They closed around me. Strong, warm, supportive. *Mine.*

Wick reached down and hoisted me up, his hands grasping my thighs in a welcome pressure. He lowered me to the bed, the pillows and comforter soft silk on my skin. He stepped back and smiled.

"Mine." His look brooked no argument and I wasn't about to make one. Especially when the next thing he did was shuck his boxer briefs. A big whoosh of air escaped my lungs at the sight and when Wick looked up to catch me staring, a smile spread across his face as he did another pelvic jiggle before sliding into the bed. Still laughing, I turned over and gave him my back. His naked body made me want to do very bad things, and I didn't trust either of us to stop if we started again.

Would that be such a bad thing? My bad self asked.

Yes, yes it would, I scolded her.

He wrapped an arm around me and swung a long heavy leg over mine—the big spoon to my little one.

"What were you saying about Vampire research?" Wick's voice cut the comforting silence of the room.

"Mmm?"

"You were going to use those mad Google skills. What for?"

"To search newspaper articles and press releases. I need to find out what Vampire hordes are visiting the area."

"Why?"

"I think one might be behind the attack."

"Explain."

My natural resistance to confide flared up like a brutal case of indigestion, but I closed my eyes and breathed through it. Wick might be able to help. I had to let down the steely gates around my heart and try to trust him—give him a shot. If he really was my true mate, he was my chance for a happy ending. So for the second time that night, I went through details with Wick, but this explanation wasn't as personal. Wick's body tensed as I spoke.

"Ethan," he spat. "It's Ethan."

I turned around in Wick's arms and raised a brow. "Ethan Monroe is a visiting Master Vampire. His emissaries started coming to us a couple days ago asking benign questions and making random requests. Nothing big. We thought it odd, but now it makes perfect sense. Ethan sent them to scout us and explain his presence in the city."

"Is this enough information to go to Lucien with?"

"No. He will want proof—some evidence that links him with your handler."

"Do you know where he's staying?"

Wick shook his head. "Somewhere in West Vancouver. His emissaries keep evading our tails. We're not sure how he's doing it."

"Magic?" Witches had an uncanny ability to wipe out all traces of scent, if the price was right or the motivation high enough.

"Maybe. There's no smell."

I frowned.

"At all. The area they disappear from is completely devoid of any scent."

Groaning, I draped a hand over my eyes. "I hate Witches."

"They smell good, though."

"They do."

"Not as good as you."

Remembering where his nose had been recently, my cheeks warmed at the same time a fire built lower down.

Wick's thumb caressed my face. "So what is your plan?"

"I'm going to hope Angie has a date with Ethan's vamps and follow her from the SeaBus terminal."

"What if she doesn't?"

"Then I scour West Van in a grid and hope to catch their scent."

"And if you don't?"

I groaned. "Aren't you Mister Negativity? If none of this works, I'll have to repeat the process."

"You do not have the luxury of time." Wick hesitated. "You know...you are not in this alone."

"Well, what do you suggest?"

"Let me send the pack to West Van to work a grid while you sit on the receptionist."

My eyes narrowed. "And if your pack catches their scent?" Wow. That came out a bit more accusatory than planned. Wick's eyes widened and something flashed in his eyes.

"We phone you?" he answered slowly.

"It's not a trick question, Wick."

"I feel like you are accusing me with something."

I let out a long breath and took a moment to stare at the ceiling. "I don't know how far I can trust you." Wick started to object, but I placed a finger on his lips. "Not because you want to betray me, but because you have to."

"You don't trust Lucien."

"Not one bit."

A pause. "Me neither."

There was a long awkward silence where we both avoided eye contact. What was there to say? We were both in a difficult position.

"Let me help you. I don't have any orders to sabotage your investigation or go running to Lucien instead of informing you."

"Lucien could have ordered you to say that."

"Yes. He could have. But if he did, I would not have offered to help. And you can smell a lie."

I dropped my head so my nose was wedged against his neck between his cheek and the pillow. Taking a deep breath, I immersed my senses in Wick's scent.

Good mate, my wolf panted. I shushed her and relaxed in the moment.

"I could get used to this." Wick rubbed my back.

"Hmm?" I took another deep breath in. His scent was addictive.

"The purring."

"Didn't realize I was doing it."

He continued to run his hands down my back. "Don't stop."

"I won't, if you won't. I love a good back rub."

"Noted." He kept his hands moving. "So?"

"Hmm?"

"Will you let me help you?"

I nodded and hoped I wasn't making a mistake I would pay for with my heart and possibly my life.

27

My phone beeped. I frantically dug it out of my pocket. Did Wick and his pack find the Vampires? Hoped so—I could get off this stupid roof and out of the chilly wind. Angie'd done nothing this evening but prance around her living room in her panties dancing—thank goodness she did it at home, because nobody should have to see that. No woman who wanted to keep some self-esteem, at least.

I looked at my phone and discovered a text from Mel. I groaned, knowing what she wanted without reading her message. She'd been on my case to go shopping with her all day. Now that everyone in Wick's pack had these smart phones, I'd gone from invisible to easily accessible. I hadn't wanted her to know how dire my circumstances were, so I'd been shaking her off with weak excuses. I needed to come clean and tell her the truth. It wasn't that I didn't want to spend time with her—I just lacked time to spend. I had three days left. My heart pounded against my chest at the thought of being Clint's play toy.

I punched in my password and read her text.

> Please say yes to breakfast and
> shopping tomorrow. I need to find a
> cute crotch for next weekend.

A cute crotch? I stared at the phone in shock. That certainly wasn't what I expected. I looked over the message again to make sure I read it right. Sure thing—she'd written crotch.

I texted back:

> Cute one? As opposed to your regular
> one?

Smiling, I waited for her response. It came quickly.

> FML! A clutch purse! I meant
> CLUTCH!

Hah! I stifled a laugh because Wereleopards weren't deaf. My fingers ran over the keys quickly to send my next message.

> I like my current crotch.

I wanted to ask what FML stood for, but it must be something I should already know.

> We should meet and talk. You're not in
> this alone, you know.

> Can't. I have three days before my ass
> is grass. When this is over, we'll talk.
> Promise.

I locked my phone and tucked it back into my pocket. I needed to focus.

I hated sitting around and waiting in human form. Without fur or feathers, the cold air slashed against my skin. But my falcon's form had limits—texting one of the main ones. I adjusted my position to let blood flow back into my numb ass.

The door to the Wereleopard's house swung open and I bit back a cheer. Angie walked out in a skin tight, hot pink dress. The square neckline emphasized her ample breasts and clung to her perky butt. Did this woman own anything casual to wear? She should buy stock in spandex brands.

I kept my eyes trained on her and watched as she sauntered to the garage. When a sleek black leopard emerged and disappeared into the shadows ten minutes later, I pulled out my phone and sent a quick text to Wick:

> Tits McGee has left the skank shack.

His reply was swift.

> You have a way with words. I'll send
> someone for your things.

I climbed out of my clothes and tucked the undies

into my sweatpants. I'd no idea who he would send and the last thing I wanted was someone like John handling my delicates. *Gross.* I placed my cell phone on top and shifted into my falcon. There'd be no more communication with Wick. I was off the grid. Spreading my wings wide, I launched into the air. There was no point following Angie through all her backtracking and switchbacks. I knew where she headed.

ANGIE DIDN'T ARRIVE ON THE NORTH SHORE from the SeaBus until well over an hour later. I couldn't track time well in falcon form, but I could count SeaBuses. One arrived every fifteen minutes and four had come and gone before Angie and her hips promenaded off the commuter ferry. She wasn't alone.

Flanking her on each side were two robust Vampires. My falcon couldn't scent things like my wolf or mountain lion, but I'd bet my government paycheque they weren't Lucien's.

Angie now wore a leopard print dress with a black fuzzy trim and a sweetheart neckline. It clung to her body, showing every curve with its tight fit—no surprise there.

When a sleek black car, probably a Mercedes, pulled up, one of the Vampires reached over and opened the door for Angie to climb in. The car pulled away and left the Vampire escort behind. They must have another car around to follow, but I wasn't going to stick around to learn insignificant details. I took to the air and trailed the car with Angie.

Night descended, and with no more SeaBuses to count, I'd no idea how long I trailed the car before they pulled up to a large building that was more of an estate than it was a house. Three more cars drew up behind it—all sleek and expensive-looking. Not being a car person, if asked to elaborate on their description, I'd say they were black and shiny with silver trim.

The house sat on the edge of a cliff overlooking the Strait of Georgia. Circling the house, I watched Angie leave the car and swivel her hips into the house guarded by large men dressed in black. One day I would like to meet a Master Vampire that outfitted his guards in a different colour, like lime green or bright fuchsia.

I recognized the area. Off Marine Drive, this neighbourhood contained the filthy rich and picturesque parks. Angling in the light wind, I banked my little falcon body toward the nearest green space. The shift to wolf was swift and not wanting to lose any more time, I loped in the direction of the house. I knew I had the right place a block before I got there. The air went from sea salt and pine to saturated with the tang of blood and death.

Lucien's unique scent was not entangled in the odour. This was the visiting horde. Pushing my excitement back, I circled the block before I dared a closer look. Sentries paced the surrounding area, but I slipped by them unseen. Although wolves weren't as common in this area as coyotes, they weren't unheard of. If the sentries caught my scent, they'd still check it out first before raising an alarm, giving me enough time to escape.

A familiar smell reached my nose when I loped closer to the house—citrus and sunshine—more specifically, the same big cat from Landen's apartment. Faint but present—and all the proof I needed. My wolf stood still and drank in the Wereleopard's essence. A rich bouquet wrapped around me with a heady effect and my mountain lion surged up, demanding a change. I stopped the shift before it could start. *What the hell was that?*

My cat hissed in frustration. She wanted out.

Shaking my wolf head to clear my senses I trotted a little closer. Now was not the time to pussy out. Pun intended. Sitting across the street, hidden by the shadow of another house and massive trees acting as a pseudo hedge, I watched the estate. Not much to see, but there was no way I'd risk going in to find the killer. I had enough information.

An unexpected sting pierced me behind the ear and my hind leg sprung up by instinct to scratch it. *Fucking mosquitoes.*

28

What is that pounding? Oh God. It's in my head. Back in human form, I forced my eyes open to slits, and then shut them quickly. *That stings!* Taking a moment to pull out of the grogginess in my mind was like swimming through dense sludge.

When I rolled onto my belly, the insides of my stomach continued to roll, even after my body stopped. I clamped down on my tongue. Taking long breaths, I swallowed repeatedly to prevent the flux of vomit threatening to surge up and escape. Counting to ten didn't work, so I continued until I reached one hundred. Carefully, I pried my eyes open to stare at the ground, which was some sort of hard metal flooring. It smelled cold and clinical. Propping my body on all fours, I closed my eyes and waited for my quaking stomach to settle before I dared move again. I sat back on my butt and splayed my legs out in front.

Another wave of nausea floored me, but I ground my teeth and refused to part with the nice dinner I had earlier. Scratching the burning itch on my neck, I replayed my actions. The last thing I remember was using my hind leg to scratch what I thought was a bite. Not a mosquito, then—a tranq dart. I hated tranquilizers. They made me nauseous.

I faced a wall, which told me nothing besides the lack of interior decorating. With a groan, I managed to shuffle around with a series of bum shimmying moves that would've made a gymnast cringe. The sinking feeling in my gut wasn't from the side effects of the drugs alone—it was also from a deepening sense of impending doom.

I'm fucked.

I sat in a six by six foot holding cell: three of the sides cement, and if I had to put money on it, thick enough to withstand a Were. Bars made up the last side of the cell and the chains attached to massive pegs in each corner of the room confirmed my suspicions—this was either an S&M room designed by some minimalist freak, or it was a Were-proof cell. Lots of packs used these to contain Weres shifting for the first time, or ones that lost control of their beast and, of course, Weres considered enemies of the pack. I knew which category I fell into, despite not being a Were.

On the other side of the bars, more cells ran off the main room. Although there were no windows and this was obviously a basement, someone had gone to the effort to make the main sitting room comfortable, equipping it with oversized couches, tables, benches and what looked like well stocked bookcases. The only exit appeared to be the staircase on the far side of the room. Escape would be difficult, if not impossible.

I looked down at my arm to find a bloody bandage. The tape holding it down pulled at my skin. I ripped it off and it took a minute for me to register the two-inch incision stitched up on my arm. *Right where my tracker had been.*

A door slammed. High heels clanked heavy on the stairs as someone walked down into the room.

Angie.

She wore a skin-tight, knee-length dress in a purple satin-like material. It looked great on her, and it told me I'd slept through at least one night since she'd changed outfits.

A growl escaped my lips.

Hers curled up in response. "Agent McNeilly."

"Angie." I kept my response stiff.

Her eyes narrowed. "It's Angelica." She moved gracefully over to the couch and sat down. "But I suppose you call me Angie to get under my skin."

I made a show of looking around my cement cube prison before I wrapped my hands around the bars. "The punishment doesn't exactly fit the crime. Overreact, much?"

The delicate trill of her laughter filled the room, and she covered her mouth as if embarrassed it escaped. When she dropped her hand, her expression transformed into something more serious. "If I were going to lock you up for annoying me, you would've been caged the moment you walked into the SRD office."

I shrugged.

"No. You're here because you botched your assignment to kill Clint."

"Pertinent information was left out."

"That human servant nonsense?" She waved a noncommittal hand in the air. "You were on a need to know basis. Besides, you should've figured it out." The look she gave me could only be described as scornful. "You're supposed to be a professional."

"There was a strict deadline." I crossed my arms in front of my chest, instinctively. I unfolded them as soon as I realized how defensive the posture looked. I didn't have to explain anything to her.

"And now you're here to redeem yourself? Scoop up information and run back to your new master like a good little pup?" The sneer transformed her face into something less attractive.

"Isn't that the pot calling the kettle black?"

Angie frowned. "What do you mean? I'm a Wereleopard."

I spread my arms and waved them around the room. "You work for a Master Vampire, too."

Angie straightened as if she was a marionette and the strings controlling her were pulled taut. "That's different."

"Because you have no choice?"

Angie nodded.

"And you think I have one?"

Angie cut her gaze away and balled her tiny hands into fists. Her body vibrated with anger, so strong the scent of it hit me in waves. "You screwed everything up!" Angie hissed. "If you had done your job, Clint would be dead and Lucien would be weakened."

"And then what? Your master would take over the city and let you go?"

A red flush spread across Angie's face. "No. He'll never let us go. But he will let our prowl leader come back to us."

"Where is he now?"

"Here...and there."

I raised an eyebrow at her vague answer.

"You should be more concerned about yourself."

"Oh, Angie. I didn't know you cared."

"I don't."

"Did you come here to gloat then?"

"To get answers. I know it will go against all of your training, but I suggest you answer them. You don't want to experience their other forms of...interrogation."

"Riiight."

She shook her head.

"Well let's summarize and save some time. You are controlled by the Master Vampire Ethan Monroe. He had you contact Landen to put a hit on Clint because he wanted to weaken Lucien in order to gain control of his territory. To clean up loose ends, Landen was killed by someone from your prowl." I stopped to gauge her reaction. Nothing. Flat eyes regarded me from across the bars. "How am I doing so far?"

Angie rolled her eyes and motioned for me to continue. *Bang on, then.*

"I took out Clint, but he didn't die. I was captured by Lucien's Werewolves and tasked with finding the person behind my orders or face eternal enslavement and some fucked up forms of torture before a long, drawn out death. I tracked Landen, discovered he was killed by a Wereleopard. I called it into the SRD, discovered he went rogue and when I came into the station to clear my name, I'm greeted by you. A Wereleopard, like Landen's killer. I followed you and discovered the connection to Ethan." I looked up at Angie. "Did I miss anything?"

"Yes." She smirked. "You missed the part where you got caught...again."

"I thought it rather obvious."

"The story doesn't end here."

"No, it doesn't," I agreed. "I hope you'll fill me in on how it ends."

"For you? Not good."

"Another loose end? Surely Ethan must realize the mess is now too big to clean up with a broom and rug."

"It's the principle. You failed him. And you might provide information crucial to his plans."

"I don't know anything important about Lucien." I chose my words carefully, not giving a direct lie Angie could smell.

Her lip quirked. "That's what I said."

A door slammed, causing us both to jump. Angie spun around and looked up the stairs. "I haven't finished." Her voice was commanding.

The soft footsteps continued down the stairs, undeterred from the icy glare on Angie's face. The waft of death and decay hit my face before the Vampire came into view. He wore all black and his dark skin tone and black wavy hair suggested a South Asian heritage. He walked up beside Angie and regarded me with cold black eyes.

I didn't register the gun until he lifted it and shot me.

29

When my vision cleared and my stomach stopped doing flips like a dolphin on crack, I drew in a deep breath and surveyed my situation. *Not good! Not good!*

Stop panicking, I ordered my brain. *Stay calm to stay safe.* I repeated the mantra until my breathing was under control and reopened my eyes. I lay naked on an operating table in a cold room that looked like a set from a hospital television drama.

My ankles and wrists, shackled to the corners of the table, splayed me out like a stunned snow angel. There was a smaller table to my left that I could barely see over my shoulder. It glinted with metallic objects I didn't want to think about.

Images of Dylan leaning over me with a sick gleam in his eye and a random utensil in his hand clogged my throat with an influx of stomach acid. *Don't puke. Don't puke. Don't...ahhhh!* I turned my head to the side and spewed the contents of my stomach until nothing was left except the dull ache and aftershocks of dry heaving. *Fucking tranquilizers.* I tried to roll over, but my arms were held down.

A noise caught my attention. Someone stood in the room with me and I peered down my body to see who.

"What the hell is going on?" I glared at Angie who stood meekly in the corner. Meekly? That wasn't right. There were all sorts of things wrong with this situation.

She didn't look up. "I'm sorry about this."

"What?"

"I don't like you." She lifted her head and her sad eyes met mine. "But I wouldn't wish this on anyone."

"Wish what?"

Angie opened her mouth to say more when the door opened. She quickly clamped her lips, dropped her gaze and rounded her shoulders inward, her body language alerting the warning bells in my brain. It didn't look right on her, this submissive, scared posture reeking of fear. It sent tiny shocks down my body as if little fish nipped at my skin. Angie didn't strike me as a person who frightened easily.

A stout man walked into the room. His greasy hair was tucked behind his gnarled ears with the exception of a portion used as a modest comb-over. His shiny scalp gleamed through the sparse cover. Despite his rotund belly, he moved with a sleek, quick grace—a Were.

His beady black eyes watched me intently as he approached. His non-existent top lip curled up into a nasty sneer. A Wererat, maybe?

My nose crinkled at the stench rolling off him—a disturbing mix of asparagus ridden piss and cooked shrimp. It took me a minute to place what caused my nose hairs to shrivel up and hide.

"Hyena," I grunted. Never met one who'd pass a sanity test.

The man dipped his head. "But the burning questions is—what are you?"

"A wolf." The truth, but not the whole truth.

"You're not a Were." The man stepped up to the table and ran a finger down the naked flesh spanning over my ribs.

"No."

"A little wolf Shifter." He picked up one of the shiny utensils from the tray near the table. I didn't want to look, but I stared at the knife. He held it up to the light as if he too was mesmerized by how the light played off the sharp edge and smooth sides.

"Yes." He'd get one word answers from me.

"Pathetic and weak." The flat of the blade was cold against the soft tissue of my stomach.

"Sure." I tightened my abs to avoid flinching, but when he dug the edge of the knife into the sensitive skin on my side below the ribcage, I jerked.

The man laughed. "That was a lie. You think you're stronger than that."

"Yup."

"Where's your fera?" He leaned over my body and ran the blade down my left cheek. He didn't apply enough pressure for it to cut deep or bleed profusely, but it left a sting. Torture by paper cuts. *Awesome.*

"Around."

"If she's in the area, we'll find her."

"Okay."

The man cocked his head. "You don't believe me."

"Should I apologize?"

"No." He focused on my skin again, his eyes widening along with his smile. The way he licked his lips, made me think of a man walking out of the desert and seeing a fountain of water for the first time.

A bead of sweat dripped down my hairline as the blade slid up my rib cage, catching on each rib in turn, over the delicate curve of my underarm, and along the soft skin tissue inside my bicep. Drawing the knife against the soft tissue of my arm, he increased the pressure until it drew blood.

"You'll be begging soon enough," he said.

Without needing to scent the air, I knew he spoke the truth. Glancing over my shoulder, I saw Angie squirm, moving her weight from one foot to the other, glancing everywhere in the room but where I lay. When our eyes finally met, she froze before casting her gaze down to her feet. She swayed back and forth, the bold smell of sweat laced with her perfume drifted across the room.

"You're not going to join in?" I asked.

Angie looked up with...sympathy?

"Angelica doesn't like this sort of play." The man made another slow slash at my skin. "I could order her to participate, of course. I have before. But she gets the shakes and last time she threw up. It's distracting and I don't like the smell."

I peered over the side of the table, eyed my spewed stomach contents and smiled. *Take that, asshole*. Hyena Piss Man dug his knife into the inside of my thigh, snapping my attention back to him. I clenched the straps holding down my wrists and strained not to cry out. Panting, I gawked at him down the length of my body, his nose inches from my crotch. He missed the femoral artery, but not my reaction; a nasty smile spread across his face as he made a matching incision on the other thigh. I bit my tongue to stop the squeal lodged in my throat from getting out. Blood oozed from the cut. After the stinging sensations dulled, I decided he needed to talk more and cut less.

"You don't get off on discomfort?"

"I get off on pain." He straightened from my thighs and waved at the puke on the floor. Angie jumped and clambered to my side. She kept her face impassive as she cleaned the area up, but I smelled the sour tang of her anxiety, and the salty, yet sickly sweet stench of her fear.

I ignored Angie and turned to the Werehyena. "Have you met Clint? The two of you have a lot in common."

"I'm nothing like that man," Hyena man's face darkened. "His tastes differ from mine."

"You're both fucked up in my opinion."

He snorted. "You have a narrow scope on life."

"I happen to like it." I fished for information. Hyena Piss Man had no intensions of killing me any time soon, but if he planned to slit my throat after all this knife play,

I'd prefer to have a ball park of when so I knew how much time I had to work with. I never counted on others to save me. Although, Wick barging through the doors right now would be nice. If I had the tracker in my arm it might've been a possibility.

"Oh, I'm not going to kill you," he said.

"Let me rephrase. I happen to like my life before I met you."

The man sighed. "Such a limited palate."

"I think a food reference in this situation is highly inappropriate."

"You joke at a time like this?" He ran the blade down the inside of my left calf.

"Who said I was joking?" Bantering acted as a coping mechanism. It kept my mind from sinking into the seriousness of the situation and panicking. He'd do whatever he liked to me, no matter what I said or did. Defiance would give me something to focus on, and if I didn't give this guy the reaction he wanted, he might lose interest and leave me alone. Or kill me. Then it would be over, and nothing more to worry about. Needless hours of torture—been there, done that, thanks to Dylan.

He didn't comment on my last statement, preferring to eye my skin like a dog salivating over its food bowl. The bite of the blade on the inside of my knee was his answer. The sting vibrated up my leg and a shriek caught in my throat.

The Werehyena leaned over me, shoving his face inches from my own. His breath smelled of chewing tobacco and ginger beef—not a good combination to his natural hyena piss and shrimp odour—and his teeth were yellow and crooked with pieces of cracked pepper wedged into the gaps. "Let me tell you how this is going to go."

"Ok." My face warped into an obedient one.

He didn't miss a beat. He wasn't looking at my face; instead he petted my skin with the flat of the blade. "I'm going to cut you. I'm going to ask you questions and then I'm going to cut you more. If I get turned on, I may fuck you. Or maybe I'll get Angie to do it with a knife. Or maybe I'll just keep cutting. If you answer my questions like a good little girl, maybe I'll let you pick what I do. But I will do you one way or another."

I was speechless from the mental picture of him hot and heavy and grunting on top of me, dredging up painful memories of my time with Dylan. Fear sliced through my body in time with his knife. I think I'd prefer Angie and the blade. If I survived this, he'd pay with a lot of pain. I'd let my wolf track him, my mountain lion play with him before ripping him apart, and my falcon carry the bits and pieces left over to smash against the rocks. The seagulls could fight over his remains. *Keep those thoughts close.*

"Do you understand?" The man leaned back, sniffing the air and considering every subtle movement of my body.

"Yes."

"Will you answer my questions?"

"Yes."

"Good." He reached over and dropped the knife in

favour of a different one. This one was a scalpel. It looked like something I used in Biology class back in high school, except this one had no cracks or rust. At least I could cross out tetanus as a torture possibility.

"You have such beautiful lips." The man leaned in again. His breath steamed up my face. I shut my eyes when the scalpel tip pressed against the corner of my mouth.

A thudding knock at the door rocked the silence of the room. I jumped. Or at least tried to—the straps held me down. The scalpel nicked the soft tissue at the corner up my mouth and I yelped. I tasted blood and my eyes watered at the sting.

The man cursed and straightened from his hunched position over me. "What?" he demanded at the closed door.

A muffled response filtered into the room.

"Fucking sound proofing." The man chucked his scalpel onto the tray. The look of disgust caused his lip to curl up in a sneer. "Why anyone would want to muffle the exquisite sounds of someone's pain is beyond me."

The muffled knock came again.

"Open the fucking door you halfwit," the man spat at Angie.

Angie jumped and stumbled to the door, flinging it open. A large male Wereleopard stood on the other side of the doorway, his skin deeply tanned and his arms rippled with muscle. From the way he stood with a slightly diminutive posture, easy to spot for a supe versed in Were dynamics, he was a sub. He looked at Angie with a question in his eyes and she replied by shaking her head in the slightest of movements.

"Well? What do you want?" Hyena Piss Man snarled at the Wereleopard.

"Master Monroe wishes to speak with you."

"Wishes or wants?" The man asked as he toyed with my hair.

"Pardon, sir?"

"Was it a request or an order? Do I have to go right away?"

"I believe so, sir."

"You believe?" The man yanked my hair so my head lifted off the table. "I'm busy. If I've been dragged away to speak with Monroe on an issue that could've waited, I will be displeased."

The Wereleopard looked nonplused. "If it was a matter that could have waited, I doubt Master Monroe would request your presence."

The man glared at the Wereleopard.

The leopard shrugged. "Better safe than sorry."

"You forget, cat. Monroe isn't my master. He can't order me around, like he does you."

"Which is why I believe he phrased it as a request."

The man clutched my hair near the scalp and used it to slam my head against the table. The room sank and closed in on itself.

"It has to be important, because he wouldn't interrupt you. Not when he knows how much you enjoy your..." The leopard trailed off, averting his eyes from the table and my strapped, vulnerable body.

Fetish? Hobby? I would've been unsure how to classify the man's perversion as well.

The Werehyena turned toward Angie. "Don't leave the room and don't touch her or unstrap her." He turned toward the door, but stopped and snapped his fingers "And leave the door open. I want the men who walk by to witness her humiliation." He walked back to the table and leaned down. Using his body weight and Were strength, he swung the table around on its wheels so I could look down my body to the open door. Anyone looking in would get a view meant only for lovers and my gynecologist.

"Mmmm. Feel that, Angie? That anger? That mortification? Can you smell it?"

"Yes," Angie bit out. The burning scent of anger hopping around the room emanated from her and her prowlmate as well, not just me.

Hyena Piss Man turned to me before leaving the room with the other Wereleopard. "Maybe I should let the men take you. One by one. Would you like that?"

"No." Not sure how I managed speech with the images of Dylan strangling my throat with invisible hands.

Dylan's powerful frame built for intimidation hovered over me. He savoured the air, my scent laced with his personal aphrodisiac of trepidation and terror. I'd loved this man. I chose him.

"Not again," I whimpered. The strong tang of his desire seared my nose. Dylan wasn't the only one who reeked of anticipation. The others did, too. "Please."

Dylan smirked, pulling his shirt over his head in one swift move, shucking his jeans off next. "Maybe if you beg, I'll keep them from you, this time."

Last night, after I refused the mate bond, he'd ordered every pack male to take a turn. Panic shook my body, urging me to flee. But there was nowhere to run. My head turned to the side to avoid looking at the men, reeking with anticipation. I would not be spared, no matter how much I begged. I'd learned that lesson.

Hyena Piss Man cocked his head and sniffed the air. "Truth." His laughter trailed him as he walked down the hall out of sight, leaving me with my day-walking nightmares.

The asshole probably had no idea he triggered these memories. When the last of the shakes racking my body dissipated, and the room cleared of my past horrors, I blinked away the tears in my eyes and surveyed the room. The Werehyena had left me alone with Angie.

"Let me go." My voice came out as a hiss.

Angie shook her head. "I've been ordered to assist Mark and he told me not to unstrap you. *I can't.*"

"Mark? Hyena Piss Man?"

Angie nodded.

"Did he order you to prevent my escape?"

Angie frowned, thinking over the Werehyena's words. "No. Not expressly. How will you get out of the cuffs?"

"Don't worry about that. Can you check the hall-way? Is there anyone there?"

Angie turned and peered out of the door. She made

sure to keep her feet inside to comply with Mark's orders.
"No."

"Any open windows?"

Angie looked over her shoulder with her eyebrow raised in question.

I raised both of mine in response.

"Yes. There's one at the end of the hallway to the right. Quite big, but it's high up."

As soon as she confirmed an open window was present, I willed the change. The shackles fell away from my petite falcon form. Angie gasped.

Stretching my wings, I took a little hop and launched into the air. Flapping wildly to maneuver through the doorway, I banked sharply to the right. Picking up speed, I flew through the empty hallway and out the open window.

30

F light time from West Vancouver to Wick's house on a bad day with horrific weather required half an hour tops. It took me several hours. I soared aimlessly in the sky, enjoying the wind as it soothed my feathers and lifted me up. Losing myself in the freedom acted as a cleanser and shook the last vestiges of fear clinging to my essence. Too hell with Lucien and his deadline. I needed to fix myself first.

After what I went through in Dylan's pack, the torture I endured under the Werehyena's ministrations seemed minor in comparison, but the fear I'd experienced dredged up a lot of unwanted memories. My skin recoiled at the thought of Mark's hands and the blades. What he planned to do—to hurt and humiliate me—boiled my blood, leaving one consistent thought running through my bird brain.

Mark was a dead man.

The sun crested the horizon by the time I landed in

Wick's room. He'd left the window open, but he wasn't there. I shifted to my human form and flopped face first onto his bed to nuzzle into his pillows and inhale his scent deep into my body, over and over and over again. I savoured the calm washing through me. My wolf relaxed, my mountain lion stopped pacing, and it would've been nice to drift to sleep surrounded by everything Wick, but there was another scent in the room. It leeched off my skin and rubbed into the sheets, prickling my nose. Mark's signature stench clung to my body, refusing to let me truly escape.

I hopped off the bed and ran to the shower, flinging the dials to full blast. The near-blistering hot water scalded my skin, burning it, but in a good way. It felt *good*. But not *enough*. I glanced down at the pink loofa Wick purchased for me a few weeks ago. It didn't scour as hard as I wanted. I leapt out of the shower and pulled items out from under the sink until I found a pumice stone.

Jumping back in the shower, I scrubbed until the top layer of my skin sloughed off and everything felt new and clean. Now only my woodsy scent mixed in with the soap and water. Pumice stones were meant for sanding off the hard layers of skin on the bottom of feet, but it was perfect for what I wanted and needed—getting rid of any trace of Mark. If only it could work on my mind as well.

Leaning against the wall, I let the water run over my head and down my back, my skin long since numb from the soothing burn. My injuries, rather minor to begin with, had healed significantly from shifting twice.

The shower curtain flung back and I jumped. My feet slipped on the slick flooring and the tiling tilted as I fell backward. Strong hands grabbed me before I struck the ground and I looked up to see Wick. He leaned into the shower stall, gripping both my arms with his hands. His eyes blazed an intense yellow, boring into my mind and my heart. The water from the shower pelted the back of his head, making his short hair plaster against his scalp. He didn't notice as his eyes remained glued to mine.

Without releasing his hold, he stepped into the shower and brought me up against him. He tucked his head against my neck and inhaled, wrapping his arms around me, not showing any concern for his soaked clothes.

Relaxing into the hardness of Wick, I released the breath caught in my throat. "How long have I been gone?"

His fingers dug into my skin. "Two days." His tone quiet, but rough, sounded like his normal husky voice had been kicked in the ribs a couple times.

"So I have one day left?" I wiggled in his grasp, but Wick's arms tightened, crushing me. I couldn't move. Something uncomfortable bubbled up into my throat. Wick posed no threat, but it didn't stop my body from tensing and my heart rate from picking up at the perceived captivity.

Wick's muscles tightened and then relaxed, quickly, like he'd smelled my fear. He kept his arms around me, but loose enough that I could push them away if I decided to bolt. He ran his hand down my hair and back.

"Shhhh," he breathed into my ear before he nuzzled my neck. "Let me hold you."

Breathing in Wick's rosemary and sugar scent, my body softened under his calming caresses. This couldn't go on forever. Wick would want answers and his wolf would need them. The unpleasantly sharp and pungent smell of his turmoil broiled in the heat of the hot shower water. It cost him to give me this—the time to calm down, to heal.

His back muscles felt smooth under my hands. *When did I slip my hands under his shirt?* I ran them up and down, enjoying the slick feel of his skin while trying to reciprocate some of the therapeutic calm. He needed to ask and I just told him without words that he could.

"Tell me." His command was gruff against my cheek. He clutched my hair with one hand and my side with another, a little harder than I think he meant to, because after a few seconds, his grip softened again.

"I will," I promised. "But let me... Let me get clothes on."

Wick stiffened. "I'm going to fucking kill him."

"You'll have to beat me to it." I pulled back, giving Wick time to let me go. He did, but he wasn't happy about it. I got out of the shower and towelled off while Wick discarded his wet clothes. How did Wick know about Mark? I'd washed his scent off me.

Wick approached from behind and wrapped me in a thick warm bathrobe. The kind found in an expensive spa. I had one once—stole it from a swanky hotel I stayed at during my SRD training. Wick didn't strike me as the five-finger discount type, so he probably paid full price for this one.

As he tied the robe up for me, Wick dipped his head into the crook of my neck again. His wolf so close, I smelled it mingling with his barely contained rage. I reached back and ran my hands over his head. Maybe it would soothe Wick. Maybe it would soothe his wolf.

And then again, maybe not.

I opened the door to the bedroom and stared in disbelief at the room I left not long ago. The bed frame thrown up against the wall and what remained of the mattress and sheets strewn across the room in shreds, told me either a tornado blasted through the room, or

Wick had unleashed his fury on the inanimate objects.

I turned slowly in Wick's arms. His eyebrows pinched together and his lips compressed. Burnt cinnamon sparked up around us.

"His scent was all over the bed," Wick whispered. It cost him to say it. His eyes flashed yellow and he shivered, holding back the shift. His wolf wanted out. "I want to hunt him down and rip him apart."

I splayed my hand against his chest and stared at my fingers, pale and small against his body. "He barely touched me."

"One touch too many."

"Agreed. But there wasn't much of his scent on me."

"Is that why you were in the shower for an hour?"

An hour? I spent more time in there than I thought.

"It was more psychological than physical cleansing."

Wick grumbled.

"You waited an hour?" That showed a lot of restraint. His wolf would've wanted confirmation and Werewolves weren't known for their patience.

Wick nodded. "I tried to wait until you came out, because I thought you might want the space."

"Thank you. I know it was difficult to wait."

Wick nodded.

"Is that when you tore up the room?"

Wick nodded again.

I stared transfixed at my fingers pressed against his chest. Wick ran his hands down my back. His chin rested on the top of my head.

"Tell me," Wick asked again. He didn't lift his head, so his voice vibrated down the length of my body. It felt nice.

I bit my lip. "Can you put some clothes on first?"

Wick stepped back and went straight for the dresser. Pulling on sweatpants in one swift motion, he stalked back to me, stepped in close and invaded my personal space. He considered my face for a few minutes, and then, as if coming to some unspoken decision, reached down and picked me up.

Holding me close, he stomped to the guest room at the end of the hall. Shifting my weight, he managed to open and close the door without setting me down or letting me go. He placed me gently on the bed before turning the lights off and clambering into the bed to sprawl out beside me.

"Tell me."

So I did. Every sordid detail, every thought, every fear. It felt liberating not to censor what I said and a crushing pressure I didn't realize was there, released my chest, allowing me to breathe. My mouth kept moving as I drifted to sleep. Maybe I talked in my sleep, too.

31

When I woke up bathed in Wick's warmth, I found my phone filled with text messages and voicemails; most of them from Wick and Mel, first worried about my progress, then frantic about my whereabouts—the stress and panic in their voices progressing as time went on. Even Booth called, demanding an update. But my last text arrived at 5:30 this morning while I blissfully slept in Wick's arms.

Tonight. Sundown

The text was from Clint and he didn't need to elaborate. Wick must've reported my return. I wanted to be pissed off about that, but he didn't have much of a choice.

Eyeing the red horizon cast by the setting sun through the window with a dual sense of trepidation and excitement, I moved quietly through the room to pick out my outfit for tonight. Wick had gone to work. Some sort of emergency he couldn't delegate. Knowing little about the world of building development, I didn't ask.

I'd wasted most of the day lounging around in bed, being able to relax for the first time since I took the hit on Clint. I knew the person responsible for the orders and where to find him, and only had to relay the information to Lucien to pay my debt.

My phone beeped with a text from Clint:

We're here.

I texted back:

I'm about to take a shower. Do you mind waiting?

I'll be right up.

Huh? I looked over my last text and cringed. Instead of waiting, I'd asked Clint if he minded watching. Damn autocorrect.

I texted as fast as I could.

Waiting! I meant waiting.

Too late—Clint's head poked through the doorway. He must've run. With the house uncharacteristically empty of wolves, there'd been no one to stop him. His phone beeped and his attention flicked down to quickly read my latest message—the one correcting my error. He raised an eyebrow and looked me up and down with a smile.

"Freudian slip?" he asked.

"You know me so well."

Clint smiled at my dry voice, and then frowned. He strode up to me, a little too close for my liking, and studied my face. When he brought his hand up, it took everything in my self-control not to flinch. That would be a mistake with Clint. He pinched my chin and used the chunk of flesh and bone to turn my head from side to side. "Who hurt you?" he demanded.

"I didn't know you cared."

He snorted. "Of course, I care."

I frowned. Maybe Clint was really an onion—full of layers. And a funky odour.

"Only I can mark you," he said.

Groaning, I looked up to the ceiling and fervently wished some deity would save me. Someone needed to write a book for this social situation: *Avoiding Sado-masochists for Dummies.*

Clint hesitated before releasing my chin. "Who?"

"A dead man." Not a complete lie.

"Good."

"I still need to shower. You can WAIT downstairs."

Instead, he sat down on the edge of the bed and rubbed his hands together like a birthday boy about to get his cake.

Well, I have a surprise for you, buddy. Clint would have to find a new toy to play with. I could tell him now, but a perverse joy in misleading him overcame my urge for honesty.

"When you're mine, privacy will be a luxury I'll permit only if you've been good." He leered and ran his eyes slowly up and down my body. "Very good."

"Uh huh." I closed the bathroom door firmly, locked it and then hopped in the shower. His laughter leaked into the room. *Good thing I'm not yours, Clint.*

I kept my shower brisk. The tiny cuts healed up, but the one on my face and the incisions on my arm and inner thighs stung under the onslaught of water and soap. Wick hadn't dared tell Lucien he lost me. He'd used the tracking device app on his phone to follow my chip, but Ethan's goons had inserted it into a mangy coyote. When Wick's pack finally tracked it down, Wick panicked, but kept quiet, lying by omission.

When we finally stumbled out of bed, Wick told me he would've let me run. Something tightened in my gut, but my feelings clashed. The idea of getting out from Lucien's control? Electrifying. But leaving Wick... That brought up a whole different mix of emotions.

I towelled off. My feelings would have to wait for examination after I cleaned up this mess. My mind needed to be on lockdown once I climbed into the car with Allan.

I swung my hair down to twist up in the towel. When I straightened, I turned to grab my clothes. *Crap!* They were in the room with Clint. I inspected the bathroom for something else to throw on, but nothing magically appeared. Taking a deep breath to curse, I ripped the towel from my head, wrapped it tightly around my body before walking back into the bedroom. Clint sat on the end of the bed, holding up my purple and black zebra print underwear with the tip of his forefinger. "Looking for these?"

"Thank you." I clutched my towel firmly as I reached out to snatch my Brazilian panties from his grasp.

"You can change out here." Clint leaned back in the bed and winked.

"I don't think so." With as much dignity I could muster, partially clothed in a skimpy towel, I collected the rest of my clothes on the bed and then stalked back to the bathroom. *Wick's going to trash this room, too, once he smells Clint on the sheets.*

A loud sigh followed behind me. "You're no fun."

My middle finger replied for me before I shut the door.

STRETCHING OUT MY FEET IN FRONT OF ME IN the limo, I watched the impassive faces of Clint and Allan. Clint had stayed in the bedroom, opting to escort me to the vehicle waiting outside, apparently not wanting to risk the possibility of me escaping. Or so he said. His scent on my dresser told me he took the opportunity to sift through my underwear drawer. Pervert.

Still stuck at work, Wick had sent a text:

luck, xx.

As cute as the message was, I wanted the Alpha with me instead.

My phone beeped. It startled me because I wasn't expecting to hear from anyone. Maybe Wick planned to meet me at Lucien's place after all. I glanced down at my phone to find a text from Mel.

> I'm glad you're ok. Have you figured everything out?

> On my way to clear my name now.

> Good. Let's get penis to celebrate.

A laugh escaped my lips before I could clamp my mouth shut. It drew raised brows from Allan and Clint. I ignored them and texted back, glad to not be the only one who struggled with new technology:

> I'm not sure the men would approve.

Five minutes passed before I got her response.

> Noooooooooooo!!! That's not what I meant! Pedis, not penis. PEDICURES. There's a perverted old man in my phone. I didn't type that!

I laughed, drawing dark stares from Clint, who had no idea what was going on and a lewd smile from Allan, who would've plucked it from my head. Hopefully that's all he picked up.

Yeah, ok. I'm down.

NO DEEP SENSE OF DREAD OR FOREBODING consumed my thoughts like the last time I pulled up Lucien's long impressive driveway, because this time I had what he wanted—Ethan's name and the evidence to back it up. The trick would be to get out again without a new trumped up charge or task to keep me in his grasp.

The guards at the door dipped their heads as we approached.

"Lucien wishes to speak to her alone," the guard said. His voice wavered a bit.

Clint and Allan stopped and exchanged a look over my head.

Allan turned to the guard that spoke. "Did he say why?"

The guard took in the glares of my escorts, clamped his mouth shut and shook his head. The men stared at one another in a silent eye game of Mexican Standoff, smelling of dead meat and nothing else. Not sure who won, but after a few seconds Clint gripped my upper arm and ushered me forward.

When we reached the doors to Lucien's court, Clint spun me around, caressing my cheek with his finger.

Bite, my wolf howled.

"I'll wait here to collect my prize."

Faking a gagging sound, I smacked Clint's hand away from my face and turned to the doors. Before I pushed them open, I glanced over at Allan whose lips turned up slightly at one corner in a determinedly amused expression.

"Any advice?" I asked.

Allan's smile grew. "Don't fuck it up."

Laughing, I pushed the doors open and stepped through, letting them swing closed behind me before striding up the long walkway. I didn't get far up the aisle to Lucien's seat of power at the end, because we weren't alone. A solid silhouette stood between me and the Vampire. Unsure of how to proceed, I stopped and waited for the vamp's cue.

Lucien, sprawled in his giant seat worthy of a king, not bothering to hide his bored expression, straightened on my arrival. Standing at the other end of the room, the weight of his gaze hit me. "Come forward."

When I hesitated, his eyes cut to the man in front of him. "Don't be shy. He's merely an envoy from a visiting horde."

Shrugging, I started forward again, only to stop a few paces away when the envoy turned at Lucien's pseudo introduction. I did a double take. The envoy had the face of an angel, but instead of making me think pure and godly thoughts, his appearance made me want to sin in every possible way. A little under six feet, he was solid muscle. Strong legs, shoulders and forearms gave him the physique of a professional rugby player—like the ones that played on the wing. Rich black hair contrasted sharply with his sapphire blue eyes and full lips curled up in a dazzling smile that revealed even white teeth.

He walked confidently down the aisle in my direction, his movement too sleek and smooth to be a norm's. Then his scent hit me. Citrus and sunshine, with something more; a hint of honeysuckle on a warm summer's day mingled, danced and rolled over my skin, making me think of mojitos, and sex on the beach. Then the familiarity of it sank in.

My eyes narrowed.

Landen's killer.

He stopped a few feet before me. His eyes closed to slits as he drew a deep breath in, savouring my scent like a fine wine. "You smell of the forest," he purred.

My mountain lion preened in response. My wolf growled. *Interesting.*

"I'm Tristan." His eyes travelled up my body and made my knees wobble. His head tilted to the side. "And you are?"

His scent swirled around me, like distracting pheromones, encouraging me to act—I've never had the urge to dry hump more than at this particular moment. More potent than what I'd detected in Landen's apartment and Ethan's Vampire lair, this man's scent called out to me, to my mountain lion. Every nuance licked my skin. Realizing my mouth hung open like a Venus flytrap, I snapped it shut.

"One of my minions," Lucien interjected. Despite what he said and what it implied, I wanted to thank the vamp for butting in. Still incapable of speech, I sniffed the air, thanking the beast goddess my mountain lion scent hadn't leaked out. Only my forest pine scent laced with attraction flittered about.

"What a shame." Tristan's eyes twinkled. He winked and walked past me.

I don't think I breathed until I heard the door click behind me.

"Have you got your libido in check yet?" Lucien leaned forward as if to help me.

I waved him off. "I'm not buckling under raging hormones like an angsty teenager."

"Could've fooled me." He sat back in his chair and steepled his fingers. "What have you learned?"

"The envoy is Ethan's, isn't he?"

Lucien's hands unlocked to grasp the armrests. "Yes." His eyes flew to my mouth, waiting for me to speak again, to elaborate.

Excitement bubbled up in my chest at the missing piece to the puzzle, causing me to blurt out the truth. "Ethan Monroe issued the attack on Clint."

"Proof?" Lucien's eyes narrowed.

"That envoy killed my handler Landen. His scent is all over Landen's apartment."

"More." Apparently, the older the Vampire, the less articulate in stressful situations.

Shrugging, I launched into a factual account of my investigation. Lucien sat back and closed his eyes, as if savouring the truth of my words in his mind. He didn't have Allan present to validate my honesty. That surprised me. But Lucien was a master. He must have other tricks up his sleeve. Shivering, I barrelled through the last of the details, not wanting to think too much about Lucien's capabilities.

"...and now I'm here," I finished.

Lucien observed me while tapping his fingers on the ends of the armrest. Aside from that minute motion, he held the rest of his body still in the eerie way older Vampires could; like the truly dead, body rigid and stiff, eyes unblinking, heart not beating. When he spoke, his words surprised me. "Clint will be disappointed."

Grunting, I placed my hand on my hip. "Not my problem."

His eyebrow rose in what I hoped was amusement.

"My debt is paid." I wanted to hear him say it.

"No." Lucien's lips turned up. "It's not."

"No?" *What the fuck?*

"No."

"But I did what you wanted." That came out whinier than I planned.

"Yes." He flipped a hand in the air, as if finding my response inconsequential. "And for that I will not give you to Clint as his new play thing *and* allow you to live." He sounded annoyed, which made no sense to me because he was the one going back on our agreement.

"That wasn't the deal."

Lucien's smile was slow and sly and I wanted to punch it off his face. "If you recall our first fateful meeting, my dear Andrea, you will realize that was precisely our deal."

About to demand to know what the hell he'd been smoking, I clamped my mouth shut and thought back to our first fateful meeting. Images from the night flittered through my memory—Lucien acting like a douchebag, Lucien threatening life and limb, Lucien revealing Clint's survival of my attack, Lucien running his cold finger down my face, Lucien saying, *And if you don't provide me with answers in a week, you will be Clint's new toy.* Fuck! I provided answers, so I wouldn't be Clint's, but that didn't mean my debt to Lucien was cleared. My vision clouded with a red haze. A growl escaped my lips when I realized he was right. "Remind me to get our next deal in writing and to go over it with an expert legal team."

"Next deal?" Lucien asked, sounding genuinely surprised.

"The deal we make for me to pay my debt to you for attacking Clint."

"And if I don't want to?"

"You have enough minions. You don't need me."

"Ah, but you are special. I enjoy collecting unique things." Lucien's lips puckered out in a pout, looking decisively child-like.

It took a lot of self-control to ignore the absurdity of that look and not comment on it, or attack him. I focused on his words instead. He collected unique things? Like Clint? As much as I wanted to solve the puzzle of "What The Fuck Is Clint," now was not the time. "Name your price, Lucien. I'm not a collector's item. I won't be chained to you. I can't be. The SRD considers it a Conflict of Interest."

Lucien sighed and inspected his nails. "If you were my minion, you'd have no need for the SRD. But if you insist..." The clock ticked and ticked after his sentence trailed off. About to say something snide, I had to shut my mouth when he spoke up, "Bring me Ethan's head." When I didn't reply right away, Lucien looked up from his manicured fingernails. My mind blanked of all thought, then slowly, white hot rage consumed every neuron in my brain. I clenched my toes in my shoes and counted to ten. Then I counted to one hundred.

"You expect me to take down an entire horde of Vampires and a prowl of Wereleopards?" I asked. I let it come out as pissed off as I felt.

"No. I only asked for Ethan's head."

I balked.

"I will send Wick to take care of the rest."

"Only Wick?"

Lucien scoffed—a condescending sound that grated against my skin. "You mortals are so outrageous. Of course not. Wick will lead his pack and Allan will accompany him with his elite crew."

"I'm sure they could take Ethan's head."

"Ah, but I want it to be you."

32

"Booth." The agent's voice scratched my ear from the other end of the line when she answered the phone with her own name.

"It's Andy."

"McNeilly." Her tone hardened. What was her problem? We weren't exactly besties, but I thought we were on better terms than her crisp speech implied.

"Is this a good time?" I asked.

"No." A long pause stretched, long enough for her to elaborate or throw me a bone for when I could call back, but she did neither.

"Okay..." Another pause.

"When would be a good time?" I asked.

"I'll call you." *Click.*

I stared at the receiver for a moment, dumbstruck the cow had hung up on me.

"What did the SRD say?" Wick's voice pierced the silence.

I slammed the phone down on its charger and whirled around to find Wick leaning against the doorway with his arms crossed and his long frame filling up the small space.

"Apparently *Agent Booth* had more pressing things to discuss, so she'll call me." I tried to imitate her voice, but I couldn't get the voice husky or deep enough.

Wick raised an eyebrow. "Does she sound that bad?"

"Worse."

Wick shuddered and unfolded his long muscular frame to step into the room. "Why don't you call your handler? What's his name? O'Donnell?"

"Yeah that's him. Wiley old coyote. I'd call him, except Booth demanded I report to her directly."

"Have you checked your phone?"

"No, why?"

"Check it." He sprawled on the bed, turned onto his side and propped his head on his hand.

I tapped my phone screen to discover I had missed a barrage of messages. Huh? I looked up at Wick. He waved me to go ahead and read them. It took me seconds to grasp the situation. "We're going in tonight?" My voice came out flat.

Wick nodded.

"Doesn't give me much time to prepare."

"What do you need?"

Sighing, I thunked my head against the carpeted floor. "Nothing. Everything."

"Not sure I can help with that."

"I need to get my thoughts straight. Mentally prepare."

"You are the big bad SRD assassin."

"I used to be. Life with your pack is making me soft." I held my hand up against Wick's brilliant smile. "That's not a compliment."

"I'm still taking it as one."

"Ugh. Alphas." I stretched and got up. "Let's hash out the details. That will help me get back into SRD mode."

Wick sat up and patted the bed beside him. "Okay."

His actions appeared innocent, but the sharp gleam in his eyes and not-quite-relaxed posture told a different story. I didn't trust him and I didn't trust myself. I pulled up a chair to sit across from him instead. "No hanky panky."

"Wouldn't dream of it," he said.

I arched a brow.

"Ok. I do dream of it. Every night." He gave me a knowing look. "Makes me hard."

Ah fuck. I crossed my legs to clamp down the sudden longing manifesting at Wick's words. "Brandon."

Wick grunted and his whole body recoiled at the sound of his first name. Good.

"Behave," I said.

He held his hands out in a supplicant gesture. "But I want you to relax and focus."

I snorted. No need to elaborate on what he meant—the musky, coconut scent of desire came off him in waves and made the air in the room heavy with tension. "Relax, yes. Focus, no. I have no intention of attacking Ethan when I've been turned into a limp noodle."

Wick's smile widened.

Oh yeah, he knew the effect he had on me. "Focus," I snapped, but I spoke more to my humming libido than to Wick.

He scooted closer. "This might be our last day together, and I wish to savour it." *I wish to savour you.* His silent words rebounded inside my head as if he spoke them out loud. Shivering, I cast my gaze down.

"If you'd prefer to *focus*, then I'll respect that." *And just dream of licking you all over. Tasting you. Loving you.* Wick's voice caressed the inside of my head.

"Stop it!"

Wick straightened, his brows drawing together. "You heard that?"

Confused, I replayed what had just happened in my mind. My eyes snapped up to meet his. "Were you thinking dirty thoughts? Maybe I imagined it." Wouldn't be the first time.

Wick frowned. *Are you imaging this?*

Leaping off the chair I cast an accusatory glare at the man on my bed. "How did you do that?"

Wick shrugged. "I don't know. You are not pack. Not yet, at least. You should not be able to hear me."

Can you hear me?

Wick smiled and nodded. *Crystal clear. I like your voice in my mind.*

What the hell is going on? Did you join me to your pack when I was injured?

Wick looked affronted at the accusation. *You know as well as I do that joining a pack has to be voluntary. The suggestion that I forced you is not only absurd, it's hurtful.*

Sorry. I didn't sound sorry. I sounded like a petulant debutant after being scolded for running up her credit card.

Have you ever spoken mind to mind before? Wick asked.

I started to deny that I had, but then I remembered Ma. Frowning, I explained what happened to Wick.

So you can mind speak to feras?

I nodded.

Maybe that means you can speak to all animals.

You're not an animal, Wick.

I am, where and when it counts. The look he cast me left little to the imagination, no, wait, it left a little too much to my vivid and overactive imagination. Images of Wick naked in bed sent a wave of pleasure and promise rippling through my body. The air in the room grew heavy.

Wick's smile widened. His eyelids lowered halfway and he leaned in to watch every movement like a predator closing in on its prey. My skin quivered.

Inhaling deeply, his gaze caught mine. *Say the word, Andy, and I'll show you.*

You're incorrigible.

Wick shrugged and slowly stretched out of his sitting position on the bed. He ran his hands up my arms as he stood in front of me. *But you like it.*

And I did. His behaviour from anyone else would've

had me running away, or kneeing him in the groin, but I understood his persistence, his need to close the gap that existed between us, because I felt it too. The mate bond. His rosemary scent curled around me like a lasso, and one tug would have me in his lap, under his control. But that extra tug would never come from Wick, because he'd never push me, not really. He'd know from Mel how I'd been treated in the past and seemed to understand my need to close the distance in my own time and on my own terms.

Wick's hand glided up behind my head and tangled in my hair. He pulled me close and pressed his mouth against mine. But the gentle seduction of our earlier encounters disappeared as his kiss deepened, along with his control. He growled into my lips, but his hold on the back of my neck loosened and he withdrew. Intoxicating. Wick used a perfect balance of soft and hard. I grabbed his shirt and pulled him back to me.

When his tongue stroked mine, I groaned and drew him closer, the feel of every hard contour of his body sending a rush of pleasure coursing through me.

The phone rang.

Get lost.

Wick chuckled, which meant I projected my thoughts. Now that I'd placed my voice in his head, it seemed I lacked a filter. That would have to change fast. Sobering, I pulled away from Wick. He grumbled and made a last ditch effort to drag me close again. I shrugged out of his grasp.

Next time a phone interrupts us, I am going to bash

that thing into the wall. His voice brushed against my thoughts. *That goes for anything or anyone else that interrupts us.* He released me and held his hands up in mock surrender.

Laughing, I answered the phone.

I'm serious, Andy.

"Hello?" I answered the phone with a shaky voice. Wick stepped in behind me—to hold me? Throttle me? To make sure I heard? I waved him off.

"It's Joyce."

The name stumped me, but the cheese grater voice helped identify the caller. "Agent Booth?"

"Yes. I have a first name." From her tone, I practically heard her eyes roll from the other end of the phone.

"First I've heard of it," I grumbled. All agents had first names, but I didn't use them, ever. Only agents who were friends referred to each other by their first name. Didn't realize Joyce and I fit into that category.

Wick crossed his arms and huffed in my ear.

I heard you!

His body relaxed, but he remained standing inches behind me. His breath hit the back of my neck. Distracted, I missed what Booth said. "Sorry. What was that?"

"There's no need for the attitude. I said it once. I'm not going to repeat myself."

"No. I missed what you said. I was distracted." I shot Wick a cold stare. His eyes widened and he took a step back.

Dead silence answered me on the other end of the

phone, as if Booth took time to contemplate whether I was sincere or not. "I apologized for my brisk manner on the phone earlier."

"I'm sorry I missed it."

"Yes, well, like I said. I'm not going to repeat myself."

I didn't bother pointing out that she kind of already did. She didn't strike me as the type to apologize often. I turned and found a comfortable position on the bed.

"I was not alone and I don't trust my work phone."

"Troubles at the SRD?"

Booth snorted. "I'm not entirely convinced Landen left the SRD without help."

"You think someone high up was involved in his going rogue?"

"And pulling his strings," she confided. "Someone cleaned up after the two of you, keeping you off the radar, feeding Landen tips whenever we got close."

"And you're sure this line secure?"

Booth snorted again. "What a silly question. I wouldn't call you on it otherwise."

"I've had a rough couple of days. Cut me some slack."

Booth paused. "Give me the full report."

"There is a Master Vampire in town with his horde by the name of Ethan Monroe. He's holed up in West Vancouver and was behind the hit on Lucien's human servant."

"The hit you botched."

I ground my teeth ground. "I ripped his throat out.

He should have died. Even as a human servant, it should have been enough."

"But it wasn't."

"No."

Another pause. "So you found out who issued the orders. Does Lucien consider your debt paid?"

It was my turn to snort. "No. He considers the insult appeased. He will no longer kill me or give me to Clint, but I still owe him."

"And let me guess, he won't name a price."

"I made him."

"And?"

"Kill Ethan."

Booth laughed, deep and throaty and not altogether unpleasant because it sounded genuine. "These Vampires never cease to amaze me. You think with immortality, they would gain some perspective on trivial matters."

"I think they lose perspective, not gain it. The older they get the more serious they take themselves."

"So you're not a vamp tramp?"

"No."

"Is that all?" She sounded like she knew more existed, but wanted to be wrong.

"Nope."

A long drawn out sigh came from the other end of the phone.

"Ethan's animal to call is the leopard."

"Angelica," Booth cursed. "I knew there was something wrong with her."

"Agreed. She's how I found him. The scent of

Landen's killer was faint, but I knew it had to be a big cat. When I met Angie, I recognized a familiarity with her scent and tracked her to Ethan. One of his envoys was the killer."

"Do you know the envoy's name?"

When I went to answer, my throat constricted. A pang of guilt lanced through my body. Why did I feel this sudden loyalty to him? Why did my mountain lion try to shred the inside of my head with her claws to prevent me from saying his name? I'd met him only once and I didn't know a thing about him. I cleared my throat. "Tristan."

"Tristan Kayne?"

I shrugged. Realizing she couldn't see me, I answered "I guess."

"Angie's prowl Alpha? God, she never stops talking about him."

"Sounds right."

"Black hair like shining ebony, eyes like cut sapphires." Booth tried to pitch her voice higher to imitate Angie, but she sounded like nails on a chalkboard. "Is he all that special?"

My immediate thought: Hell yeah. But conscious Wick lurked in the room and followed the entire conversation like an overprotective mother hen I considered my answer before speaking. Crap, could he hear my thoughts now? I glanced at him over my shoulder. He kept his arms crossed and remained silent, a good sign. "He's a good looking man," I said.

Wick growled.

I threw both my arms up, including the one that

clutched the phone. I would've missed Booth's reply if I didn't possess Shifter hearing. "That's too bad. I'd hoped Angie loved a mutant."

"Will the SRD pursue him?" I asked.

"Unlikely. I would have to file a report and cite my sources. Besides, Landen was a wanted fugitive, there was an open bounty on his head. Yours, too. The SRD will be pleased no one will come forth to claim the reward."

I breathed a sigh of relief.

"Tristan most likely had no choice in the matter."

I nodded at the phone. "I have reason to believe the Wereleopards are not content being controlled by Monroe. I hope they find a loophole and avoid interfering with our siege. That's how I escaped."

"What do you mean?"

"Let me tell you the whole story..." And for what felt like the fiftieth time that day, I launched into the story of my investigation like a war veteran recounting the good ol' days. Booth remained silent, either rendered speechless or asleep. As much as I would love to believe my storytelling abilities improved to the point of taking her breath away, she probably drifted off. As a glorified assassin for the SRD, I had little practice talking about myself, so it came out stilted and factual. If I threw in bigger words, which I didn't, it would sound like I read from a scientific research paper. People got paid to research the north Atlantic honeybee's average wing beat speed. *Blows. My. Mind.*

When I tore out throats of supernatural delinquents, it soothed my soul to know researchers were out there getting paid big bucks to produce research papers that would greatly impact my life.

"Andy?"

I shook my head to clear my thoughts, like my mind was one of those Etch-A-Sketches. "Sorry. Lost in thought."

"I said, it looks like Angie's not as evil as we'd like to believe. You might have to be cordial to her next time you're in."

"I hate being nice to people when I really just want to punch them in the face." I blew at some hair that had fallen into my face.

"What will you do now?"

"I'm about to meet with the Alpha of the Werewolf pack to discuss a plan of attack."

Booth shuffled through some papers. I heard it through the phone. "Brandon Wickard?"

I glanced over at Wick. His lips curled up into a smug smile as if to say, 'Who's the big dog?'

I rolled my eyes. "Yeah, that's him all right."

"Mmmm." Booth made the same sound I did when I engulfed chocolate ice cream. I stared at the receiver in shock. That sounded wrong coming from Booth—someone I was fairly sure up to now was an asexual organism. But what really bothered me was the ferocious surge of jealousy rearing its ugly head, making me want to travel through the phone and dig my claws into Agent Booth's neck. I caught the growl before it escaped my lips, but the bitter stench of cat pee flared out of my pores and filled the room. Jealousy—an ugly emotion, and an even uglier smell.

Wick chuckled.

"Have *fun*." Her tone implied that she didn't refer to the G-rated playground variety.

"Um. Ok. Sure."

"And keep me updated."

Click. She hung up before I thought of anything witty to say.

"Don't say it." I didn't need to turn around to know Wick wore one of his wide smiles. What he planned to say, I had no idea, but it would be cheeky. I heard his mouth clamp shut after his words stopped in his throat. When I did turn around, Wick leaned against the wall again with his arms crossed, eyes averted, and an innocent expression plastered on his face.

"Ok. Fine," I huffed. "What were you going to say?"

He slanted his gaze to meet mine. "Not a thing."

"Out with it." I waved him on in encouragement.

He shook his head. "Let me show you."

"Down boy." My hand on his chest stopped him in his tracks. "We need to strategize."

Wick growled and stepped closer, making my arm bend. "I don't want to behave. You can't dodge me forever, Andy."

"We need to go over the attack logistics." I shook my head at him. "We go in tonight."

Wick flopped on the bed and draped an arm over his eyes. "You're going to be the death of me, woman."

"I think you've mentioned that already. Twice. But cheer up, if we don't have a good game plan, a Wereleopard or Vampire might snatch the honour from me."

Wick grumbled under his arm before he launched into a detailed plan for a tactical assault. I listened with my mouth open and mentally cursed my lack of a notepad.

It took me a few moments in the silence following Wick's lengthy explanation to digest what he'd said. "So basically, you're going to swarm the house from all possible entrances, while you blow up stuff with bombs and grenades?"

"Pretty much. We have better numbers and the time-line doesn't give us much of an opportunity to plan something subtle or elegant."

"Where do I fit in?"

"Could you wait in the car?" Wick looked hopeful.

I snorted. "No."

Wick straightened up and stared at the ceiling. "Well I would prefer the next best thing."

"And what's that?"

"At least wait in the car until the takeover is complete and we have Ethan pinned."

"And then what? I sweep in and take his life?"

"Well, his head to be more precise."

My hands twitched and my jaw tightened. I had to take a deep breath before I voiced my objection. "I'm not helpless, Wick."

"Never said you were."

"Then why are you treating me like a defenceless puppy?"

"Is it so wrong that I want to keep you safe?"

"Yes."

Wick grumbled and looked around as if trying to find back-up. "Fine. How do you want to play it?"

I sat back in the lounge chair across from Wick. "I'd like to waltz in after the initial wave, find Ethan and chop his head off." Not a lie. It's what I'd like to do, not what I'd actually do, but Wick didn't need to know that.

He laughed; a great sound that warmed my heart, but not enough to drown out the guilty feeling deep in my chest. What came over me? Why couldn't I tell Wick what I planned? Independence didn't go poof after years of becoming an ingrained habit, but I'd opened up. A bit. My strategy for tonight wasn't that devious—I just didn't plan to wait. I would enter the house during the initial surge and use the commotion and confusion as camouflage to search out Ethan. I learned long ago not to count on others to do my job for me. My hands would be dirty before the end of the night and that was okay with me.

If someone took Ethan's head before I had a chance, either intentional or accidental, I'd still belong to Lucien. Still trapped. Still *owned*. I couldn't let that happen.

I looked up in time to get a close view of Wick's lips before they pressed into mine. Well, maybe I'd enjoy this for a little longer. I'd forget the job we had tonight and my intentions to get as far from Lucien and the Were-wolves he controlled. The tension in my muscles released, flowing from my limbs. And then I tensed again. I couldn't let Wick get attached if I planned to leave. Stealing the last of my resolve, I pulled away.

"Let me guess? You need to mentally prepare?" Wick grumbled.

"How'd you know?"

Wick's lip quirked. "You're running out of excuses."

"It's not an excuse."

"A badass assassin like you." He brushed my cheek with his thumb. "Should not need to meditate before a job."

My mouth opened to say something, anything, to deny his accusation. His thumb pressed against my lips, effectively silencing me.

"I'll give you tonight, Andy. But after this job..." He leaned down to draw in my scent by the crook of my neck. He let his words hang in the air and smiled at my gaping expression before stepping away and leaving me to my thoughts.

When I came downstairs, I found Wick and a number of the pack curled up on the couches and chairs around the television. It took me two seconds of looking at the screen filled with atrophied humans to figure out what they watched.

"This is how you prepare for a raid?" I turned away

with a grunt. Obviously, not everyone could be a professional.

"Not joining us?" Jess asked.

"Definitely not."

"What's your beef with zombies?" John demanded, coming across a little defensive, like he found it insulting I wasn't jumping up and down screaming "yay" like a little girl.

"You mean, besides hearing my brain cells die every minute I watch?"

"It's not that bad." Wick looked over his shoulder to wink.

"Yes it is. I don't understand this fetish for everything zombie. The plot line for each show is the same."

"Is not." John frowned.

"Is too. 'Oh no. The zombies are coming to get us. We could easily outrun them, but somehow we run in circles and can't outwit lobotomized humans. Oh no! I've been infected. But I won't tell my group because I'll be different...'" John and Wick didn't look impressed. Maybe I overdid it with the theatrical hand gestures and fake damsel in distress fainting.

"So you don't like zombie movies?" Jess asked with a dry voice.

"No." My hands went to my hips on reflex. "If there's ever a zombie apocalypse, I'm going to hole up somewhere with my guns and knives and stay away from all the dumbasses."

"And these dumbasses would be?" Jess asked.

"Everyone else."

"A bit of an exaggeration." John's voice pinched the air as he crossed his arms.

"Say what you want, but there appears to be something about zombie apocalypses that renders the non-infected terminally stupid," I said. John looked about to say something, but I overrode him. "Case in point!" I pointed my damning finger at the television screen and waved it around a little.

One of the female actors pulled back her sleeve to look at a zombie inflicted wound, before covering it back up and glancing back and forth to see if anyone saw. Dramatic music followed and then the show cut to commercial.

No one spoke. Everyone looked at either me or John.

"Okay. Maybe you have a point," John conceded. "But before you start doing your happy dance, know that your attempt to ruin this show for me failed. I'll still watch it." He popped a chip in his mouth. "And I'll love it even more knowing it pisses you off."

"Ugh." Though tempting to tell him to chew with his mouth closed, it would come across as petty. I'd already won the argument.

"What's everyone else's motive?"

"Same as John's," Ryan quipped. He looked away immediately to avoid contact. A dig, but given that he voluntarily spoke in my direction for the first time, I took it as progress.

Jess shrugged. "I'm outnumbered."

"I like that they have guns and shoot stuff. There tends to be a lot of things blown up, too. That's good."

Wick smiled. "Besides, it makes me want to smash things. It's perfect motivation before a raid."

"Are you a seven-year-old boy trapped in a man's body?" Did they take nothing serious?

John laughed along with Wick. "We're all seven-year-old boys at heart."

The door slammed and by the time I turned around, Steve ran around the corner into the living room. He carried a case of beer in one hand and cradled four bags of chips with his other arm. "Did I miss anything?"

"No…" Jess's lie stank up the room. She looked away.

Steve halted. "Oh man! You started without me?"

"Relax bud." John relieved him of the case of beer.

"It's saved. We'll start at the beginning."

The groan escaped my mouth before I could clamp it shut.

Steve eyed me suspiciously.

"Don't," John warned, shaking his head at his packmate.

Steve turned to John. "Zombie hater?"

John nodded and they both shot me disgusted looks.

I held their stares. "I feel like I've justified my stance on this matter." Looking at the couches, I considered my options. "Think I might join you."

John groaned. "You can't stay if all you're going to do is sit there and make bitchy comments."

No point denying I intended to do exactly what he accused me of. I turned to everyone else and gave them a sympathetic look. "Fine, then. I'm going to do a little reading, to improve my mind."

"Good luck with that," Steve shot as he opened a bag of chips. He misjudged his strength and ripped the bag open, sending chips flying across the room and eliciting a string of curses and barbs from the others. He shrugged, picked some off the coffee table and popped them in his mouth.

Frowning, I considered how at home Steve seemed with Wick's inner circle, yet the first time I met him, he'd been at that awful gas station. The words escaped before I could filter. "How come you weren't around when Wick first imprisoned me in this house and now you're here *all the time*?"

Steve turned to me with a mouth full of potato chips. He started to speak and then, realizing exactly how full his mouth was, thought better of it.

Wick placed a hand on Steve's shoulder. "Steve is one of my enforcers. He was out of town on pack business during your...confinement."

Steve gave me a wide, close-mouthed smile. He looked like my childhood pet hamster when he shoved all the food in his mouth. Didn't look the enforcer type at all. My eyes narrowed.

"Why were you at the gas station that day?"

Steve gulped down the contents in his mouth and shrugged. "Duh. It's a gas station."

"But you didn't buy anything. Why were you there?"

Steve shifted in his seat and glanced at Wick, which answered my question—Steve had been following me on Wick's orders. Their faces looked apprehensive, as if bracing for a thunderous reaction. They wouldn't get one. If I'd been in Wick's position, I'd have me followed too.

Shaking my head with a chuckle, I turned back to the stairs. "I'll be in my room."

"Want some company later?" Steve called out. A low growl vibrated the air behind me, followed by a thump. When I looked over my shoulder, Steve rubbed his shoulder with a smile and Wick looked murderous.

"Sorry, it's a zombie-lover free zone." I smiled.

He's baiting you, I sent to Wick.

I know.

I never heard anyone huff in my head before. It felt interesting, to say the least; like my brain cells were candles and he blew them out, but only for a moment, because then they were back up and running.

Steve pretended to pout, but his eyes sparkled.

Wick's grin spread across his face and he gave his enforcer a triumphant look.

I couldn't help it. "Don't look so pleased, Wick. Same rule applies to you." I spun on my heel to everyone's laughter. Everyone's but Wick's.

We'll see, he shot back. *We'll see.*

33

S andwiched between Clint and Allan, I couldn't shake the feeling I was a donut being delivered to the police station. When we piled into the SUV earlier for the drive to Ethan's mansion, I tried to call shotgun so I could sit in the front with Wick. It took one shake of Allan's head to stop Wick from agreeing, and Allan pulled me into the back with him instead.

"I'm surprised you're here," I said, and turned to Clint. Seeing him for the first time since I thwarted his attempt to enslave me as a pet, I expected him to be more upset about the whole thing, yet nothing about his demeanour implied hostility. In fact I couldn't get *any* impressions of his mood. Relaxing back into his seat with loose limbs and slow easy breaths, he looked like he should be wearing yoga pants and chanting "Om." Why wasn't he pissed off? Should I be worried? My scalp prickled and my stomach felt like a snow globe being shook by a five year old. What was he up to?

Earlier tonight, I'd been relieved to be free of Clint. But now? Now this empty feeling in the depths of my stomach kept expanding, the mere presence of Clint reminding me of how close I'd come to enslavement.

"Why's that?" Clint asked.

"You're too valuable to Lucien."

Clint shrugged. "Ethan tried to assassinate me. It's not something I can ignore."

"Ego can't take it?"

Clint laughed and shook his head.

Allan's lip twisted, the movement small, and almost imperceptible, but I managed to catch it from the corner of my eye. I guessed correctly, then, or close enough.

"But if something were to happen..." I let my voice trail off.

Clint smirked. "Worried for me? I'm not without my own skills. Something Ethan should've realized. If he had known, he would've left me alone."

"Known what?"

Clint's smile widened and he shook his head. "Nice try, kitten. I'm sure you'll figure it out soon enough."

"Allan gets to call me kitten. Not you." I said. When did I become okay with the Japanese Hulk using that nickname?

"It fits." Clint reached to do something to my face, caress it maybe? I batted his hand away before it reached me, and not in a playful way. Who knew where it had been.

"Being your sex slave was taken off the table."

Clint looked away.

"Are you pouting?"

He turned back toward me and gave me a flat stare.

"I'm guessing yes."

"I will have you, Andy," Clint said. "You will screw up and I will be there ready to claim you."

The intensity of his eyes bore into mine. I cleared my throat and looked away, and my wolf, not liking the submissive move, growled so deep and low in my subconscious that I didn't realize right away Wick snarled from the front seat.

Clint's eyes glanced to the tense Werewolf before returning to me. "And no one will do a goddamn thing about it."

THE WIND SLICED PAST MY SKIN LIKE A butcher's knife through a chicken bone, so strong it hacked against my exposed flesh.

The men had already parked and ambled out of the vehicles. The community playground, downwind from Ethan's mansion, filled with naked pre-shift Werewolves and Vampires, all milling about finalizing plans. More cavalry occupied the other parks surrounding the house, far enough away to be undetectable to the Wereleopards' noses and sentries. Not only would it be too late to run, but by the time Ethan sensed the attack, there'd be nowhere to run to.

"Remember, you're going to wait," Wick said to me. "When we give the signal for you to come in, stay behind me. Let me and my wolves take care of Ethan for you."

I shot him a quick smile and nodded. Wick planned to immobilize Ethan for me, so I'd only have to waltz in and sever his head from his body. I couldn't let Wick do that. No way would I let someone else do my fighting, or chance something going wrong. Clint and Allan's presence made my skin itch. I also didn't want Wick to put himself in unnecessary danger. Not for me.

Wick growled when I yanked off my shirt.

"I said I'd wait, not *how* I would wait," I said. I crossed my arms over my bra.

He shut his mouth and stalked off. Only to stop twenty paces away before marching back to stand in front of me. Planting his feet in a wide stance inches from mine, he gripped both my arms and loomed over me. "Be careful," he said with a gruff voice, as if his vocal cords sprouted coarse wolf hair. He leaned down and pressed his lips tenderly against mine before whirling around and running off to join his pack. *Fucking alphas.* He didn't even give me a chance to slip him some tongue.

When the assault team spread out, turning their backs on me, I shucked off the rest of my clothes and willed the change. Skin folded in on itself, feathers sprouted, my body condensed. I launched into the air.

Circling the mansion, I made out the wolves and Vampires moving into position. Team Lucien easily maneuvered around Ethan's sentries, having scouted them out beforehand. Angling closer to the house, I searched for an open window. There were several. But which one would lead to Ethan? And what did he look like? I didn't know because no one had a picture.

I'd look for the pompous ass who ordered everyone around with a flick of his wrist—a stereotype, sure, but it hadn't led me wrong yet.

A grand ballroom with giant floor to ceiling windows faced the ocean. Long black out curtains were pulled to the side, but the edges still showed to the outside world. Seeing nothing to perch on outside, I battled the offshore wind to do a number of fly-bys. A few vamps sauntered about, but the large, red velour chair at the end of the room, looking an awful lot like a throne, remained empty. I couldn't make this stuff up. Who had a chair like that? Ethan. That's who. It practically screamed Vampire Master because without fail, they were all over the top and easy to spot. Lucien had a similar chair.

If Ethan wasn't sitting in his throne, lording over his minions, where was he?

I kept looking. If Ethan wasn't a permanent fixture in the area, how did he have a posh place like this, outfitted with dungeons and his own special home décor? Vampires must have their own definition for a visit. Then again, being so old, a few years would be a short-term stay in comparison to their age. Something weird about the whole situation, but regardless, Ethan must've been pretty sneaky with his set-up to not raise any alarms with Lucien's horde until now.

The volatile winds fought me as I pumped my wings harder to gain elevation. The master suite had to be the room on the top floor with a wall of windows. I quickly circled around and careened toward the patio. Wick's group would attack soon and I needed to be poised to strike at the right time.

Light flickered in the otherwise dark room. Candles? Some of the older Vampires couldn't evolve well to the changing times despite the horde of money they made over the years. The dull light reflected off two intertwined bodies. Good thing I wasn't in wolf form. Vampire sex reeked of mildew and the dregs of a wine barrel. I'd never choose to bottle that fragrance. *Gross.*

The only windows open on this level were tiny— more vents than entrances—and even if I dropped a few pounds, I'd never fit through them. A screech threatened to erupt from my throat. I clamped down on it and flew around to the second floor, circling, desperately looking for an opening.

Casting my gaze to the surrounding foliage, I made out dark shapes moving toward the mansion.

There! A larger window on the second floor level, open just enough for me to fit. I pulled my wings in and barrelled through the opening just as cries of alarm rose in the house. Chaos reigned.

34

S hifting quickly to human form, my feet barely touched the floor when a large force smashed against my head, sending me reeling into the wall. Dazed, I turned around to see a fuzzy Mark, the Were-hyena, holding what looked like a baseball bat. Certainly felt like one.

"Overcompensating?" I squared off, ignoring the thumping of my brain inside my skull. Maybe having a smart mouth would be useful for once and buy me time to get my eyes to focus.

He laughed and my vision cleared enough to see him stroke the baseball bat with a jerky pump motion. "I'm going to have fun with you."

"Mmhmm," I stalled, willing my eyes to see only one of him. The three swirling Marks solidified into one just in time to see him swinging the bat at my head.

I ducked.

"I hope you like this bat." Mark circled me. "I plan to

give you splinters." He made a thrusting motion with his hips, giving little doubt to *where* he referred.

"That's disgusting." I dodged another swing of the bat.

Mark licked his lips. A waft of his saliva coursed through the air and smacked me in the face. A nastier weapon than the bat.

"Ugh." I fanned the air away from my nose, and caught Mark's tensing muscles too late. He shot out and tackled me.

Slammed to the ground, I had little time to appreciate the inlaid stonework as I battled for position against the Werehyena's heavy body. Sparring with Wick had its advantages—my ground game had improved.

Gripping one of his legs with both of mine, I prevented Mark from moving to a more dangerous position. Let him get distracted with dry humping my leg. It beat a bat to the head or getting choked out.

A large bang downstairs rattled the floor. Mark and I froze. Some screaming and hissing erupted below and I took Mark's renewed ardour as my signal.

I thrust a hip up and yanked my arm to the side and threw Mark off-balance. Pressing my advantage, I used my momentum and rolled until I straddled Mark. I met his smug smile with my own.

His grin faltered.

"My sole regret is that I don't have more time for this." My smiled widened. I enjoyed the deep set frown on his face as I willed the changed.

The scent of his confusion turned to fear, his eyes big

and round, took in the sight of a large mountain lion pinning him to the floor instead of a five foot ten slender woman. My tail twitched from side to side as memories of what this man did to me and the stuff he planned to do.

Another outburst of screaming spiralled up the staircase from the first floor.

No time!

With no warning, I dipped my feline head and clamped my jaws around Mark's neck. With a quick jerk of my head, I heard a snap and Mark's body went limp beneath me. Not dead, not yet. Some Weres could heal an injury even this intense. I quickly sank my teeth into the soft tissue of his throat and ripped it out. Ugh. The taste! Hacking, I spat out chunks of cartilage, artery, muscle and a whole slew of other tissues. When that didn't rid the taste, I wiped my tongue off on my paw.

"Eric!" A man's voice shouted from the floor above me. "Dammit, answer your phone."

I followed the sound of his voice and slunk up the staircase, ignoring the battle waging below.

"What's wrong, Ethan?" The sound of a whimpering female voice flittered to my position. Even from a distance the high pitched whine irritated and grated my nerves. I bit back a hiss.

"Not now."

"But Ethan, I'm scared," she simpered.

The pounding of feet followed by a sharp snap made me poke my head around the corner to find out what the hell just happened. A naked woman's body lay crumpled on the floor, her head twisted at an unnatural angle.

I guess her voice irritated Ethan, too.

Ethan stood over her prone body, also naked, and ran a hand through his thick wavy hair before turning away from the staircase. Moving at vamp speed, he changed into clothes. Too fast to track. Too fast for me to attack. My advantage was the element of surprise. I waited.

He was in the middle of throwing various articles into a bag when he froze. His head turned to the side and his nostrils flared.

Fuck!

Coiling my muscles, I sprung forward as he swivelled around to face me with fangs barred. My claws swiped empty air. The weight of my body would have felled any norm and most supes on impact, but Ethan only staggered back a step. His cold fingers, strong as metal, grasped my front limbs.

He held me at arms-length, my feet dangling off the ground, and smiled, a slow, calculating smile. "They sent a pathetic Shifter? After me?" His hands tightened. "I'm going to enjoy sending a message."

His face surged forward like a striking cobra, going in for the bite.

I shifted.

My limbs slipped out of his grasp as they formed wings. The moment my talons touched the floor, I shifted again. Back to cat, I twisted around Ethan and used the bed to launch onto his back. This time, my claws sank into cold flesh. I plunged my teeth into the back of his neck. And raked his skin with my hind legs. Ethan howled, but his skin closed up after each lash of my claws. Freshly fed, he had the energy to heal quickly. He whirled around the room with Vampire speed and slammed me against the wall.

My vision went black.

I hit the floor. A heavy numb feeling spread through my body and I staggered to my feet in time for Ethan to clutch my hide and fling me across the room. This wall was as hard and unforgiving as the last; my body bounced off and fell to the cold hardwood.

Ethan tackled me before my brain could process the need to move. He flipped me over and pinned my back to the ground. An awkward and uncomfortable position for a mountain lion. His knees dug into my thighs so I couldn't use my legs or my sharp claws to rip open his body.

"Full of surprises." His head plunged down.

His teeth punctured my skin. The draw of blood sent a cold shiver through my body...and then he stopped.

My eyes fluttered opened and I struggled to maintain the cat form unsuccessfully. I groaned as my fur folded and I lay in my human body, limp under Ethan's control. Ethan pulled back, his face inches from mine, his mouth dripping blood onto my cheek.

"What are you?" His voice softly hit my face.

My chest felt hollow as aches and pains hammered my nerve cells, and heavy, fatigued muscles remained unresponsive. Developing a new super power right now would be helpful. Or what about an old one? A power so raw and furious, it remained buried deep inside after the night I broke Dylan's hold. I reached for it. Hidden in the depths of my core, it waited, coiled and poised to strike. Something monstrous answered my call and rose up within me. The beast.

Like hot lava flowing over fields, it consumed my centre.

No! What was I thinking? It took years to find my humanity after the last time. I doubt I'd find it a second time, if it happened again. And that kind of vacuous life wasn't worth living. I tried to push the monster back, but fluid fury bathed my cells, overpowering my will.

My mountain lion responded first. Pressing down on the feral monster within, she stemmed the flow. The wolf and falcon joined, containing it, leashing it.

When my eyes opened, the vision my own. The control, my own. What seemed like an eternal battle lasting hours, must've passed in mere seconds because Ethan still watched me in wonder. Where was Wick? I could use him right about now.

A shard of glass glinted from the corner of my eye. I snaked my hand out and clutched it. Ethan blocked my arm and pinned my hand behind my head. He squeezed until I let the glass go.

My muscles tensed as Ethan's face dipped closer. I shut my eyes, but the second bite never came.

Looking up, I found Ethan still, in that freaky way Vampires were capable of. His eyes shifted to the right, where I caught a blur of motion. What the heck was that?

Whirling around in his crouched position, Ethan avoided the decapitating swing of Clint's sword. It glanced off his shoulder.

My breath hitched, caught in my throat. A flush of adrenaline tingled through my body, moving in waves, revitalizing my energy. Clint! I watched him move around the room, dodging and weaving to avoid Ethan's grasp. I stood up and whispered *thank you*. He'd saved my life. Now, I might have to return the favour. In a movement, too quick for the human or cat eye to follow, Ethan disarmed and pinned Clint.

Ethan hovered over Clint, eyes glinting. "I'm going to enjoy this."

I threw myself on his back and forced my body to change back to the mountain lion. Legs pumping, I used them to shred at the lower half of his body. Ethan grunted and straightened up, releasing Clint.

Ethan reached around and grabbed me by the scruff off the neck. Tearing me off his back, he flung me across the room. Again.

Dazed, I looked up from my curled, fetal position in time to see Ethan drive the sword through Clint's body.

No!

Staggering to an upright position, I limped up to Ethan's exposed back while he dropped his head back and relished the glory of his kill. He licked the sword.

"Are you going to try again, little kitty?" He spoke with a calm voice without turning around. "Third time's the charm?"

I hissed and sat back on my haunches. He had a

point. Attacking his back had already proven fruitless twice. Maybe a frontal assault would work? Maybe I could use his confidence against him.

Maybe my death would be quicker.

Ethan glanced over his shoulder with a smirk before he turned around and studied me.

My tail swished back and forth with a mind of its own.

A dark figure moved silently up the stairs behind Ethan.

On all fours, I barred my teeth and let out a yowl that would raise the hairs of any wild animal in a five mile radius. Ethan blinked and then smiled before taking a step closer.

"I wish I had more time to play with my food, but there's a battle going on downstairs. I don't think my team's winning." He shrugged. "It's of little consequence. Progeny is easy to make. But you..." His head tilted to the side. "You are rare, unique. I wish I could keep you."

The dark figure materialized behind Ethan. Allan.

Not daring to make eye contact or look over Ethan's shoulder, I projected my thoughts to Allan. *On the count of three?*

I didn't wait for a response I wouldn't get. Could Allan even hear me? Swishing my tail like a pendulum, I counted to three.

One.
Two.
Three.

On three, I leapt at Ethan. His arms moved up instinctively to block my claws. But he had no defence for my jaws clamping on his face.

Ethan dropped my forelimbs and grasped my head, preventing me from ripping his own off. Then Ethan's body jolted. Again and again. The sick sound of metal slipping into his body reverberated in the room. Something pricked my belly.

Ethan's grip relaxed and he fell forward, landing on top of me. Unlocking my jaw, I rolled out from underneath the dead weight.

Allan stood over us with a katana sword, its curved, slender single edge coated with blood.

"Make it quick." He tossed the sword before my shift fully finished. I caught the hilt mid-flight and brought the blade down on the back of Ethan's neck.

Young vamps turned to ash when staked or beheaded. The older ones would too, eventually, but I had a few hours to get his head to Lucien. Already shrivelling, it looked like an old bloodless corpse instead of something that had kicked my ass moments ago.

"Don't suppose you want to carry that for me?" Looking down at the gray, emaciated head, I shivered.

Allan held out a handkerchief and shook his head.

"I have to carry Clint."

My head whipped around to where the human servant lay in a pool of blood. His glazed eyes, open and unblinking.

Allan waved the handkerchief in my face. Frowning, I snatched it from him. "You're bleeding," he explained.

Sure enough, when I cast my eyes down at my bare navel, an ugly gash oozed blood. I clamped the cloth on it and pressed to stem the flow.

"I thought you were offering it to me to pick up the head. That or to cover up."

"It would take more than that flimsy piece of cloth to cover your ass."

Flicking him the bird, I reached down and picked up Ethan's head by the hair. Good thing these old European vamps tended to grow their hair out—never met one with a crew cut. No idea how I'd pick his head up if he had short hair.

Allan walked over to Clint and hoisted him over his shoulders in one swift move.

"He saved my life." *So did you.*

Allan glanced over. His smile widened and his fangs punched out. "Maybe you can thank him later."

My head tilted to the side. "A bit beyond saving, isn't he?"

Somehow Allan conveyed a shrug with Clint draped around his shoulders. He glanced down at Ethan's withering head. "We need to go."

With my heart stuck in my throat like a dry hairball, I ran into the grand foyer with Allan close behind me. And stopped, nearly causing Allan to collide into my back. In front of us, two figures squared off to fight in the middle of the otherwise empty room, making the space seem enormous. Wick and Tristan in Were form.

I recognized both instantly. Wick's sweet rosemary scent and Tristan's citrus and sunshine slammed into my pores and set my mountain lion and wolf grappling with each other for control. I staggered and gripped Allan's arm as he came to stand beside me.

Settle. I pulled my falcon up close to the surface, so close, my eyes tingled, partially shifting into the bird's. Using the heightened vision, and newly cleared mind, I scanned the room.

Where was the rest of the pack? Allan's elite vamp legion? My hearing sharpened, letting in sounds of yelling and bodies crashing into one another beyond the doors. The main fighting had moved outside, then, leaving the two leaders to battle it out here. Wick limped and oozed blood, looking more damaged than Tristan. My chest tightened at the sight and I swallowed. In nature a lone wolf couldn't compete with a leopard and the same held true for Weres. It didn't matter how strong and big Wick was on his own, his power diminished without his pack and his Alpha dominance held no advantage because Tristan had the feline equivalent. The power they emanated clashed together in the air, a torrent of authority sent my heartbeat racing. I saw the truth, even if I didn't want to believe it: if no one stepped in, Wick would lose this fight.

My gaze snapped back and forth as they circled each other.

"We need to go," Allan repeated.

Without another thought, I tossed the decaying head at Allan. He caught it and frowned.

"Hold that for me?" My expression must've conveyed my desperation, because he nodded, shifted Clint's weight across his shoulders and grasped the stringy hair harder.

"I'll meet you there. When you're done, fly to Lucien's. I'll wait outside as long as possible. After that, you're on your own."

I nodded, not wanting to dwell on the inner work-ings of Allan's mind or why he'd become so eager to help me. I turned toward the circling Weres as Allan jogged out of the building. I couldn't best a Wereleopard one on one. But I could buy Wick time to heal. With a sudden burst of manic energy and no time to think, I ran across the room and willed the change.

Flying across the room, my feline body slammed into Tristan's sleek black fur before he could deliver a devastating blow to Wick. We rolled, slashing at one another.

Andy! Wick shouted in my head.

Heal, I snarled back at him. *Quickly!*

Tristan shifted his weight and tossed me off. My body sailed through the air and came down hard against the floor. My head snapped back and I slid to the floor. *Oh God, that hurts.* I stood on wobbly legs, but the room wavered and I keeled over. Before everything went black, my muscles and skin folded, shifting back to human form.

Maybe Tristan really was an angel. It would explain why this one looked so much like him. I stared into the familiar sapphire eyes and frowned at his wrinkled brow and stooped posture. Why would an angel worry?

"Hang on." His silken voice smoothed over my skin and rolled down my body. It awakened other sensations, less pleasant ones. The pain came slamming back. *I'm not dead.*

I moved my head and regretted it.

"Shhh..." Strong hands stroked my hair back. I looked up to see Wick bending over me. My head cradled in his lap.

My eyebrows bunched together as I looked back at Tristan. He kneeled by my waist, one hand resting on my hip and the other gently held my wrist as if taking my pulse. My attention flicked again to Wick's upside down face. They were both alive. "Why aren't you fighting?"

"You interrupted us, love." Tristan ran a crooked finger down my cheek. He paused and then snatched his blood covered hand back. My blood. Wick growled.

Tristan looked away from my face and started to say something to Wick when the door across the room slammed open.

"Tristan!" A naked Angie ran into the room. "Do you feel it? Ethan's dead. We're free!" Her ecstatic expression soured when she saw both men bent over me.

Turn that frown upside down. Why would she be upset? She didn't like me.

Wick's worried expression turned back to my face.

What? he asked.

I must have spoken that out loud, or in Wick's head. *He probably thinks I'm losing it. Maybe I am. Maybe my brain is leaking out with my blood.* I didn't have much left. Not after Ethan.

"Her mountain lion has retreated. I can't reach it. But her wolf..." Tristan's hand pressed firmer against my wound. "Heal her," he hissed at Wick.

Wick didn't need to be asked twice. He leaned down

and hefted me into his arms. Tristan kept the pressure on the wound and moved with Wick.

"Why do you care?" Wick asked.

Tristan stared down at my face, his intense blue eyes met mine. "My cat has seen hers."

Wick's arms stiffened beneath me.

Tristan must have seen it. "We can fight over her later." Tristan glanced back to my face. "We need her to survive first."

Whatever he said after that became lost in the foggy gray void my mind slipped into. My last lucid thought contained regret that I had two naked Weres hovering over me and I hadn't thought to *look*. Pity.

36

"We have to stop meeting like this." Wick's voice acted as a cool salve to the burning pain flowing through my body. The nerve endings in my skin screamed from the multiple shifts and felt so raw, the high thread-count sheet covering me may as well have been a coarse wool blanket used for horses.

"It hurts." I opened my eyes to find Wick's face inches from mine. He lay on his side on top of the sheets, resting his head on his hand. I'd woken up in this bed before. Wick's bed. His room still smelled of man, wolf and floral dryer sheets. I inhaled deeply and let the comforting scent soothe away some of the pain.

"I know." Wick moved a strand of hair out of my face, giving me a better view of the small crease between his eyes and the slight tightness to his mouth. He hesitated, as if to say something more, but a small smile appeared instead.

"Crap!" I bolted upright in bed. Ignoring the pain lancing through my body, I grabbed the sheets to throw aside. "The head!"

Wick's hand dwarfed mine as he laid it across my fingers. "Allan presented it on your behalf."

My lip quivered so I bit down on it. "Did Lucien accept it as payment?"

Wick let a breath out and his gaze cut away. "He said he'd deliberate on the matter and pass judgment after you're healed."

I groaned and flopped back into bed.

"It will be okay, Andy." Wick's voice encouraged me to look back up. Waves of emotion emanated from his skin and percolated in my nose. My brows knit together as I analyzed his scent—a hint of fresh cut grass on a summer morning, poking through his normal rosemary, spoke of happiness; happy because I was safe, happy because it was over? But the pungent stench of canned ham and the skin of a snake soiled his otherwise joyful aroma. Why the despair? The turmoil?

Our gazes met and all coherent thoughts ran away. Wick's irises flashed yellow, his wolf close and despite many shifts and the damage I sustained, mine howled in response. My mountain lion, recessed deep in my psyche for recovery, couldn't act as a referee, couldn't prevent my wolf from rushing up and simmering just beneath the surface.

Wick inched closer, dropping his head to mine. His fingers tangled in my hair as he pulled my face to his. Soft lips pressed in a kiss that could only be described as delicious.

More. I reached up and pulled Wick closer, wanting the weight of his body against mine, to hell with my injuries. He groaned and strong arms enveloped me as he deepened the kiss, his tongue stroking mine. Heat pooled in my body, making me ache in all the right places as he ran his large hands up my rib cage to cup my breasts. His hot mouth trailed kisses along my jaw and neck. He paused, hovering over the sensitive skin between my neck and shoulder, where the carotid artery pumped fast to keep up with my galloping heart. His warm peppermint breath brushed my nerve endings while he waited, wordlessly asking a question.

I pulled back. I wanted him to keep going, to keep touching, kissing and holding me, but I also wanted to take things slow, get to know him under more normal circumstances before the ultimate supe commitment. "No mating bond?"

"Not yet," he agreed, his lips twisting into a smile. He slowly looked my body over. "I honestly don't think you could handle it right now."

"Is that a challenge?"

"No." Wick shook his head. His rich whiskey and cream voice rolled over my skin and sank into my pores with his next words. "It's a promise."

EPILOGUE

A knock on the door interrupted our teenaged make-out session on the couch. The air hummed with silence before a subtle creaking sound of working hinges shattered it. Someone walked into Wick's house without waiting for an invitation. Must be pack.

Pushing Wick and his glorious mouth away, I sat up on the couch to greet our visitor. A woozy feeling in the pit of my stomach bubbled up and I swallowed. It had only been a week since I woke up in Wick's bed after the Ethan takedown, and if I moved too fast, my body gave me a good bitch slap to remind me I still needed to mend.

Clint strutted into the room.

My stomach rolled. I swallowed again and squeezed my eyelids shut against the waves of nausea. Maybe hallucination. It couldn't be Clint...could it? He might be a human servant, but he *died*. Glazed eyes and all. I'd seen it.

My stomach settled and I pried my eyelids open enough to squint through them. There, on the other side of the living room, stood a smug-looking Clint, smiling at me as if my confusion amused the heck out of him.

Holy crap!

My response came out in one breath. "*Whatthefuck*?"

"Allan said you had something to say to me?" He crossed his arms.

Wick moved off the couch and stood up. I averted my gaze to avoid the questions in his. I couldn't explain the war of emotions going through my head right now anyway. On a normal day, I despised Clint and everything he stood for, but then he saved my life, interrupting Ethan long enough for me to recuperate and for Allan to arrive. The action cost him his life. Or so I thought. I'd wanted to thank him. But now...

"What the hell are you?" I asked. So much for voicing my gratitude. I would've been Ethan's last meal if not for Clint. Well, Ethan had fed on me before he died, so technically I was his last—"And where do you buy your spinach?"

Clint smirked and stepped around to face me on the couch. "I told you I wasn't without resources." He leered down at me. "Did you miss me?"

"Only when I thought you were dead," I grumbled.

"Well, your fun time is over. You've been summoned."

BEAST

J. C. McKENZIE

They call me BEAST...

As an assassin for the Supernatural Regulatory Division, I possess several unique and deadly skills.

But dancing in a bedazzled thong has never been one of them.

When an unknown entity starts wreaking havoc on the Lower Mainland, though, I find myself in a precarious position. The Master Vampire has threatened the local werewolf alpha's life if I don't hunt down and find the supernatural being. So here I am, willing to employ a den of witches, work with the Vancouver Police Department and jiggle my booty to save my potential mate—even if I'm not speaking to him right now.

And though I will succeed, I might still lose everything. This conflict has awakened something else within me, a raging beast I have never learned to control.

And she's pissed.

Don't miss this fast-paced, addictive urban fantasy with sugar and spice and everything not-nice by international bestselling author, J. C. McKenzie.

Previously published as *Beast Coast* by the Wild Rose Press.

Acknowledgments

This was my debut novel, originally published in 2014. I'm forever grateful to the Wild Rose Press for starting my journey as an author. Though this book has been editing and revised since then, I want to thank all those who helped get this book to where it is today.

Thank you to my critique partners and beta readers: Jo-Ann Carson, Kelly Atkins, Loyd A. Meeker, Hannah Myles, Jackelyn Ford and Anna Kearie. Thank you to Olga Sauchenia for the beautiful cover. Thank you to my editor, Lara Parker, who has been with me since day one with the original version, *Shift Happens*, and stayed with me for all the books that followed. Thank you to my friends and family for their love and support.

And finally, the biggest thank you of all goes to my readers for continuing to support me and enjoy the worlds I create.

J. C.

About the Author

J. C. McKenzie is a book loving, gumboot-wearing, unapologetic science geek. She predominantly writes urban fantasy and post-apocalyptic dystopian fantasy with strong romantic elements. When she's not spinning tales, she's in the classroom sharing her passion for science and mathematics while secretly warping the young, impressionable minds of our future to carry out her evil plans for world domination. She lives in the Pacific Northwest with her family.

Visit her at jcmckenzie.ca

facebook.com/j.c.mckenzie.author

instagram.com/j.c.mckenzie

tiktok.com/@jcmckenzie0

bookbub.com/authors/j-c-mckenzie

www.ingramcontent.com/pod-product-compliance
Lightning Source LLC
Chambersburg PA
CBHW030635020726
47493CB00006B/1722